2 ∞

ACKNOWLEDGMENT:

Oxford University Press, London, for "Master and Man" by Leo Tolstoy, translated by Louise and Aylmer Maude.

The Vedanta Society of Southern California for "Bhagavad–Gita." Copyright 1944, 1951. Translated by Swami Prabhavananda and Christopher Isherwood.

LEO TOLSTOY *was born at the family estate in Russia in 1828. His mother and father died while he was still a boy. After a short period at a university, Tolstoy tried agriculture, city life, the army, writing, travel in Europe, education, social reform, magazine publishing, and arbitration between the nobles and serfs. At thirty-four he married and retired to his estate, where his wife bore him thirteen children. He became absorbed in research for a historical novel which he published as War and Peace in 1869. Its appearance made a reputation for Tolstoy, who only busied himself with new occupations and studies. Master and Man appeared in 1895. Religion slowly became his chief interest and he evolved a doctrine of poverty, celibacy, and manual labor. Tolstoy died in 1910.*

MASTER AND MAN

I

It happened in the 'seventies in winter, on the day after St. Nicholas's Day. There was a fête in the parish and the innkeeper, Vasíli Andréevich Brekhunóv, a Second Guild merchant, being a church elder had to go to church, and had also to entertain his relatives and friends at home.

But when the last of them had gone he at once began to prepare to drive over to see a neighbouring proprietor about a grove which he had been bargaining over for a long time. He was now in a hurry to start, lest buyers from the town might forestall him in making a profitable purchase.

The youthful landowner was asking ten thousand rubles for the grove simply because Vasíli Andréevich was offering seven thousand. Seven thousand was, however, only a third of its real value. Vasíli Andréevich might perhaps have got it down to his own price, for the woods were in his district and he had a long-standing agreement with the other village dealers that no one should run up the price in another's district, but he had now learnt that some timber dealers from town meant to bid for the Goryáchkin grove and he resolved to go at once and get the matter settled. So as soon as the feast was over, he took seven hundred rubles from his strong box, added to them two thousand three hundred rubles of church money he had in his keeping, so as to make up the sum to three thousand; carefully counted the notes, and having put them into his pocketbook made haste to start.

Nikíta, the only one at Vasíli Andréevich's labourers who was not drunk that day, ran to harness the horse. Nikíta, though an habitual drunkard, was not drunk that day because since the last day before the fast, when he had drunk his coat and leather boots, he had sworn off drink and had kept his vow for two months, and was still keeping it despite the temptation of the vodka that had been drunk everywhere during the first two days of the feast.

Nikíta was a peasant of about fifty from a neighbouring village, 'not a manager' as the peasants said of him, meaning that he was not the thrifty head of a household but lived most of his time away from home as a labourer. He was valued everywhere for his industry, dexterity, and strength at work, and still more for his kindly and pleasant temper. But he never settled down anywhere for long because about twice a year, or even oftener, he had a drinking bout, and then besides spending all his clothes on drink he became turbulent and quarrelsome. Vasíli Andréevich himself had turned him away several times, but had afterwards taken him back again—valuing his honesty, his kindness to animals, and especially his cheapness. Vasíli Andréevich did not pay Nikíta the eighty rubles a year such a man was worth, but only about forty, which he gave him haphazard, in small sums, and even that mostly not in cash but in goods from his own shop and at high prices.

Nikíta's wife Martha, who had once been a handsome vigorous woman, managed the homestead with the help of her son and two daughters, and did not urge Nikíta to live at home: first because she had been living for some twenty years already with a cooper, a peasant from another village who lodged in their house; and secondly because though she managed her husband as she pleased when he was sober, she feared him like fire when he was drunk. Once when he had got drunk at home, Nikíta, probably to make up for his submissiveness when sober, broke open her box, took out her best clothes, snatched up an axe, and chopped all her undergarments and dresses to bits. All the wages Nikíta earned went to his wife, and he raised no objection to that. So now, two days before the holiday, Martha had been twice to see Vasíli Andréevich and had got from him wheat flour, tea, sugar, and a quart of vodka, the lot costing three rubles, and also five rubles in cash, for which she thanked him as for a special favour, though he owed Nikíta at least twenty rubles.

'What agreement did we ever draw up with you?' said Vasíli Andréevich to Nikíta. 'If you need anything, take it; you will work it off. I'm not like others to keep you waiting, and making up accounts and reckoning fines. We deal straightforwardly. You serve me and I don't neglect you.'

And when saying this Vasíli Andréevich was honestly convinced that he was Nikíta's benefactor, and he knew how to put it so plausibly that all those who depended on him for their money, beginning with Nikíta, confirmed him in the conviction that he was their benefactor and did not overreach them.

'Yes, I understand, Vasíli Andréevich. You know that I serve you and take as much pains as I would for my own father. I understand very well!' Nikíta would reply. He was quite aware that Vasíli Andréevich was cheating him, but at

the same time he felt that it was useless to try to clear up his
accounts with him or explain his side of the matter, and that
as long as he had nowhere to go he must accept what he could
get.

Now, having heard his master's order to harness, he went as
usual cheerfully and willingly to the shed, stepping briskly and
easily on his rather turned-in feet; took down from a nail the
heavy tasselled leather bridle, and jingling the rings of the bit
went to the closed stable where the horse he was to harness
was standing by himself.

'What, feeling lonely, feeling lonely, little silly?' said Nikíta
in answer to the low whinny with which he was greeted by
the good-tempered, medium-sized bay stallion, with a rather
slanting crupper, who stood alone in the shed. 'Now then, now
then, there's time enough. Let me water you first,' he went on,
speaking to the horse just as to someone who understood the
words he was using, and having whisked the dusty, grooved
back of the well-fed young stallion with the skirt of his coat,
he put a bridle on his handsome head, straightened his ears
and forelock, and having taken off his halter led him out to
water.

Picking his way out of the dung-strewn stable, Mukhórty
frisked, and making play with his hind leg pretended that he
meant to kick Nikíta, who was running at a trot beside him to
the pump.

'Now then, now then, you rascal!' Nikíta called out, well
knowing how carefully Mukhórty threw out his hind leg just
to touch his greasy sheepskin coat but not to strike him—a
trick Nikíta much appreciated.

After a drink of the cold water the horse sighed, moving his
strong wet lips, from the hairs of which transparent drops fell

into the trough; then standing still as if in thought, he suddenly gave a loud snort.

'If you don't want any more, you needn't. But don't go
asking for any later,' said Nikíta quite seriously and fully
explaining his conduct to Mukhórty. Then he ran back to the
shed pulling the playful young horse, who wanted to gambol
all over the yard, by the rein.

There was no one else in the yard except a stranger, the
cook's husband, who had come for the holiday.

'Go and ask which sledge is to be harnessed—the wide one
or the small one—there's a good fellow!'

The cook's husband went into the house, which stood on an
iron foundation and was iron-roofed, and soon returned saying
that the little one was to be harnessed. By that time Nikíta
had put the collar and brass-studded bellyband on Mukhórty
and, carrying a light, painted shaftbow in one hand, was
leading the horse with the other up to two sledges that stood
in the shed.

'All right, let it be the little one!' he said, backing the
intelligent horse, which all the time kept pretending to bite
him, into the shafts, and with the aid of the cook's husband he
proceeded to harness. When everything was nearly ready and
only the reins had to be adjusted, Nikíta sent the other man to
the shed for some straw and to the barn for a drugget.

'There, that's all right! Now, now, don't bristle up!' said
Nikíta, pressing down into the sledge the freshly threshed oat
straw the cook's husband had brought. 'And now let's spread
the sacking like this, and the drugget over it. There, like that it
will be comfortable sitting,' he went on, suiting the action to
the words and tucking the drugget all round over the straw to
make a seat.

'Thank you, dear man. Things always go quicker with two working at it!' he added. And gathering up the leather reins fastened together by a brass ring, Nikíta took the driver's seat and started the impatient horse over the frozen manure which lay in the yard, towards the gate.

'Uncle Nikíta! I say, Uncle, Uncle!' a high-pitched voice shouted, and a seven-year-old boy in a black sheepskin coat, new white felt boots, and a warm cap, ran hurriedly out of the house into the yard. 'Take me with you!' he cried, fastening up his coat as he ran.

'All right, come along, darling!' said Nikíta and stopping the sledge he picked up the master's pale thin little son, radiant with joy, and drove out into the road.

It was past two o'clock and the day was windy, dull, and cold, with more than twenty degrees Fahrenheit of frost. Half the sky was hidden by a lowering dark cloud. In the yard it was quiet, but in the street the wind was felt more keenly. The snow swept down from a neighbouring shed and whirled about in the corner near the bath-house.

Hardly had Nikíta driven out of the yard and turned the horse's head to the house, before Vasíli Andréevich emerged from the high porch in front of the house with a cigarette in his mouth and wearing a cloth-covered sheepskin coat tightly girdled low at his waist, and stepped onto the hard-trodden snow which squeaked under the leather soles of his felt boots, and stopped. Taking a last whiff of his cigarette he threw it down, stepped on it, and letting the smoke escape through his moustache and looking askance at the horse that was coming up, began to tuck in his sheepskin collar on both sides of his ruddy face, clean-shaven except for the moustache, so that his breath should not moisten the collar.

'See now! The young scamp is there already!' he exclaimed
when he saw his little son in the sledge. Vasíli Andréevich was
excited by the vodka he had drunk with his visitors, and so he
was even more pleased than usual with everything that was
his and all that he did. The sight of his son, whom he always
thought of as his heir, now gave him great satisfaction. He
looked at him, screwing up his eyes and showing his long
teeth.

His wife—pregnant, thin and pale, with her head and
shoulders wrapped in a shawl so that nothing of her face could
be seen but her eyes—stood behind him in the vestibule to see
him off.

'Now really, you ought to take Nikíta with you,' she said
timidly, stepping out from the doorway.

Vasíli Andréevich did not answer. Her words evidently
annoyed him and he frowned angrily and spat.

'You have money on you,' she continued in the same plain-
tive voice. 'What if the weather gets worse! Do take him, for
goodness' sake!'

'Why? Don't I know the road that I must needs take a
guide?' exclaimed Vasíli Andréevich, uttering every word very
distinctly and compressing his lips unnaturally, as he usually
did when speaking to buyers and sellers.

'Really you ought to take him. I beg you in God's name!' his
wife repeated, wrapping her shawl more closely round her
head.

'There, she sticks to it like a leech! ... Where am I to take
him?'

'I'm quite ready to go with you, Vasíli Andréevich,' said
Nikíta cheerfully. 'But they must feed the horses while I am
away,' he added, turning to his master's wife.

'I'll look after them, Nikíta dear. I'll tell Simon,' replied the mistress.

'Well, Vasíli Andréevich, am I to come with you?' said Nikíta, awaiting a decision.

'It seems I must humour my old woman. But if you're coming you'd better put on a warmer cloak,' said Vasíli Andréevich, smiling again as he winked at Nikíta's short sheepskin coat, which was torn under the arms and at the back, was greasy and out of shape, frayed to a fringe round the skirt, and had endured many things in its lifetime.

'Hey, dear man, come and hold the horse!' shouted Nikíta to the cook's husband, who was still in the yard.

'No, I will myself, I will myself!' shrieked the little boy, pulling his hands, red with cold, out of his pockets, and seizing the cold leather reins.

'Only don't be too long dressing yourself up. Look alive!' shouted Vasíli Andréevich, grinning at Nikíta.

'Only a moment, Father, Vasíli Andréevich!' replied Nikíta, and running quickly with his inturned toes in his felt boots with their soles patched with felt, he hurried across the yard and into the workmen's hut.

'Arínushka! Get my coat down from the stove. I'm going with the master,' he said, as he ran into the hut and took down his girdle from the nail on which it hung.

The workmen's cook, who had had a sleep after dinner and was now getting the samovar ready for her husband, turned cheerfully to Nikíta, and infected by his hurry began to move as quickly as he did, got down his miserable worn-out cloth coat from the stove where it was drying, and began hurriedly shaking it out and smoothing it down.

'There now, you'll have a chance of a holiday with your good man,' said Nikíta, who from kindhearted politeness always said something to anyone he was alone with.

Then, drawing his worn narrow girdle round him, he drew in his breath, pulling in his lean stomach still more, and girdled himself as tightly as he could over his sheepskin.

'There now,' he said addressing himself no longer to the cook but the girdle, as he tucked the ends in at the waist, 'now you won't come undone!' And working his shoulders up and down to free his arms, he put the coat over his sheepskin, arched his back more strongly to ease his arms, poked himself under the armpits, and took down his leather-covered mittens from the shelf. 'Now we're all right!'

'You ought to wrap your feet up, Nikíta. Your boots are very bad.'

Nikíta stopped as if he had suddenly realized this.

'Yes, I ought to. . . . But they'll do like this. It isn't far!' and he ran out into the yard.

'Won't you be cold, Nikíta?' said the mistress as he came up to the sledge.

'Cold? No, I'm quite warm,' answered Nikíta as he pushed some straw up to the forepart of the sledge so that it should cover his feet, and stowed away the whip, which the good horse would not need, at the bottom of the sledge.

Vasíli Andréevich, who was wearing two fur-lined coats one over the other, was already in the sledge, his broad back filling nearly its whole rounded width, and taking the reins he immediately touched the horse. Nikíta jumped in just as the sledge started, and seated himself in front on the left side, with one leg hanging over the edge.

II

The good stallion took the sledge along at a brisk pace over the smooth-frozen road through the village, the runners squeaking slightly as they went.

'Look at him hanging on there! Hand me the whip, Nikíta!' shouted Vasíli Andréevich, evidently enjoying the sight of his 'heir,' who standing on the runners was hanging on at the back of the sledge. 'I'll give it you! Be off to mamma, you dog!'

The boy jumped down. The horse increased his amble and, suddenly changing foot, broke into a fast trot.

The Crosses, the village where Vasíli Andréevich lived, consisted of six houses. As soon as they had passed the black-smith's hut, the last in the village, they realized that the wind was much stronger than they had thought. The road could hardly be seen. The tracks left by the sledge-runners were immediately covered by snow and the road was only distin-guished by the fact that it was higher than the rest of the ground. There was a whirl of snow over the fields and the line where sky and earth met could not be seen. The Telyátin forest, usually clearly visible, now only loomed up occasionally and dimly through the driving snowy dust. The wind came from the left, insistently blowing over to one side the mane on Mukhórty's sleek neck and carrying aside even his fluffy tail, which was tied in a simple knot. Nikíta's wide coat-collar, as he sat on the windy side, pressed close to his cheek and nose.

'This road doesn't give him a chance—it's too snowy,' said Vasíli Andréevich, who prided himself on his good horse. 'I once drove to Pashútino with him in half an hour.'

'What?' asked Nikíta, who could not hear on account of his collar.

'I say I once went to Pashútino in half an hour,' shouted Vasíli Andréevich.

'It goes without saying that he's a good horse,' replied Nikíta.

They were silent for a while. But Vasíli Andréevich wished to talk.

'Well, did you tell your wife not to give the cooper any vodka?' he began in the same loud tone, quite convinced that Nikíta must feel flattered to be talking with so clever and important a person as himself, and he was so pleased with his jest that it did not enter his head that the remark might be unpleasant to Nikíta.

The wind again prevented Nikíta's hearing his master's words.

Vasíli Andréevich repeated the jest about the cooper in his loud, clear voice.

'That's their business, Vasíli Andréevich. I don't pry into their affairs. As long as she doesn't ill-treat our boy—God be with them.'

'That so,' said Vasíli Andréevich. 'Well, and will you be buying a horse in spring?' he went on, changing the subject.

'Yes, I can't avoid it,' answered Nikíta, turning down his collar and leaning back towards his master.

The conversation now became interesting to him and he did not wish to lose a word.

'The lad's growing up. He must begin to plough for himself, but till now we've always had to hire someone,' he said.

'Well, why not have the lean-cruppered one. I won't charge much for it,' shouted Vasíli Andreéevich, feeling animated, and consequently starting on his favourite occupation—that of horse-dealing—which absorbed all his mental powers.

'Or you might let me have fifteen rubles and I'll buy one at the horse-market,' said Nikíta, who knew that the horse Vasíli Andréevich wanted to sell him would be dear at seven rubles, but that if he took it from him it would be charged at twenty-five, and then he would be unable to draw any money for half a year.

'It's a good horse. I think of your interest as of my own— according to conscience. Brekhunóv isn't a man to wrong anyone. Let the loss be mine. I'm not like others. Honestly!' he shouted in the voice in which he hypnotized his customers and dealers. 'It's a real good horse.'

'Quite so!' said Nikíta with a sigh, and convinced that there was nothing more to listen to, he again released his collar, which immediately covered his ear and face.

They drove on in silence for about half an hour. The wind blew sharply onto Nikíta's side and arm where his sheepskin was torn.

He huddled up and breathed into the collar which covered his mouth, and was not wholly cold.

'What do you think—shall we go through Karamýshevo or by the straight road?' asked Vasíli Andréevich.

The road through Karamýshevo was more frequented and was well marked with a double row of high stakes. The straight road was nearer but little used and had no stakes, or only poor ones covered with snow.

Nikíta thought awhile.

'Though Karamýshevo is farther, it is better going,' he said.

'But by the straight road, when once we get though the hollow by the forest, it's good going—sheltered,' said Vasíli Andréevich, who wished to go the nearest way.

'Just as you please,' said Nikíta, and again let go of his collar.

Vasíli Andréevich did as he had said, and having gone about half a verst came to a tall oak stake which had a few dry leaves still dangling on it, and there he turned to the left.

On turning they faced directly against the wind, and snow was beginning to fall. Vasíli Andréevich, who was driving, inflated his cheeks, blowing the breath out through his moustache. Nikíta dosed.

So they went on in silence for about ten minutes. Suddenly Vasíli Andréevich began saying something.

'Eh, what?' asked Nikíta, opening his eyes.

Vasíli Andréevich did not answer, but bent over, looking behind them and then ahead of the horse. The sweat had curled Mukhórty's coat between his legs and on his neck. He went at a walk.

'What is it?' Nikíta asked again.

'What is it? What is it?' Vasíli Andréevich mimicked him angrily. 'There are no stakes to be seen! We must have got off the road!'

'Well, pull up then, and I'll look for it,' said Nikíta, and jumping down lightly from the sledge and taking the whip from under the straw, he went off to the left from his own side of the sledge.

The snow was not deep that year, so that it was possible to walk anywhere, but still in places it was knee-deep and got into Nikíta's boots. He went about feeling the ground with his feet and the whip, but could not find the road anywhere.

'Well, how is it?' asked Vasíli Andréevich when Nikíta came back to the sledge.

'There is no road this side. I must go to the other side and try there,' said Nikíta.

'There's something there in front. Go and have a look.'

Nikíta went to what had appeared dark, but found that it was earth which the wind had blown from the bare fields of winter oats and had strewn over the snow, colouring it. Having searched to the right also, he returned to the sledge, brushed the snow from his coat, shook it out of his boots, and seated himself once more.

'We must go to the right,' he said decidedly. 'The wind was blowing on our left before, but now it is straight in my face. Drive to the right,' he repeated with decision.

Vasíli Andréevich took his advice and turned to the right, but still there was no road. They went on in that direction for some time. The wind was as fierce as ever and it was snowing lightly.

'It seems, Vasíli Andréevich, that we have gone quite astray,' Nikíta suddenly remarked, as if it were a pleasant thing. 'What is that?' he added, pointing to some potato vines that showed up from under the snow.

Vasíli Andréevich stopped the perspiring horse, whose deep sides were heaving heavily.

'What is it?'

'Why, we are on the Zakhárov lands. See where we've got to!'

'Nonsense!' retorted Vasíli Andréevich.

'It's not nonsense, Vasíli Andréevich. It's the truth,' replied Nikíta. 'You can feel that the sledge is going over a potato-field, and there are the heaps of vines which have been carted here. It's the Zakhárov factory land.'

'Dear me, how we have gone astray!' said Vasíli Andréevich. 'What are we to do now?'

'We must go straight on, that's all. We shall come out
somewhere—if not at Zakhárova, then at the proprietor's
farm,' said Nikíta.

Vasíli Andréevich agreed, and drove as Nikíta had indicated. So they went on for a considerable time. At times they
came onto bare fields and the sledge-runners rattled over
frozen lumps of earth. Sometimes they got onto a winter-rye
field, or a fallow field on which they could see stalks of
wormwood, and straws sticking up through the snow and
swaying in the wind; sometimes they came onto deep and
even white snow, above which nothing was to be seen.

The snow was falling from above and sometimes rose from
below. The horse was evidently exhausted, his hair had all
curled up from sweat and was covered with hoarfrost, and he
went at a walk. Suddenly he stumbled and sat down in a ditch
or water-course. Vasíli Andréevich wanted to stop, but Nikíta
cried to him:

'Why stop? We've got in and must get out. Hey, pet! Hey,
darling! Gee up, old fellow!' he shouted in a cheerful tone to
the horse, jumping out of the sledge and himself getting stuck
in the ditch.

The horse gave a start and quickly climbed out onto the
frozen bank. It was evidently a ditch that had been dug there.

'Where are we now?' asked Vasíli Andréevich.

'We'll soon find out!' Nikíta replied. 'Go on, we'll get
somewhere.'

'Why, this must be the Goryáchkin forest!' said Vasíli Andréevich, pointing to something dark that appeared amid the
snow in front of them.

'We'll see what forest it is when we get there,' said Nikíta.

He saw that beside the black thing they had noticed, dry, oblong willow-leaves were fluttering, and so he knew it was not a forest but a settlement, but he did not wish to say so. And in fact they had not gone twenty-five yards beyond the ditch before something in front of them, evidently trees, showed up black, and they heard a new and melancholy sound. Nikíta had guessed right: it was not a wood, but a row of tall willows with a few leaves still fluttering on them here and there. They had evidently been planted along the ditch round a threshing-floor. Coming up to the willows, which moaned sadly in the wind, the horse suddenly planted his forelegs above the height of the sledge, drew up his hind legs also, pulling the sledge onto higher ground, and turned to the left, no longer sinking up to his knees in snow. They were back on a road.

'Well, here we are, but heaven only knows where!' said Nikíta.

The horse kept straight along the road through the drifted snow, and before they had gone another hundred yards the straight line of the dark wattle wall of a barn showed up black before them, its roof heavily covered with snow which poured down from it. After passing the barn the road turned to the wind and they drove into a snow-drift. But ahead of them was a lane with houses on either side, so evidently the snow had been blown across the road and they had to drive through the drift. And so in fact it was. Having driven through the snow they came out into a street. At the end house of the village some frozen clothes hanging on a line—shirts, one red and one white, trousers, leg-bands, and a petticoat—fluttered wildly in the wind. The white shirt in particular struggled desperately, waving its sleeves about.

'There now, either a lazy woman or a dead one has not taken her clothes down before the holiday,' remarked Nikíta, looking at the fluttering shirts.

III

At the entrance to the street the wind still raged and the road was thickly covered with snow, but well within the village it was calm, warm, and cheerful. At one house a dog was barking, at another a woman, covering her head with her coat, came running from somewhere and entered the door of a hut, stopping on the threshold to have a look at the passing sledge. In the middle of the village girls could be heard singing.

Here in the village there seemed to be less wind and snow, and the frost was less keen.

'Why, this is Gríshkino,' said Vasíli Andréevich.

'So it is,' responded Nikíta.

It really was Gríshkino, which meant that they had gone too far to the left and had travelled some six miles, not quite in the direction they aimed at, but towards their destination for all that.

From Gríshkino to Goryáchkin was about another four miles.

In the middle of the village they almost ran into a tall man walking down the middle of the street.

'Who are you?' shouted the man, stopping the horse, and recognizing Vasíli Andréevich he immediately took hold of the shaft, went along it hand over hand till he reached the sledge, and placed himself on the driver's seat.

He was Isáy, a peasant of Vasíli Andréevich's acquaintance, and well known as the principal horse-thief in the district.

'Ah, Vasíli Andréevich! Where are you off to?' said Isáy, enveloping Nikíta in the odour of the vodka he had drunk.

'We were going to Goryáchkin.'

'And look where you've got to! You should have gone through Molchánovka.'

'Should have, but didn't manage it,' said Vasíli Andréevich, holding in the horse.

'That's a good horse,' said Isáy, with a shrewd glance at Mukhórty, and with a practised hand he tightened the loosened knot high in the horse's bushy tail.

'Are you going to stay the night?'

'No, friend, I must get on.'

'Your business must be pressing. And who is this? Ah, Nikíta Stepánych!'

'Who else?' replied Nikíta. 'But I say, good friend, how are we to avoid going astray again?'

'Where can you go astray here? Turn back straight down the street and then when you come out keep straight on. Don't take to the left. You will come out onto the high road, and then turn to the right.'

'And where do we turn off the high road? As in summer, or the winter way?' asked Nikíta.

'The winter way. As soon as you turn off you'll see some bushes, and opposite them there is a way-mark—a large oak, one with branches—and that's the way.'

Vasíli Andréevich turned the horse back and drove through the outskirts of the village.

'Why not stay the night?' Isáy shouted after them.

But Vasíli Andréevich did not answer and touched up the horse. Four miles of good road, two of which lay through the forest, seemed easy to manage, especially as the wind was apparently quieter and the snow had stopped.

Having driven along the trodden village street, darkened here and there by fresh manure, past the yard where the clothes hung out and where the white shirt had broken loose and was now attached only by one frozen sleeve, they again came within sound of the weird moan of the willows, and again emerged on the open fields. The storm, far from ceasing, seemed to have grown yet stronger. The road was completely covered with drifting snow, and only the stakes showed that they had not lost their way. But even the stakes ahead of them were not easy to see, since the wind blew in their faces.

Vasíli Andréevich screwed up his eyes, bent down his head, and looked out for the way-marks, but trusted mainly to the horse's sagacity, letting it take its own way. And the horse really did not lose the road but followed its windings, turning now to the right and now to the left and sensing it under his feet, so that though the snow fell thicker and the wind strengthened they still continued to see way-marks now to the left and now to the right of them.

So they travelled on for about ten minutes, when suddenly, through the slanting screen of wind-driven snow, something black showed up which moved in front of the horse.

This was another sledge with fellow-travellers. Mukhórty overtook them, and struck his hoofs against the back of the sledge in front of him.

'Pass on . . . hey there . . . get in front!' cried voices from the sledge.

Vasíli Andréevich swerved aside to pass the other sledge. In it sat three men and a woman, evidently visitors returning from a feast. One peasant was whacking the snow-covered croup of their little horse with a long switch, and the other two sitting in front waved their arms and shouted something. The woman, completely wrapped up and covered with snow, sat drowsing and bumping at the back.

'Who are you?' shouted Vasíli Andréevich.

'From A-a-a . . .' was all that could be heard.

'I say, where are you from?'

'From A-a-a-a!' one of the peasants shouted with all his might, but still it was impossible to make out who they were.

'Get along! Keep up!' shouted another, ceaselessly beating his horse with the switch.

'So you're from a feast, it seems?'

'Go on, go on! Faster, Simon! Get in front! Faster!'

The wings of the sledges bumped against one another, almost got jammed but managed to separate, and the peasants' sledge began to fall behind.

Their shaggy, big-bellied horse, all covered with snow, breathed heavily under the low shaft-bow and, evidently using the last of its strength, vainly endeavoured to escape from the switch, hobbling with its short legs through the deep snow which it threw up under itself.

Its muzzle, young-looking, with the nether lip drawn up like that of a fish, nostrils distended and ears pressed back from fear, kept up for a few seconds near Nikíta's shoulder and then began to fall behind.

'Just see what liquor does!' said Nikíta. 'They've tired that little horse to death. What pagans!'

For a few minutes they heard the panting of the tired little horse and the drunken shouting of the peasants. Then the panting and the shouts died away, and around them nothing could be heard but the whistling of the wind in their ears and now and then the squeak of their sledge-runners over a wind-swept part of the road.

This encounter cheered and enlivened Vasíli Andréevich, and he drove on more boldly without examining the way-marks, urging on the horse and trusting to him.

Nikíta had nothing to do, and as usual in such circum-stances he drowsed, making up for much sleepless time. Sud-denly the horse stopped and Nikíta nearly fell forward onto his nose.

'You know we're off the track again!' said Vasíli André-evich.

'How's that?'

'Why, there are no way-marks to be seen. We must have got off the road again.'

'Well, if we've lost the road we must find it,' said Nikíta curtly, and getting out and stepping lightly on his pigeon-toed feet he started once more going about on the snow.

He walked about for a long time, now disappearing and now reappearing, and finally he came back.

'There is no road here. There may be farther on,' he said, getting into the sledge.

It was already growing dark. The snow-storm had not in-creased but had also not subsided.

'If we could only hear those peasants!' said Vasíli André-evich.

'Well they haven't caught us up. We must have gone far astray. Or maybe they have lost their way too.'

'Where are we to go then?' asked Vasíli Andréevich.

'Why, we must let the horse take its own way,' said Nikíta. 'He will take us right. Let me have the reins.'

Vasíli Andréevich gave him the reins, the more willingly because his hands were beginning to feel frozen in his thick gloves.

Nikíta took the reins, but only held them, trying not to shake them and rejoicing at his favourite's sagacity. And indeed the clever horse, turning first one ear and then the other now to one side and then to the other, began to wheel round.

'The one thing he can't do is to talk,' Nikíta kept saying. 'See what he is doing! Go on, go on! You know best. That's it, that's it!'

The wind was now blowing from behind and it felt warmer.

'Yes, he's clever,' Nikíta continued, admiring the horse. 'A Kirgiz horse is strong but stupid. But this one—just see what he's doing with his ears! He doesn't need any telegraph. He can scent a mile off.'

Before another half-hour had passed they saw something dark ahead of them—a wood or a village—and stakes again appeared to the right. They had evidently come out onto the road.

'Why, that's Gríshkino again!' Nikíta suddenly exclaimed.

And indeed, there on their left was that same barn with the snow flying from it, and farther on the same line with the frozen washing, shirt and trousers, which still fluttered desperately in the wind.

Again they drove into the street and again it grew quiet, warm, and cheerful, and again they could see the manure-stained street and hear voices and songs and the barking of a dog. It was already so dark that there were lights in some of the windows.

Half-way through the village Vasíli Andréevich turned the
horse towards a large double-fronted brick house and stopped
at the porch.

Nikíta went to the lighted snow-covered window, in the
rays of which flying snow-flakes glittered, and knocked at it
with his whip.

'Who is there?' a voice replied to his knock.

'From Krestý, the Brekhunóvs, dear fellow,' answered Nikíta. 'Just come out for a minute.'

Someone moved from the window, and a minute or two
later there was the sound of the passage door as it came
unstuck, then the latch of the outside door clicked and a tall
white-bearded peasant, with a sheepskin coat thrown over his
white holiday shirt, pushed his way out holding the door
firmly against the wind, followed by a lad in a red shirt and
high leather boots.

'Is that you, Andréevich?' asked the old man.

'Yes, friend, we've gone astray,' said Vasíli Andréevich. 'We
wanted to get to Goryáchkin but found ourselves here. We
went a second time but lost our way again.'

'Just see how you have gone astray!' said the old man.
'Petrúshka, go and open the gate!' he added, turning to the lad
in the red shirt.

'All right,' said the lad in a cheerful voice, and ran back into
the passage.

'But we're not staying the night,' said Vasíli Andréevich.

'Where will you go in the night? You'd better stay!'

'I'd be glad to, but I must go on. It's business, and it can't
be helped.'

'Well, warm yourself at least. The samovar is just ready.'

'Warm myself? Yes, I'll do that,' said Vasíli Andréevich. 'It won't get darker. The moon will rise and it will be lighter. Let's go in and warm ourselves, Nikíta.'

'Well, why not? Let us warm ourselves,' replied Nikíta, who was stiff with cold and anxious to warm his frozen limbs.

Vasíli Andréevich went into the room with the old man, and Nikíta drove through the gate opened for him by Petrúshka, by whose advice he backed the horse under the penthouse. The ground was covered with manure and the tall bow over the horse's head caught against the beam. The hens and the cock had already settled to roost there, and clucked peevishly, clinging to the beam with their claws. The disturbed sheep shied and rushed aside trampling the frozen manure with their hooves. The dog yelped desperately with fright and anger and then burst out barking like a puppy at the stranger.

Nikíta talked to them all, excused himself to the fowls and assured them that he would not disturb them again, rebuked the sheep for being frightened without knowing why, and kept soothing the dog, while he tied up the horse.

'Now that will be all right,' he said, knocking the snow off his clothes. 'Just hear how he barks!' he added, turning to the dog. 'Be quiet, stupid! Be quiet. You are only troubling yourself for nothing. We're not thieves, we're friends. . . . '

'And these are, it's said, the three domestic counsellors,' remarked the lad, and with his strong arms he pushed under the pent-roof the sledge that had remained outside.

'Why counsellors?' asked Nikíta.

'That's what is printed in Paulson. A thief creeps to a house—the dog barks, that means, "Be on your guard!" The cock crows, that means, "Get up!" The cat licks herself—that means, "A welcome guest is coming. Get ready to receive him!" ' said the lad with a smile.

Petrúshka could read and write and knew Paulson's primer, his only book, almost by heart, and he was fond of quoting sayings from it that he thought suited the occasion, especially when he had had something to drink, as to-day.

'That's so,' said Nikíta.

'You must be chilled through and through,' said Petrúshka.

'Yes, I am rather,' said Nikíta, and they went across the yard and the passage into the house.

IV

The household to which Vasíli Andréevich had come was one of the richest in the village. The family had five allotments, besides renting other land. They had six horses, three cows, two calves, and some twenty sheep. There were twenty-two members belonging to the homestead: four married sons, six grandchildren (one of whom, Petrúshka, was married), two great-grandchildren, three orphans, and four daughters-in-law with their babies. It was one of the few homesteads that remained still undivided, but even here the dull internal work of disintegration which would inevitably lead to separation had already begun, starting as usual among the women. Two sons were living in Moscow as water-carriers, and one was in the army. At home now were the old man and his wife, their second son who managed the homestead, the eldest who had come from Moscow for the holiday, and all the women and children. Besides these members of the family there was a visitor, a neighbour who was godfather to one of the children.

Over the table in the room hung a lamp with a shade,

which brightly lit up the tea-things, a bottle of vodka, and some refreshments, besides illuminating the brick walls, which in the far corner were hung with icons on both sides of which were pictures. At the head of the table sat Vasíli Andréevich in a black sheepskin coat, sucking his frozen moustache and observing the room and the people around him with his prominent hawk-like eyes. With him sat the old, bald, white-bearded master of the house in a white homespun shirt, and next him the son home from Moscow for the holiday—a man with a sturdy back and powerful shoulders and clad in a thin print shirt—then the second son, also broad-shouldered, who acted as head of the house, and then a lean red-haired peasant—the neighbour.

Having had a drink of vodka and something to eat, they were about to take tea, and the samovar standing on the floor beside the brick oven was already humming. The children could be seen in the top bunks and on the top of the oven. A woman sat on a lower bunk with a cradle beside her. The old housewife, her face covered with wrinkles which wrinkled even her lips, was waiting on Vasíli Andréevich.

As Nikíta entered the house she was offering her guest a small tumbler of thick glass which she had just filled with vodka.

'Don't refuse, Vasíli Andréevich, you mustn't! Wish us a merry feast. Drink it, dear!' she said.

The sight and smell of vodka, especially now when he was chilled through and tired out, much disturbed Nikíta's mind. He frowned, and having shaken the snow off his cap and coat, stopped in front of the icons as if not seeing anyone, crossed himself three times, and bowed to the icons. Then, turning to the old master of the house and bowing first to him, then to all those at table, then to the women who stood by the oven, and muttering: 'A merry holiday!' he began taking off his outer things without looking at the table.

'Why, you're all covered with hoar-frost, old fellow!' said the eldest brother, looking at Nikíta's snow-covered face, eyes, and beard.

Nikíta took off his coat, shook it again, hung it up beside the oven, and came up to the table. He too was offered vodka. He went through a moment of painful hesitation and nearly took up the glass and emptied the clear fragrant liquid down his throat, but he glanced at Vasíli Andréevich, remembered his oath and the boots that he had sold for drink, recalled the cooper, remembered his son for whom he had promised to buy a horse by spring, sighed, and declined it.

'I don't drink, thank you kindly,' he said frowning, and sat down on a bench near the second window.

'How's that?' asked the eldest brother.

'I just don't drink,' replied Nikíta without lifting his eyes but looking askance at his scanty beard and moustache and getting the icicles out of them.

'It's not good for him,' said Vasíli Andréevich, munching a cracknel after emptying his glass.

'Well, then, have some tea,' said the kindly old hostess. 'You must be chilled through, good soul. Why are you women dawdling so with the samovar?'

'It is ready,' said one of the young women, and after flicking with her apron the top of the samovar which was now boiling over, she carried it with an effort to the table, raised it, and set it down with a thud.

Meanwhile Vasíli Andréevich was telling how he had lost his way, how they had come back twice to this same village,

and how they had gone astray and had met some drunken
peasants. Their hosts were surprised, explained where and
why they had missed their way, said who the tipsy people they
had met were, and told them how they ought to go.

'A little child could find the way to Molchánovka from
here. All you have to do is to take the right turning from the
high road. There's a bush you can see just there. But you
didn't even get that far!' said the neighbour.

'You'd better stay the night. The women will make up beds
for you,' said the old woman persuasively.

'You could go on in the morning and it would be pleasan-
ter,' said the old man, confirming what his wife had said.

'I can't, friend. Business!' said Vasíli Andréevich. 'Lose an
hour and you can't catch it up in a year,' he added, remembering the grove and the dealers who might snatch that deal from
him. 'We shall get there, shan't we?' he said, turning to Nikíta.

Nikíta did not answer for some time, apparently still intent
on thawing out his beard and moustache.

'If only we don't go astray again,' he replied gloomily.

He was gloomy because he passionately longed for some
vodka, and the only thing that could assuage that longing was
tea and he had not yet been offered any.

'But we have only to reach the turning and then we shan't
go wrong. The road will be through the forest the whole way,'
said Vasíli Andréevich.

'It's just as you please, Vasíli Andréevich. If we're to go, let
us go,' said Nikíta, taking the glass of tea he was offered.

'We'll drink our tea and be off.'

Nikíta said nothing but only shook his head, and carefully
pouring some tea into his saucer began warming his hands, the
fingers of which were always swollen with hard work, over the

steam. Then, biting off a tiny bit of sugar, he bowed to his hosts, said, 'Your health!' and drew in the steaming liquid.

'If somebody would see us as far as the turning,' said Vasíli Andréevich.

'Well, we can do that,' said the eldest son. 'Petrúshka will harness and go that far with you.'

'Well, then, put in the horse, lad, and I shall be thankful to you for it.'

'Oh, what for, dear man?' said the kindly old woman. 'We are heartily glad to do it.'

'Petrúshka, go and put in the mare,' said the eldest brother.

'All right,' replied Petrúshka with a smile, and promptly snatching his cap down from a nail he ran away to harness.

While the horse was being harnessed the talk returned to the point at which it had stopped when Vasíli Andréevich drove up to the window. The old man had been complaining to his neighbour, the village elder, about his third son who had not sent him anything for the holiday though he had sent a French shawl to his wife.

'The young people are getting out of hand,' said the old man.

'And how they do!' said the neighbour. 'There's no managing them! They know too much. There's Demóchkin now, who broke his father's arm. It's all from being too clever, it seems.'

Nikíta listened, watched their faces, and evidently would have liked to share in the conversation, but he was too busy drinking his tea and only nodded his head approvingly. He emptied one tumbler after another and grew warmer and warmer and more and more comfortable. The talk continued on the same subject for a long time—the harmfulness of a household dividing up—and it was clearly not an abstract discussion but concerned the question of a separation in that house; a separation demanded by the second son who sat there morosely silent.

It was evidently a sore subject and absorbed them all, but out of propriety they did not discuss their private affairs before strangers. At last, however, the old man could not restrain himself, and with tears in his eyes declared that he would not consent to a break-up of the family during his lifetime, that his house was prospering, thank God, but that if they separated they would all have to go begging.

'Just like the Matvéevs,' said the neighbour. 'They used to have a proper house, but now they've split up none of them has anything.'

'And that is what you want to happen to us,' said the old man, turning to his son.

The son made no reply and there was an awkward pause. The silence was broken by Petrúshka, who having harnessed the horse had returned to the hut a few minutes before this and had been listening all the time with a smile.

'There's a fable about that in Paulson,' he said. 'A father gave his sons a broom to break. At first they could not break it, but when they took it twig by twig they broke it easily. And it's the same here,' and he gave a broad smile. 'I'm ready!' he added.

'If you're ready, let's go,' said Vasíli Andéevich. 'And as to separating, don't you allow it, Grandfather. You got everything together and you're the master. Go to the Justice of the Peace. He'll say how things should be done.'

'He carries on so, carries on so,' the old man continued in a whining tone. 'There's no doing anything with him. It's as if the devil possessed him.'

Nikíta having meanwhile finished his fifth tumbler of tea laid it on its side instead of turning it upside down, hoping to be offered a sixth glass. But there was no more water in the samovar, so the hostess did not fill it up for him. Besides, Vasíli Andréevich was putting his things on, so there was nothing for it but for Nikíta to get up too, put back into the sugar-basin the lump of sugar he had nibbled all round, wipe his perspiring face with the skirt of his sheepskin, and go to put on his overcoat.

Having put it on he sighed deeply, thanked his hosts, said good-bye, and went out of the warm bright room into the cold dark passage, through which the wind was howling and where snow was blowing through the cracks of the shaking door, and from there into the yard.

Petrúshka stood in his sheepskin in the middle of the yard by his horse, repeating some lines from Paulson's primer. He said with a smile:

> 'Storms with mist the sky conceal,
> Snowy circles wheeling wild.
> Now like savage beast 'twill howl,
> And now 'tis wailing like a child.'

Nikíta nodded approvingly as he arranged the reins.

The old man, seeing Vasíli Andréevich off, brought a lantern into the passage to show him a light, but it was blown out at once. And even in the yard it was evident that the snowstorm had become more violent.

'Well, this is weather!' thought Vasíli Andréevich. 'Perhaps

we may not get there after all. But there is nothing to be done.
Business! Besides, we have got ready, our host's horse has
been harnessed, and we'll get there with God's help!'

Their aged host also thought they ought not to go, but he
had already tried to persuade them to stay and had not been
listened to.

'It's no use asking them again. Maybe my age makes me
timid. They'll get there all right, and at least we shall get to
bed in good time and without any fuss,' he thought.

Petrúshka did not think of danger. He knew the road and
the whole district so well, and the lines about 'snowy circles
wheeling wild' described what was happening outside so aptly
that it cheered him up. Nikíta did not wish to go at all, but he
had been accustomed not to have his own way and to serve
others for so long that there was no one to hinder the departing travellers.

V

Vasíli Andréevich went over to his sledge, found it with
difficulty in the darkness, climbed in and took the reins.

'Go on in front!' he cried.

Petrúshka kneeling in his low sledge started his horse. Mukhórty, who had been neighing for some time past, now scent-
ing a mare ahead of him started after her, and they drove out
into the street. They drove again through the outskirts of the
village and along the same road, past the yard where the
frozen linen had hung (which, however, was no longer to be
seen), past the same barn, which was now snowed up almost
to the roof and from which the snow was still endlessly pouring, past the same dismally moaning, whistling, and swaying

willows, and again entered into the sea of blustering snow raging from above and below. The wind was so strong that when it blew from the side and the travellers steered against it, it tilted the sledges and turned the horses to one side. Petrúshka drove his good mare in front at a brisk trot and kept shouting lustily. Mukhórty pressed after her.

After travelling so for about ten minutes, Petrúshka turned round and shouted something. Neither Vasíli Andréevich nor Nikíta could hear anything because of the wind, but they guessed that they had arrived at the turning. In fact Petrúshka had turned to the right, and now the wind that had blown from the side blew straight in their faces, and through the snow they saw something dark on their right. It was the bush at the turning.

'Well now, God speed you!'

'Thank you, Petrúshka!'

'Storms with mist the sky conceal!' shouted Petrúshka as he disappeared.

'There's a poet for you!' muttered Vasíli Andréevich, pulling at the reins.

'Yes, a fine lad—a true peasant,' said Nikíta.

They drove on.

Nikíta, wrapping his coat closely about him and pressing his head down so close to his shoulders that his short beard covered his throat, sat silently, trying not to lose the warmth he had obtained while drinking tea in the house. Before him he saw the straight lines of the shafts which constantly deceived him into thinking they were on a well-travelled road, and the horse's swaying crupper with his knotted tail blown to one side, and farther ahead the high shaft-bow and the swaying head and neck of the horse with its waving mane. Now

and then he caught sight of a way-sign, so that he knew they
were still on a road and that there was nothing for him to be
concerned about.

Vasíli Andréevich drove on, leaving it to the horse to keep
to the road. But Mukhórty, though he had had a breathing-
space in the village, ran reluctantly, and seemed now and then
to get off the road, so that Vasíli Andréevich had repeatedly to
correct him.

'Here's a stake to the right, and another, and here's a third,'
Vasíli Andréevich counted, 'and here in front is the forest,'
thought he, as he looked at something dark in front of him.
But what had seemed to him a forest was only a bush. They
passed the bush and drove on for another hundred yards but
there was no fourth way-mark nor any forest.

'We must reach the forest soon,' thought Vasíli Andréevich,
and animated by the vodka and the tea he did not stop but
shook the reins, and the good obedient horse responded, now
ambling, now slowly trotting in the direction in which he was
sent, though he knew that he was not going the right way. Ten
minutes went by, but there was still no forest.

'There now, we must be astray again,' said Vasíli Andréevich, pulling up.

Nikíta silently got out of the sledge and holding his coat,
which the wind now wrapped closely about him and now
almost tore off, started to feel about in the snow, going first to
one side and then to the other. Three or four times he was
completely lost to sight. At last he returned and took the reins
from Vasíli Andréevich's hand.

'We must go to the right,' he said sternly and peremptorily,
as he turned the horse.

'Well, if it's to the right, go to the right,' said Vasíli André-

evich, yielding up the reins to Nikíta and thrusting his freezing
hands into his sleeves.

Nikíta did not reply.

'Now then, friend, stir yourself!' he shouted to the horse,
but in spite of the shake of the reins Mukhórty moved only at
a walk.

The snow in places was up to his knees, and the sledge
moved by fits and starts with his every movement.

Nikíta took the whip that hung over the front of the sledge
and struck him once. The good horse, unused to the whip,
sprang forward and moved at a trot, but immediately fell back
into an amble and then to a walk. So they went on for five
minutes. It was dark and the snow whirled from above and
rose from below, so that sometimes the shaft-bow could not be
seen. At times the sledge seemed to stand still and the field to
run backwards. Suddenly the horse stopped abruptly, evidently aware of something close in front of him. Nikíta again
sprang lightly out, throwing down the reins, and went ahead
to see what had brought him to a standstill, but hardly had he
made a step in front of the horse before his feet slipped and he
went rolling down an incline.

'Whoa, whoa, whoa!' he said to himself as he fell, and he
tried to stop his fall but could not, and only stopped when his
feet plunged into a thick layer of snow that had drifted to the
bottom of the hollow.

The fringe of a drift of snow that hung on the edge of the
hollow, disturbed by Nikíta's fall, showered down on him and
got inside his collar.

'What a thing to do!' said Nikíta reproachfully, addressing
the drift and the hollow and shaking the snow from under his
collar.

'Nikíta! Hey, Nikíta!' shouted Vasíli Andréevich from
above.

But Nikíta did not reply. He was too occupied in shaking
out the snow and searching for the whip he had dropped
when rolling down the incline. Having found the whip he
tried to climb straight up the bank where he had rolled down,
but it was impossible to do so: he kept rolling down again, and
so he had to go along at the foot of the hollow to find a way
up. About seven yards farther on he managed with difficulty
to crawl up the incline on all fours, then he followed the edge
of the hollow back to the place where the horse should have
been. He could not see either horse or sledge, but as he
walked against the wind he heard Vasíli Andréevich's shouts
and Mukhórty's neighing, calling him.

'I'm coming! I'm coming! What are you cackling for?' he
muttered.

Only when he had come up to the sledge could he make out
the horse, and Vasíli Andréevich standing beside it and looking gigantic.

"Where the devil did you vanish to? We must go back, if
only to Gríshkino,' he began reproaching Nikíta.

'I'd be glad to get back, Vasíli Andréevich, but which way
are we to go? There is such a ravine here that if we once get
in it we shan't get out again. I got stuck so fast there myself
that I could hardly get out.'

'What shall we do, then? We can't stay here! We must go
somewhere!' said Vasíli Andréevich.

Nikíta said nothing. He seated himself in the sledge with his
back to the wind, took off his boots, shook out the snow that
had got into them, and taking some straw from the bottom of
the sledge, carefully plugged with it a hole in his left boot.

Vasíli Andréevich remained silent, as though now leaving everything to Nikíta. Having put his boots on again, Nikíta drew his feet into the sledge, put on his mittens and took up the reins, and directed the horse along the side of the ravine. But they had not gone a hundred yards before the horse again stopped short. The ravine was in front of him again.

Nikíta again climbed out and again trudged about in the snow. He did this for a considerable time and at last appeared from the opposite side to that from which he had started.

'Vasíli Andréevich, are you alive?' he called out.

'Here!' replied Vasíli Andréevich. 'Well, what now?'

'I can't make anything out. It's too dark. There's nothing but ravines. We must drive against the wind again.'

They set off once more. Again Nikíta went stumbling through the snow, again he fell in, again climbed out and trudged about, and at last quite out of breath he sat down beside the sledge.

'Well, how now?' asked Vasíli Andréevich.

'Why, I am quite worn out and the horse won't go.'

'Then what's to be done?'

'Why, wait a minute.'

Nikíta went away again but soon returned.

'Follow me!' he said, going in front of the horse.

Vasíli Andréevich no longer gave orders but implicitly did what Nikíta told him.

'Here, follow me!' Nikíta shouted, stepping quickly to the right, and seizing the rein he led Mukhórty down towards a snow-drift.

At first the horse held back, then he jerked forward, hoping to leap the drift, but he had not the strength and sank into it up to his collar.

'Get out!' Nikíta called to Vasíli Andréevich who still sat in
the sledge, and taking hold of one shaft he moved the sledge
closer to the horse. 'It's hard, brother!' he said to Mukhórty,
'but it can't be helped. Make an effort! Now, now, just a little
one!' he shouted.

The horse gave a tug, then another, but failed to clear
himself and settled down again as if considering something.

'Now, brother, this won't do!' Nikíta admonished him. 'Now
once more!'

Again Nikíta tugged at the shaft on his side, and Vasíli
Andréevich did the same on the other.

Mukhórty lifted his head and then gave a sudden jerk.

'That's it! That's it!' cried Nikíta. 'Don't be afraid—you
won't sink!'

One plunge, another, and a third, and at last Mukhórty was
out of the snow-drift, and stood still, breathing heavily and
shaking the snow off himself. Nikíta wished to lead him farther, but Vasíli Andréevich, in his two fur coats, was so out of
breath that he could not walk farther and dropped into the
sledge.

'Let me get my breath!' he said, unfastening the kerchief
with which he had tied the collar of his fur coat at the village.

'It's all right here. You lie there,' said Nikíta. 'I will lead
him along.' And with Vasíli Andréevich in the sledge he led
the horse by the bridle about ten paces down and then up a
slight rise, and stopped.

The place where Nikíta had stopped was not completely in
the hollow where the snow sweeping down from the hillocks
might have buried them altogether, but still it was partly
sheltered from the wind by the side of the ravine. There were
moments when the wind seemed to abate a little, but that did

not last long and as if to make up for that respite the storm swept down with tenfold vigour and tore and whirled the more fiercely. Such a gust struck them at the moment when Vasíli Andréevich, having recovered his breath, got out of the sledge and went up to Nikíta to consult him as to what they should do. They both bent down involuntarily and waited till the violence of the squall should have passed. Mukhórty too laid back his ears and shook his head discontentedly. As soon as the violence of the blast had abated a little, Nikíta took off his mittens, stuck them into his belt, breathed onto his hands, and began to undo the straps of the shaft-bow.

'What's that you are doing there?' asked Vasíli Andréevich.

'Unharnessing. What else is there to do? I have no strength left,' said Nikíta as though excusing himself.

'Can't we drive somewhere?'

'No, we can't. We shall only kill the horse. Why, the poor beast is not himself now,' said Nikíta, pointing to the horse, which was standing submissively waiting for what might come, with his steep wet sides heaving heavily. 'We shall have to stay the night here,' he said, as if preparing to spend the night at an inn, and he proceeded to unfasten the collar-straps. The buckles came undone.

'But shan't we be frozen?' remarked Vasíli Andréevich.

'Well, if we are we can't help it,' said Nikíta.

VI

Although Vasíli Andréevich felt quite warm in his two fur coats, especially after struggling in the snow-drift, a cold shiver ran down his back on realizing that he must really

spend the night where they were. To calm himself he sat
down in the sledge and got out his cigarettes and matches.

Nikíta meanwhile unharnessed Mukhórty. He unstrapped
the belly-band and the back-band, took away the reins, loosened the collar-strap, and removed the shaft-bow, talking to
him all the time to encourage him.

'Now come out! come out!' he said, leading him clear of the
shafts. 'Now we'll tie you up here and I'll put down some
straw and take off your bridle. When you've had a bite you'll
feel more cheerful.'

But Mukhórty was restless and evidently not comforted by
Nikíta's remarks. He stepped now on one foot and now on
another, and pressed close against the sledge, turning his back
to the wind and rubbing his head on Nikíta's sleeve. Then, as
if not to pain Nikíta by refusing his offer of the straw he put
before him, he hurriedly snatched a wisp out of the sledge, but
immediately decided that it was now no time to think of straw
and threw it down, and the wind instantly scattered it, carried
it away, and covered it with snow.

'Now we will set up a signal,' said Nikíta, and turning the
front of the sledge to the wind he tied the shafts together with
a strap and set them up on end in front of the sledge. 'There
now, when the snow covers us up, good folk will see the shafts
and dig us out,' he said, slapping his mittens together and
putting them on. 'That's what the old folk taught us!'

Vasíli Andréevich meanwhile had unfastened his coat, and
holding its skirts up for shelter, struck one sulphur match after
another on the steel box. But his hands trembled, and one
match after another either did not kindle or was blown out by
the wind just as he was lifting it to the cigarette. At last a
match did burn up, and its flame lit up for a moment the fur

of his coat, his hand with the gold ring on the bent forefinger, and the snow-sprinkled oat-straw that stuck out from under the drugget. The cigarette lighted, he eagerly took a whiff or two, inhaled the smoke, let it out through his moustache, and would have inhaled again, but the wind tore off the burning tobacco and whirled it away as it had done the straw.

But even these few puffs had cheered him.

'If we must spend the night here, we must!' he said with decision. 'Wait a bit, I'll arrange a flag as well,' he added, picking up the kerchief which he had thrown down in the sledge after taking it from round his collar, and drawing off his gloves and standing up on the front of the sledge and stretching himself to reach the strap, he tied the handkerchief to it with a tight knot.

The kerchief immediately began to flutter wildly, now clinging round the shaft, now suddenly streaming out, stretching and flapping.

'Just see what a fine flag!' said Vasíli Andréevich, admiring his handiwork and letting himself down into the sledge. 'We should be warmer together, but there's not room enough for two,' he added.

'I'll find a place,' said Nikíta. 'But I must cover up the horse first—he sweated so, poor thing. Let go!' he added, drawing the drugget from under Vasíli Andréevich.

Having got the drugget he folded it in two, and after taking off the breechband and pad, covered Mukhórty with it.

'Anyhow it will be warmer, silly!' he said, putting back the breechband and the pad on the horse over the drugget. Then having finished that business he returned to the sledge, and addressing Vasíli Andréevich, said: 'You won't need the sack-cloth, will you? And let me have some straw.'

And having taken these things from under Vasíli Andréevich, Nikíta went behind the sledge, dug out a hole for
himself in the snow, put straw into it, wrapped his coat well
round him, covered himself with the sackcloth, and pulling his
cap well down seated himself on the straw he had spread, and
leant against the wooden back of the sledge to shelter himself
from the wind and the snow.

Vasíli Andréevich shook his head disapprovingly at what
Nikíta was doing, as in general he disapproved of the peasant's
stupidity and lack of education, and he began to settle himself
down for the night.

He smoothed the remaining straw over the bottom of the
sledge, putting more of it under his side. Then he thrust his
hands into his sleeves and settled down, sheltering his head in
the corner of the sledge from the wind in front.

He did not wish to sleep. He lay and thought: thought ever
of the one thing that constituted the sole aim, meaning, pleasure, and pride of his life—of how much money he had made
and might still make, of how much other people he knew had
made and possessed, and of how those others had made and
were making it, and how he, like them, might still make much
more. The purchase of the Goryáchkin grove was a matter of
immense importance to him. By that one deal he hoped to
make perhaps ten thousand rubles. He began mentally to
reckon the value of the wood he had inspected in autumn, and
on five acres of which he had counted all the trees.

'The oaks will go for sledge-runners. The undergrowth will
take care of itself, and there'll still be some thirty sázheens of
fire-wood left on each desyatín,' said he to himself. 'That
means there will be at least two hundred and twenty-five
rubles' worth left on each desyatín. Fifty-six desyatíns means

fifty-six hundreds, and fifty-six hundreds, and fifty-six tens, and another fifty-six tens, and then fifty-six fives . . .' He saw that it came out to more than twelve thousand rubles, but could not reckon it up exactly without a counting-frame. 'But I won't give ten thousand, anyhow. I'll give about eight thousand with a deduction on account of the glades. I'll grease the surveyor's palm—give him a hundred rubles, or a hundred and fifty, and he'll reckon that there are some five desyatíns of glade to be deducted. And he'll let it go for eight thousand. Three thousand cash down. That'll move him, no fear!' he thought, and he pressed his pocket-book with his forearm.

'God only knows how we missed the turning. The forest ought to be there, and a watchman's hut, and dogs barking. But the damned things don't bark when they're wanted.' He turned his collar down from his ear and listened, but as before only the whistling of the wind could be heard, the flapping and fluttering of the kerchief tied to the shafts, and the pelting of the snow against the woodwork of the sledge. He again covered up his ear.

'If I had known I would have stayed the night. Well, no matter, we'll get there to-morrow. It's only one day lost. And the others won't travel in such weather.' Then he remembered that on the 9th he had to receive payment from the butcher for his oxen. 'He meant to come himself, but he won't find me, and my wife won't know how to receive the money. She doesn't know the right way of doing things,' he thought, recalling how at their party the day before she had not known how to treat the police-officer who was their guest. 'Of course she's only a woman! Where could she have seen anything? In my father's time what was our house like? Just a rich peasant's house: just an oatmill and an inn—that was the whole property. But what have I done in these fifteen years? A shop, two taverns, a flour-mill, a grain-store, two farms leased out, and a house with an iron-roofed barn,' he thought proudly. 'Not as it was in Father's time! Who is talked of in the whole district now? Brekhunóv! And why? Because I stick to business. I take trouble, not like others who lie abed or waste their time on foolishness while I don't sleep of nights. Blizzard or no blizzard I start out. So business gets done. They think money-making is a joke. No, take pains and rack your brains! You get overtaken out of doors at night, like this, or keep awake night after night till the thoughts whirling in your head make the pillow turn,' he meditated with pride. 'They think people get on through luck. After all, the Mirónovs are now millionaires. And why? Take pains and God gives. If only He grants me health!'

The thought that he might himself be a millionaire like Mirónov, who began with nothing, so excited Vasíli André-evich that he felt the need of talking to somebody. But there was no one to talk to ... If only he could have reached Goryáchkin he would have talked to the landlord and shown him a thing or two.

'Just see how it blows! It will snow us up so deep that we shan't be able to get out in the morning!' he thought, listening to a gust of wind that blew against the front of the sledge, bending it and lashing the snow against it. He raised himself and looked round. All he could see through the whirling darkness was Mukhórty's dark head, his back covered by the fluttering drugget, and his thick knotted tail; while all round, in front and behind, was the same fluctuating whity darkness, sometimes seeming to get a little lighter and sometimes growing denser still.

'A pity I listened to Nikíta,' he thought. 'We ought to have driven on. We should have come out somewhere, if only back to Gríshkino and stayed the night at Tarás's. As it is we must sit here all night. But what was I thinking about? Yes, that God gives to those who take trouble, but not to loafers, lie-abeds, or fools. I must have a smoke!'

He sat down again, got out his cigarette-case, and stretched himself flat on his stomach, screening the matches with the skirt of his coat. But the wind found its way in and put out match after match. At last he got one to burn and lit a cigarette. He was very glad that he had managed to do what he wanted, and though the wind smoked more of the cigarette than he did, he still got two or three puffs and felt more cheerful. He again leant back, wrapped himself up, started reflecting and remembering, and suddenly and quite unexpectedly lost consciousness and fell asleep.

Suddenly something seemed to give him a push and awoke him. Whether it was Mukhórty who had pulled some straw from under him, or whether something within him had startled him, at all events it woke him, and his heart began to beat faster and faster so that the sledge seemed to tremble under him. He opened his eyes. Everything around him was just as before. 'It looks lighter,' he thought. 'I expect it won't be long before dawn.' But he at once remembered that it was lighter because the moon had risen. He sat up and looked first at the horse. Mukhórty still stood with his back to the wind, shivering all over. One side of the drugget, which was completely covered with snow, had been blown back, the breeching had slipped down and the snow-covered head with its waving forelock and mane were now more visible. Vasíli Andréevich leant over the back of the sledge and looked behind. Nikíta still sat in the same position in which he had settled himself. The sacking with which he was covered, and his legs, were thickly covered with snow.

'If only that peasant doesn't freeze to death! His clothes are so wretched. I may be held responsible for him. What shiftless people they are—such a want of education,' thought Vasíli Andréevich, and he felt like taking the drugget off the horse and putting it over Nikíta, but it would be very cold to get out and move about and, moreover, the horse might freeze to death. 'Why did I bring him with me? It was all her stupidity!' he thought, recalling his unloved wife, and he rolled over into his old place at the front part of the sledge. 'My uncle once spent a whole night like this,' he reflected, 'and was all right.' But another case came at once to his mind. 'But when they dug Sebastian out he was dead—stiff like a frozen carcass. If I'd only stopped the night in Gríshkino all this would not have happened!'

And wrapping his coat carefully round him so that none of the warmth of the fur should be wasted but should warm him all over, neck, knees, and feet, he shut his eyes and tried to sleep again. But try as he would he could not get drowsy, on the contrary he felt wide awake and animated. Again he began counting his gains and the debts due to him, again he began bragging to himself and feeling pleased with himself and his position, but all this was continually disturbed by a stealthily approaching fear and by the unpleasant regret that he had not remained in Gríshkino.

'How different it would be to be lying warm on a bench!' He turned over several times in his attempts to get into a more comfortable position more sheltered from the wind, he wrapped up his legs closer, shut his eyes, and lay still. But either his

legs in their strong felt boots began to ache from being bent in
one position, or the wind blew in somewhere, and after lying
still for a short time he again began to recall the disturbing
fact that he might now have been lying quietly in the warm
hut at Gríshkino. He again sat up, turned about, muffled
himself up, and settled down once more.

Once he fancied that he heard a distant cock-crow. He felt
glad, turned down his coat-collar and listened with strained
attention, but in spite of all his efforts nothing could be heard
but the wind whistling between the shafts, the flapping of the
kerchief, and the snow pelting against the frame of the sledge.

Nikíta sat just as he had done all the time, not moving and
not even answering Vasíli Andréevich who had addressed him
a couple of times. 'He doesn't care a bit—he's probably
asleep!' thought Vasíli Andréevich with vexation, looking behind the sledge at Nikíta who was covered with a thick layer
of snow.

Vasíli Andréevich got up and lay down again some twenty
times. It seemed to him that the night would never end. 'It
must be getting near morning,' he thought, getting up and
looking around. 'Let's have a look at my watch. It will be cold
to unbutton, but if I only know that it's getting near morning I
shall at any rate feel more cheerful. We could begin harness-
ing.'

In the depth of his heart Vasíli Andréevich knew that it
could not yet be near morning, but he was growing more and
more afraid, and wished both to get to know and yet to
deceive himself. He carefully undid the fastening of his
sheepskin, pushed in his hand, and felt about for a long time
before he got to his waistcoat. With great difficulty he managed to draw out his silver watch with its enamelled flower

design, and tried to make out the time. He could not see anything without a light. Again he went down on his knees and elbows as he had done when he lighted a cigarette, got out his matches, and proceeded to strike one. This time he went to work more carefully, and feeling with his fingers for a match with the largest head and the greatest amount of phosphorus, lit it at the first try. Bringing the face of the watch under the light he could hardly believe his eyes. . . . It was only ten minutes past twelve. Almost the whole night was still before him.

'Oh, how long the night is!' he thought, feeling a cold shudder run down his back, and having fastened his fur coats again and wrapped himself up, he snuggled into a corner of the sledge intending to wait patiently. Suddenly, above the monotonous roar of the wind, he clearly distinguished another new and living sound. It steadily strengthened, and having become quite clear diminished just as gradually. Beyond all doubt it was a wolf, and he was so near that the movement of his jaws as he changed his cry was brought down the wind. Vasíli Andréevich turned back the collar of his coat and listened attentively. Mukhórty too strained to listen, moving his ears, and when the wolf had ceased its howling he shifted from foot to foot and gave a warning snort. After this Vasíli Andréevich could not fall asleep again or even calm himself. The more he tried to think of his accounts, his business, his reputation, his worth and his wealth, the more and more was he mastered by fear, and regrets that he had not stayed the night at Gríshkino dominated and mingled in all his thoughts.

'Devil take the forest! Things were all right without it, thank God. Ah, if we had only put up for the night!' he said to himself. 'They say it's drunkards that freeze,' he thought, 'and

I have had some drink.' And observing his sensations he noticed that he was beginning to shiver, without knowing whether it was from cold or from fear. He tried to wrap himself up and lie down as before, but could no longer do so. He could not stay in one position. He wanted to get up, to do something to master the gathering fear that was rising in him and against which he felt himself powerless. He again got out his cigarettes and matches, but only three matches were left and they were bad ones. The phosphorus rubbed off them all without lighting.

'The devil take you! Damned thing! Curse you!' he muttered, not knowing whom or what he was cursing, and he flung away the crushed cigarette. He was about to throw away the matchbox too, but checked the movement of his hand and put the box in his pocket instead. He was seized with such unrest that he could no longer remain in one spot. He climbed out of the sledge and standing with his back to the wind began to shift his belt again, fastening it lower down in the waist and tightening it.

'What's the use of lying and waiting for death? Better mount the horse and get away!' The thought suddenly occurred to him. 'The horse will move when he has someone on his back. As for him,' he thought of Nikíta—'it's all the same to him whether he lives or dies. What is his life worth? He won't grudge his life, but I have something to live for, thank God.'

He untied the horse, threw the reins over his neck and tried to mount, but his coats and boots were so heavy that he failed. Then he clambered up in the sledge and tried to mount from there, but the sledge tilted under his weight, and he failed again. At last he drew Mukhórty nearer to the sledge, cautiously balanced on one side of it, and managed to lie on his stomach across the horse's back. After lying like that for a while he shifted forward once and again, threw a leg over, and finally seated himself, supporting his feet on the loose breeching-straps. The shaking of the sledge awoke Nikíta. He raised himself, and it seemed to Vasíli Andréevich that he said something.

'Listen to such fools as you! Am I to die like this for nothing?' exclaimed Vasíli Andréevich. And tucking the loose skirts of his fur coat in under his knees, he turned the horse and rode away from the sledge in the direction in which he thought the forest and the forester's hut must be.

VII

From the time he had covered himself with the sackcloth and seated himself behind the sledge, Nikíta had not stirred. Like all those who live in touch with nature and have known want, he was patient and could wait for hours, even days, without growing restless or irritable. He heard his master call him, but did not answer because he did not want to move or talk. Though he still felt some warmth from the tea he had drunk and from his energetic struggle when clambering about in the snowdrift, he knew that this warmth would not last long and that he had no strength left to warm himself again by moving about, for he felt as tired as a horse when it stops and refuses to go further in spite of the whip, and its master sees that it must be fed before it can work again. The foot in the boot with a hole in it had already grown numb, and he could no longer feel his big toe. Besides that, his whole body began to feel colder and colder.

The thought that he might, and very probably would, die

that night occurred to him, but did not seem particularly unpleasant or dreadful. It did not seem particularly unpleasant, because his whole life had been not a continual holiday, but on the contrary an unceasing round of toil of which he was beginning to feel weary. And it did not seem particularly dreadful, because besides the masters he had served here, like Vasíli Andréevich, he always felt himself dependent on the Chief Master, who had sent him into this life, and he knew that when dying he would still be in that Master's power and would not be ill-used by Him. 'It seems a pity to give up what one is used to and accustomed to. But there's nothing to be done, I shall get used to the new things.'

'Sins?' he thought, and remembered his drunkenness, the money that had gone on drink, how he had offended his wife, his cursing, his neglect of church and of the fasts, and all the things the priest blamed him for at confession. 'Of course they are sins. But then, did I take them on of myself? That's evidently how God made me. Well, and the sins? Where am I to escape to?'

So at first he thought of what might happen to him that night, and then did not return to such thoughts but gave himself up to whatever recollections came into his head of themselves. Now he thought of Martha's arrival, of the drunkenness among the workers and his own renunciation of drink, then of their present journey and of Tarás's house and the talk about the breaking-up of the family, then of his own lad, and of Mukhórty now sheltered under the drugget, and then of his master who made the sledge creak as he tossed about in it. 'I expect you're sorry yourself that you started out, dear man,' he thought. 'It would seem hard to leave a life such as his! It's not like the likes of us.'

Then all these recollections began to grow confused and got mixed in his head, and he fell asleep.

But when Vasíli Andréevich, getting on the horse, jerked the sledge, against the back of which Nikíta was leaning, and it shifted away and hit him in the back with one of its runners, he awoke and had to change his position whether he liked it or not. Straightening his legs with difficulty and shaking the snow off them he got up, and an agonizing cold immediately penetrated his whole body. On making out what was happening he called to Vasíli Andréevich to leave him the drugget which the horse no longer needed, so that he might wrap himself in it.

But Vasíli Andréevich did not stop, but disappeared amid the powdery snow.

Left alone, Nikíta considered for a moment what he should do. He felt that he had not the strength to go off in search of a house. It was no longer possible to sit down in his old place— it was by now all filled with snow. He felt that he could not get warmer in the sledge either, for there was nothing to cover himself with, and his coat and sheepskin no longer warmed him at all. He felt as cold as though he had nothing on but a shirt. He became frightened. 'Lord, heavenly Father!' he muttered, and was comforted by the consciousness that he was not alone but that there was One who heard him and would not abandon him. He gave a deep sigh, and keeping the sackcloth over his head he got inside the sledge and lay down in the place where his master had been.

But he could not get warm in the sledge either. At first he shivered all over, then the shivering ceased and little by little he began to lose consciousness. He did not know whether he was dying or falling asleep, but felt equally prepared for the one as for the other.

VIII

Meanwhile Vasíli Andréevich, with his feet and the ends of the reins, urged the horse on in the direction in which for some reason he expected the forest and forester's hut to be. The snow covered his eyes and the wind seemed intent on stopping him, but bending forward and constantly lapping his coat over and pushing it between himself and the cold harness pad which prevented him from sitting properly, he kept urging the horse on. Mukhórty ambled on obediently though with difficulty, in the direction in which he was driven.

Vasíli Andréevich rode for about five minutes straight ahead, as he thought, seeing nothing but the horse's head and the white waste, and hearing only the whistle of the wind about the horse's ears and his coat collar.

Suddenly a dark patch showed up in front of him. His heart beat with joy, and he rode towards the object, already seeing in imagination the walls of village houses. But the dark patch was not stationary, it kept moving; and it was not a village but some tall stalks of wormwood sticking up through the snow on the boundary between two fields, and desperately tossing about under the pressure of the wind which beat it all to one side and whistled through it. The sight of that wormwood tormented by the pitiless wind made Vasíli Andréevich shudder, he knew not why, and he hurriedly began urging the horse on, not noticing that when riding up to the wormwood he had quite changed his direction and was now heading the opposite way, though still imagining that he was riding towards where the hut should be. But the horse kept making towards the right, and Vasíli Andréevich kept guiding it to the left.

Again something dark appeared in front of him. Again he rejoiced, convinced that now it was certainly a village. But once more it was the same boundary line overgrown with wormwood, once more the same wormwood desperately tossed by the wind and carrying unreasoning terror to his heart. But its being the same wormwood was not all, for beside it there was a horse's track partly snowed over. Vasíli Andréevich stopped, stooped down and looked carefully. It was a horse-track only partially covered with snow, and could be none but his own horse's hoofprints. He had evidently gone round in a small circle. 'I shall perish like that!' he thought, and not to give way to his terror he urged on the horse still more, peering into the snowy darkness in which he saw only flitting and fitful points of light. Once he thought he heard the barking of dogs or the howling of wolves, but the sounds were so faint and indistinct that he did not know whether he heard them or merely imagined them, and he stopped and began to listen intently.

Suddenly some terrible, deafening cry resounded near his ears, and everything shivered and shook under him. He seized Mukhórty's neck, but that too was shaking all over and the terrible cry grew still more frightful. For some seconds Vasíli Andréevich could not collect himself or understand what was happening. It was only that Mukhórty, whether to encourage himself or to call for help, had neighed loudly and resonantly. 'Ugh, you wretch! How you frightened me, damn you!' thought Vasíli Andréevich. But even when he understood the cause of his terror he could not shake it off.

'I must calm myself and think things over,' he said to himself, but yet he could not stop, and continued to urge the horse on, without noticing that he was now going with the wind instead of against it. His body, especially between his legs where it touched the pad of the harness and was not covered by his overcoats, was getting painfully cold, especially when the horse walked slowly. His legs and arms trembled and his breathing came fast. He saw himself perishing amid this dreadul snowy waste, and could see no means of escape.

Suddenly the horse under him tumbled into something and, sinking into a snow-drift, began to plunge and fell on his side. Vasíli Andréevich jumped off, and in so doing dragged to one side the breechband on which his foot was resting, and twisted round the pad to which he held as he dismounted. As soon as he had jumped off, the horse struggled to his feet, plunged forward, gave one leap and another, neighed again, and dragging the drugget and the breechband after him, disappeared, leaving Vasíli Andréevich alone on the snow-drift.

The latter pressed on after the horse, but the snow lay so deep and his coats were so heavy that, sinking above his knees at each step, he stopped breathless after taking not more than twenty steps. 'The copse, the oxen, the leasehold, the shop, the tavern, the house with the iron-roofed barn, and my heir,' thought he. 'How can I leave all that? What does this mean? It cannot be!' These thoughts flashed through his mind. Then he thought of the wormwood tossed by the wind, which he had twice ridden past, and he was seized with such terror that he did not believe in the reality of what was happening to him. 'Can this be a dream?' he thought, and tried to wake up but could not. It was real snow that lashed his face and covered him and chilled his right hand from which he had lost the glove, and this was a real desert in which he was now left alone like that wormwood, awaiting an inevitable, speedy, and meaningless death.

'Queen of Heaven! Holy Father Nicholas, teacher of temperance!' he thought, recalling the service of the day before and the holy icon with its black face and gilt frame, and the tapers which he sold to be set before that icon and which were almost immediately brought back to him scarcely burnt at all, and which he put away in the storechest. He began to pray to that same Nicholas the Wonder-Worker to save him, promising him a thanksgiving service and some candles. But he clearly and indubitably realized that the icon, its frame, the candles, the priest, and the thanksgiving service, though very important and necessary in church, could do nothing for him here, and that there was and could be no connexion between those candles and services and his present disastrous plight. 'I must not despair,' he thought. 'I must follow the horse's track before it is snowed under. He will lead me out, or I may even catch him. Only I must not hurry, or I shall stick fast and be more lost than ever.'

But in spite of his resolution to go quietly, he rushed foward and even ran, continually falling, getting up and falling again. The horse's track was already hardly visible in places where the snow did not lie deep. 'I am lost!' thought Vasíli Andréevich. 'I shall lose the track and not catch the horse.' But at that moment he saw something black. It was Mukhórty, and not only Mukhórty, but the sledge with the shafts and the kerchief. Mukhórty, with the sacking and the breechband twisted round to one side, was standing not in his former place but nearer to the shafts, shaking his head which the reins he was stepping on drew downwards. It turned out that Vasíli Andréevich had sunk in the same ravine Nikíta had previously

fallen into, and that Mukhórty had been bringing him back to
the sledge and he had got off his back no more than fifty paces
from where the sledge was.

IX

Having stumbled back to the sledge Vasíli Andréevich
caught hold of it and for a long time stood motionless, trying
to calm himself and recover his breath. Nikíta was not in his
former place, but something, already covered with snow, was
lying in the sledge and Vasíli Andréevich concluded that this
was Nikíta. His terror had now quite left him, and if he felt
any fear it was lest the dreadful terror should return that he
had experienced when on the horse and especially when he
was left alone in the snow-drift. At any cost he had to avoid
that terror, and to keep it away he must do something—oc-
cupy himself with something. And the first thing he did was to
turn his back to the wind and open his fur coat. Then, as soon
as he recovered his breath a little, he shook the snow out of his
boots and out of his left-hand glove (the right-hand glove was
hopelessly lost and by this time probably lying somewhere
under a dozen inches of snow); then as was his custom when
going out of his shop to buy grain from the peasants, he pulled
his girdle low down and tightened it and prepared for action.
The first thing that occurred to him was to free Mukhórty's leg
from the rein. Having done that, and tethered him to the iron
cramp at the front of the sledge where he had been before, he
was going round the horse's quarters to put the breechband
and pad straight and cover him with the cloth, but at that
moment he noticed that something was moving in the sledge
and Nikíta's head rose up out of the snow that covered it.

Nikíta, who was half frozen, rose with great difficulty and sat up, moving his hand before his nose in a strange manner just as if he were driving away flies. He waved his hand and said something, and seemed to Vasíli Andréevich to be calling him. Vasíli Andréevich left the cloth unadjusted and went up to the sledge.

'What is it?' he asked. 'What are you saying?'

'I'm dy . . . ing, that's what,' said Nikíta brokenly and with difficulty. 'Give what is owing to me to my lad, or to my wife, no matter.'

'Why, are you really frozen?' asked Vasíli Andréevich.

'I feel it's my death. Forgive me for Christ's sake . . .' said Nikíta in a tearful voice, continuing to wave his hand before his face as if driving away flies.

Vasíli Andréevich stood silent and motionless for half a minute. Then suddenly, with the same resolution with which he used to strike hands when making a good purchase, he took a step back and turning up his sleeves began raking the snow off Nikíta and out of the sledge. Having done this he hurriedly undid his girdle, opened out his fur coat, and having pushed Nikíta down, lay down on top of him, covering him not only with his fur coat but with the whole of his body, which glowed with warmth. After pushing the skirts of his coat between Nikíta and the sides of the sledge, and holding down its hem with his knees, Vasíli Andréevich lay like that face down, with his head pressed against the front of the sledge. Here he no longer heard the horse's movements or the whistling of the wind, but only Nikíta's breathing. At first and for a long time Nikíta lay motionless, then he sighed deeply and moved.

'There, and you say you are dying! Lie still and get warm, that's our way . . .' began Vasíli Andréevich.

But to his great surprise he could say no more, for tears came to his eyes and his lower jaw began to quiver rapidly. He stopped speaking and only gulped down the risings in his throat. 'Seems I was badly frightened and have gone quite weak,' he thought. But this weakness was not only not unpleasant, but gave him a peculiar joy such as he had never felt before.

'That's our way!' he said to himself, experiencing a strange and solemn tenderness. He lay like that for a long time wiping his eyes on the fur of his coat and tucking under his knee the right skirt, which the wind kept turning up.

But he longed so passionately to tell somebody of his joyful condition that he said: 'Nikíta!'

'It's comfortable, warm!' came a voice from beneath.

'There, you see, friend, I was going to perish. And you would have been frozen, and I should have . . .'

But again his jaws began to quiver and his eyes to fill with tears, and he could say no more.

'Well, never mind,' he thought. 'I know about myself what I know.'

He remained silent and lay like that for a long time.

Nikíta kept him warm from below and his fur coats from above. Only his hands, with which he kept his coatskirts down round Nikíta's sides, and his legs which the wind kept uncovering, began to freeze, especially his right hand which had no glove. But he did not think of his legs or of his hands but only of how to warm the peasant who was lying under him. He looked out several times at Mukhórty and could see that his back was uncovered and the drugget and breeching lying on the snow, and that he ought to get up and cover him, but he could not bring himself to leave Nikíta and disturb even for a moment the joyous condition he was in. He no longer felt any kind of terror.

'No fear, we shan't lose him this time!' he said to himself, referring to his getting the peasant warm with the same boast-fulness with which he spoke of his buying and selling.

Vasíli Andréevich lay in that way for one hour, another, and a third, but he was unconscious of the passage of time. At first impressions of the snow-storm, the sledge-shafts, and the horse with the shaft-bow shaking before his eyes, kept passing through his mind, then he remembered Nikíta lying under him, then recollections of the festival, his wife, the police-officer, and the box of candles, began to mingle with these; then again Nikíta, this time lying under that box, then the peasants, customers and traders, and the white walls of his house with its iron roof with Nikíta lying underneath, pre-sented themselves to his imagination. Afterwards all these impressions blended into one nothingness. As the colours of the rainbow unite into one white light, so all these different impressions mingled into one, and he fell asleep.

For a long time he slept without dreaming, but just before dawn the visions recommenced. It seemed to him that he was standing by the box of tapers and that Tíkhon's wife was asking for a five-kopek taper for the Church fête. He wished to take one out and give it to her, but his hands would not lift, being held tight in his pockets. He wanted to walk round the box but his feet would not move and his new clean goloshes had grown to the stone floor, and he could neither lift them nor get his feet out of the goloshes. Then the taper-box was no longer a box but a bed, and suddenly Vasíli Andréevich saw himself lying in his bed at home. He was lying in his bed and could not get up. Yet it was necessary for him to get up because Iván Matvéich, the police-officer, would soon call for him and he had to go with him—either to bargain for the forest or to put Mukhórty's breeching straight.

He asked his wife: 'Nikoláevna, hasn't he come yet?' 'No, he hasn't,' she replied. He heard someone drive up to the front steps. 'It must be him.' 'No, he's gone past.' 'Nikoláevna! I say, Nikoláevna, isn't he here yet?' 'No.' He was still lying on his bed and could not get up, but was always waiting. And this waiting was uncanny and yet joyful. Then suddenly his joy was completed. He whom he was expecting came; not Iván Matvéich the police-officer, but someone else—yet it was he whom he had been waiting for. He came and called him; and it was he who had called him and told him to lie down on Nikíta. And Vasíli Andréevich was glad that that one had come for him.

'I'm coming!' he cried joyfully, and that cry awoke him, but woke him up not at all the same person he had been when he fell asleep. He tried to get up but could not, tried to move his arm and could not, to move his leg and also could not, to turn his head and could not. He was surprised but not at all disturbed by this. He understood that this was death, and was not at all disturbed by that either. He remembered that Nikíta was lying under him and that he had got warm and was alive, and it seemed to him that he was Nikíta and Nikíta was he, and that his life was not in himself but in Nikíta. He strained his ears and heard Nikíta breathing and even slightly snoring. 'Nikíta is alive, so I too am alive!' he said to himself triumphantly.

And he remembered his money, his shop, his house, the

buying and selling, and Mirónov's millions, and it was hard for him to understand why that man, called Vasíli Brekhunóv, had troubled himself with all those things with which he had been troubled.

'Well, it was because he did not know what the real thing was,' he thought, concerning that Vasíli Brekhunóv. 'He did not know, but now I know and know for sure. Now I know!' And again he heard the voice of the one who had called him before. 'I'm coming! Coming!' he responded gladly, and his whole being was filled with joyful emotion. He felt himself free and that nothing could hold him back any longer.

After that Vasíli Andréevich neither saw, heard, nor felt anything more in this world.

All around the snow still eddied. The same whirlwinds of snow circled about, covering the dead Vasíli Andréevich's fur coat, the shivering Mukhórty, the sledge, now scarcely to be seen, and Nikíta lying at the bottom of it, kept warm beneath his dead master.

X

Nikíta awoke before daybreak. He was aroused by the cold that had begun to creep down his back. He had dreamt that he was coming from the mill with a load of his master's flour and when crossing the stream had missed the bridge and let the cart get stuck. And he saw that he had crawled under the cart and was trying to lift it by arching his back. But strange to say the cart did not move, it stuck to his back and he could neither lift it nor get out from under it. It was crushing the whole of his loins. And how cold it felt! Evidently he must crawl out. 'Have done!' he exclaimed to whoever was pressing the cart down on him. 'Take out the sacks!' But the cart pressed down colder and colder, and then he heard a strange knocking, awoke completely, and remembered everything. The cold cart was his dead and frozen master lying upon him. And the knock was produced by Mukhórty, who had twice struck the sledge with his hoof.

'Andréevich! Eh, Andréevich!' Nikíta called cautiously, beginning to realize the truth, and straightening his back. But Vasíli Andréevich did not answer and his stomach and legs were stiff and cold and heavy like iron weights.

'He must have died! May the Kingdom of Heaven be his!' thought Nikíta.

He turned his head, dug with his hand through the snow about him and opened his eyes. It was daylight; the wind was whistling as before between the shafts, and the snow was falling in the same way, except that it was no longer driving against the frame of the sledge but silently covered both sledge and horse deeper and deeper, and neither the horse's movements nor his breathing were any longer to be heard.

'He must have frozen too,' thought Nikíta of Mukhórty, and indeed those hoof knocks against the sledge, which had awakened Nikíta, were the last efforts the already numbed Mukhórty had made to keep on his feet before dying.

'O Lord God, it seems Thou art calling me too!' said Nikíta. 'Thy Holy Will be done. But it's uncanny. . . . Still, a man can't die twice and must die once. If only it would come soon!'

And he again drew in his head, closed his eyes, and became unconscious, fully convinced that now he was certainly and finally dying.

It was not till noon that day that peasants dug Vasíli Andréevich and Nikíta out of the snow with their shovels, not
more than seventy yards from the road and less than half a
mile from the village.

The snow had hidden the sledge, but the shafts and the
kerchief tied to them were still visible. Mukhórty, buried up to
his belly in snow, with the breeching and drugget hanging
down, stood all white, his dead head pressed against his frozen
throat: icicles hung from his nostrils, his eyes were covered
with hoar-frost as though filled with tears, and he had grown
so thin in that one night that he was nothing but skin and
bone.

Vasíli Andréevich was stiff as a frozen carcass, and when
they rolled him off Nikíta his legs remained apart and his arms
stretched out as they had been. His bulging hawk eyes were
frozen, and his open mouth under his clipped moustache was
full of snow. But Nikíta though chilled through was still alive.
When he had been brought to, he felt sure that he was already
dead and that what was taking place with him was no longer
happening in this world but in the next. When he heard the
peasants shouting as they dug him out and rolled the frozen
body of Vasíli Andréevich from off him, he was at first surprised that in the other world peasants should be shouting in
the same old way and had the same kind of body, and then
when he realized that he was still in this world he was sorry
rather than glad, especially when he found that the toes on
both his feet were frozen.

Nikíta lay in hospital for two months. They cut off three of
his toes, but the others recovered so that he was still able to
work and went on living for another twenty years, first as a
farm-labourer, then in his old age as a watchman. He died at

home as he had wished, only this year, under the icons with a
lighted taper in his hands. Before he died he asked his wife's
forgiveness and forgave her for the cooper. He also took leave
of his son and grandchildren, and died sincerely glad that he
was relieving his son and daughter-in-law of the burden of
having to feed him, and that he was now really passing from
this life of which he was weary into that other life which every
year and every hour grew clearer and more desirable to him.
Whether he is better or worse off there where he awoke after
his death, whether he was disappointed or found there what
he expected, we shall all soon learn.

BHAGAVAD-GITA, *or Song of God, is generally supposed to have been written between the fifth and second centuries B.C. Nothing is known of its origin.*

CONTENTS

I.	The Sorrow of Arjuna	1
II.	The Yoga of Knowledge	6
III.	Karma Yoga	16
IV.	Renunciation Through Knowledge	21
V.	The Yoga of Renunciation	28
VI.	The Yoga of Meditation	35
VII.	Knowledge and Experience	42
VIII.	The Way to Eternal Brahman	46
IX.	The Yoga of Mysticism	51
X.	Divine Glory	58
XI.	The Vision of God in His Universal Form	63
XII.	The Yoga of Devotion	69
XIII.	The Field and Its Knower	72
XIV.	The Three Gunas	78
XV.	Devotion to the Supreme Spirit	82
XVI.	Divine and Demonic Tendencies	86
XVII.	Three Kinds of Faith	88
XVIII.	The Yoga of Renunciation	91

I. The Sorrow of Arjuna*

Tell me, Sanjaya, what my sons and the sons of Pandu did, when they gathered on the sacred field of Kurukshetra eager for battle?

(In the following verses, Sanjaya describes how Duryodhana, seeing the opposing army of Pandavas in array, went to Drona, his teacher, and expressed his fear that their own army was the weaker of the two, although numerically larger. He named the leading warriors on either side. This is one of the catalogue-passages to be found in nearly all epics. It need not be translated in full.

In order to raise Duryodhana's failing courage, Bhisma, the commander-in-chief, sounded his conch-shell horn. But this was ill-advised—for the enemy chieftains immediately blew their horns in reply, and made much more noise. The trumpeting 'resounded through heaven and earth,' we are told.

Arjuna now addresses Krishna, his friend and charioteer.)

ARJUNA:
Krishna the changeless,
Halt my chariot
There where the warriors,
Bold for the battle,
Face their foemen.
Between the armies

* The accent is on the first syllable.

1

There let me see them,
The men I must fight with,
Gathered together
Now at the bidding
Of him their leader,
Blind Dhritarashtra's
Evil offspring:
Such are my foes
In the war that is coming.

SANJAYA (TO DHRITARASHTRA):

Then Krishna, subduer of the senses, thus requested by
Arjuna, the conqueror of sloth,* drove that most splendid
of chariots into a place between the two armies, confronting
Bhisma, Drona and all those other rulers of the earth. And
he said: 'O Prince, behold the assembled Kurus!'

Then the prince looked on the array, and in both armies
he recognized fathers and grandfathers, teachers, uncles,
sons, brothers, grandsons, fathers-in-law, dear friends, and
many other familiar faces.

When Kunti's son saw all those ranks of kinsmen he
was filled with deep compassion, and he spoke despairingly,
as follows:

ARJUNA:

Krishna, Krishna,
Now as I look on
These my kinsmen
Arrayed for battle,
My limbs are weakened,

---

* Arjuna is traditionally supposed to have lived entirely without
sleep. We may take this to mean that he had overcome all forms of
laziness.

My mouth is parching,
My body trembles,
My hair stands upright,
My skin seems burning,
The bow Gandiva
Slips from my hand,
My brain is whirling
Round and round,
I can stand no longer:
Krishna, I see such
Omens of evil!
What can we hope from
This killing of kinsmen?
What do I want with
Victory, empire,
Or their enjoyment?
O Govinda,*
How can I care for
Power or pleasure,
My own life, even,
When all these others,
Teachers, fathers,
Grandfathers, uncles,
Sons and brothers,
Husbands of sisters,
Grandsons and cousins,
For whose sake only
I could enjoy them
Stand here ready
To risk blood and wealth
In war against us?

* One of the names of Sri Krishna, meaning Giver of Enlightenment.

Knower of all things,
Though they should slay me
How could I harm them?
I cannot wish it:
Never, never,
Not though it won me
The throne of the three worlds;
How much the less for
Earthly lordship!

Krishna, hearing
The prayers of all men,
Tell me how can
We hope to be happy
Slaying the sons
Of Dhritarashtra?
Evil they may be,
Worst of the wicked,
Yet if we kill them
Our sin is greater.
How could we dare spill
The blood that unites us?
Where is joy in
The killing of kinsmen?

Foul their hearts are
With greed, and blinded:
They see no evil
In breaking of blood-bonds,
See no sin
In treason to comrades.
But we, clear-sighted,
Scanning the ruin
Of families scattered,

Should we not shun
This crime, O Krishna?

We know what fate falls
On families broken:
The rites are forgotten,
Vice rots the remnant
Defiling the women,
And from their corruption
Comes mixing of castes:
The curse of confusion
Degrades the victims
And damns the destroyers.
The rice and the water
No longer are offered;
The ancestors also
Must fall dishonoured
From home in heaven.

Such is the crime
Of the killers of kinsmen:
The ancient, the sacred,
Is broken, forgotten.
Such is the doom
Of the lost, without caste-rites:
Darkness and doubting
And hell for ever.

What is this crime
I am planning, O Krishna?
Murder most hateful,
Murder of brothers!
Am I indeed
So greedy for greatness?

Rather than this
Let the evil children
Of Dhritarashtra
Come with their weapons
Against me in battle:
I shall not struggle,
I shall not strike them.
Now let them kill me,
That will be better.

SANJAYA:

Having spoken thus, Arjuna threw aside his arrows and his bow in the midst of the battlefield. He sat down on the seat of the chariot, and his heart was overcome with sorrow.

II. *The Yoga of Knowledge*

SANJAYA:

Then his eyes filled with tears, and his heart grieved and was bewildered with pity. And Sri Krishna spoke to him, saying:

SRI KRISHNA:

Arjuna, is this hour of battle the time for scruples and fancies? Are they worthy of you, who seek enlightenment? Any brave man who merely hopes for fame or heaven would despise them.

What is this weakness? It is beneath you. Is it for nothing men call you the foe-consumer? Shake off this cowardice, Arjuna. Stand up.

ARJUNA:

Bhisma and Drona are noble and ancient, worthy of the deepest reverence. How can I greet them with arrows, in battle? If I kill them, how can I ever enjoy my wealth, or any other pleasure? It will be cursed with blood-guilt. I would much rather spare them, and eat the bread of a beggar.

Which will be worse, to win this war, or to lose it? I scarcely know. Even the sons of Dhritarashtra stand in the enemy ranks. If we kill them, none of us will wish to live.

Is this real compassion that I feel, or only a delusion? My mind gropes about in darkness. I cannot see where my duty lies. Krishna, I beg you, tell me frankly and clearly what I ought to do. I am your disciple. I put myself into your hands. Show me the way.

> Not this world's kingdom,
> Supreme, unchallenged,
> No, nor the throne
> Of the gods in heaven,
> Could ease this sorrow
> That numbs my senses!

SANJAYA:

When Arjuna, the foe-consuming, the never-slothful, had spoken thus to Govinda, ruler of the senses, he added: 'I will not fight,' and was silent.

Then to him who thus sorrowed between the two armies, the ruler of the senses spoke, smiling:

SRI KRISHNA:

Your words are wise, Arjuna, but your sorrow is for nothing. The truly wise mourn neither for the living nor for the dead.

There was never a time when I did not exist, nor you, nor any of these kings. Nor is there any future in which we shall cease to be.

Just as the dweller in this body passes through childhood,

youth and old age, so at death he merely passes into another kind of body. The wise are not deceived by that.

Feelings of heat and cold, pleasure and pain, are caused by the contact of the senses with their objects. They come and they go, never lasting long. You must accept them.

A serene spirit accepts pleasure and pain with an even mind, and is unmoved by either. He alone is worthy of immortality.

That which is non-existent can never come into being, and that which is can never cease to be. Those who have known the inmost Reality know also the nature of *is* and *is not*.

That Reality which pervades the universe is indestructible. No one has power to change the Changeless.

Bodies are said to die, but That which possesses the body is eternal. It cannot be limited, or destroyed. Therefore you must fight.

> Some say this Atman*
> Is slain, and others
> Call It the slayer:
> They know nothing.
> How can It slay
> Or who shall slay It?
>
> Know this Atman
> Unborn, undying,
> Never ceasing,
> Never beginning,
> Deathless, birthless,
> Unchanging for ever.
> How can It die
> The death of the body?

* The Godhead that is within every being.

Knowing It birthless,
Knowing It deathless,
Knowing It endless,
For ever unchanging,
Dream not you do
The deed of the killer,
Dream not the power
Is yours to command it.

Worn-out garments
Are shed by the body:
Worn-out bodies
Are shed by the dweller
Within the body.
New bodies are donned
By the dweller, like garments.

Not wounded by weapons,
Not burned by fire,
Not dried by the wind,
Not wetted by water:
Such is the Atman,
Not dried, not wetted,
Not burned, not wounded,
Innermost element,
Everywhere, always,
Being of beings,
Changeless, eternal,
For ever and ever.

This Atman cannot be manifested to the senses, or thought about by the mind. It is not subject to modification. Since you know this, you should not grieve.

But if you should suppose this Atman to be subject to

constant birth and death, even then you ought not to be sorry.

Death is certain for the born. Rebirth is certain for the dead. You should not grieve for what is unavoidable.

Before birth, beings are not manifest to our human senses. In the interim between birth and death, they are manifest. At death they return to the unmanifest again. What is there in all this to grieve over?

There are some who have actually looked upon the Atman, and understood It, in all Its wonder. Others can only speak of It as wonderful beyond their understanding. Others know of Its wonder by hearsay. And there are others who are told about It and do not understand a word.

He Who dwells within all living bodies remains for ever indestructible. Therefore, you should never mourn for any one.

Even if you consider this from the standpoint of your own caste-duty, you ought not to hesitate; for, to a warrior, there is nothing nobler than a righteous war. Happy are the warriors to whom a battle such as this comes: it opens a door to heaven.

But if you refuse to fight this righteous war, you will be turning aside from your duty. You will be a sinner, and disgraced. People will speak ill of you throughout the ages. To a man who values his honour, that is surely worse than death. The warrior-chiefs will believe it was fear that drove you from the battle; you will be despised by those who have admired you so long. Your enemies, also, will slander your courage. They will use the words which should never be spoken. What could be harder to bear than that?

Die, and you win heaven. Conquer, and you enjoy the earth. Stand up now, son of Kunti, and resolve to fight. Realize that pleasure and pain, gain and loss, victory and defeat, are all one and the same: then go into battle. Do this and you cannot commit any sin.

I have explained to you the true nature of the Atman. Now listen to the method of Karma Yoga.* If you can understand and follow it, you will be able to break the chains of desire which bind you to your actions.

In this yoga, even the abortive attempt is not wasted. Nor can it produce a contrary result. Even a little practise of this yoga will save you from the terrible wheel of re-birth and death.

In this yoga, the will is directed singly toward one ideal. When a man lacks this discrimination, his will wanders in all directions, after innumerable aims. Those who lack discrimination may quote the letter of the scripture, but they are really denying its inner truth. They are full of worldly desires, and hungry for the rewards of heaven. They use beautiful figures of speech. They teach elaborate rituals which are supposed to obtain pleasure and power for those who perform them. But, actually, they understand nothing except the law of Karma, that chains men to rebirth.

Those whose discrimination is stolen away by such talk grow deeply attached to pleasure and power. And so they are unable to develop that concentration of the will which leads a man to absorption in God.

* Karma: (1) Work, a deed.
        (2) Effect of a deed.
        (3) Law of causation governing action and its effects in the physical and psychological plane.

Yoga: (1) Union with God.
       (2) A prescribed path of spiritual life. The various yogas are, therefore, different paths to union with God. Karma Yoga is the path of selfless, God-dedicated action.

Yogi: One who practises yoga.

The Vedas* teach us about the three gunas† and their functions. You, Arjuna, must overcome the three gunas. You must be free from the pairs of opposites.‡ Poise your mind in tranquillity. Take care neither to acquire nor to hoard. Be established in the consciousness of the Atman, always.

When the whole country is flooded, the reservoir becomes superfluous. So, to the illumined seer, the Vedas are all superfluous.

paul "beyond the law"

You have the right to work, but for the work's sake only. You have no right to the fruits of work. Desire for the fruits of work must never be your motive in working. Never give way to laziness, either.

Perform every action with your heart fixed on the Supreme Lord. Renounce attachment to the fruits. Be even-tempered in success and failure; for it is this evenness of temper which is meant by yoga.

Work done with anxiety about results is far inferior to work done without such anxiety, in the calm of self-surrender. Seek refuge in the knowledge of Brahman.§ They who work selfishly for results are miserable.

In the calm of self-surrender you can free yourself from the bondage of virtue and vice during this very life. Devote yourself, therefore, to reaching union with Brahman. To unite the heart with Brahman and then to act: that is the secret of non-attached work. In the calm of self-surrender, the seers renounce the fruits of their actions, and so reach

* Revealed scriptures of the Hindus. The reference here is to the ritualistic portion of the Vedas.

† The three forces or substances composing the universe of mind and matter. They are sattwa, rajas and tamas.

‡ Heat and cold, pleasure and pain, etc. The seeming contradictions of the relative world.

§ The Godhead.

enlightenment. Then they are free from the bondage of rebirth, and pass to that state which is beyond all evil.

When your intellect has cleared itself of its delusions, you will become indifferent to the results of all action, present or future. At present, your intellect is bewildered by conflicting interpretations of the scriptures. When it can rest, steady and undistracted, in contemplation of the Atman, then you will reach union with the Atman.

ARJUNA:

Krishna, how can one identify a man who is firmly established and absorbed in Brahman? In what manner does an illumined soul speak? How does he sit? How does he walk?

SRI KRISHNA:

He knows bliss in the Atman
And wants nothing else.
Cravings torment the heart:
He renounces cravings.
I call him illumined.

Not shaken by adversity,
Not hankering after happiness:
Free from fear, free from anger,
Free from the things of desire.
I call him a seer, and illumined.
The bonds of his flesh are broken.
He is lucky, and does not rejoice:
He is unlucky, and does not weep.
I call him illumined.

The tortoise can draw in his legs:
The seer can draw in his senses.
I call him illumined.

The abstinent run away from what they desire
But carry their desires with them.
When a man enters Reality,
He leaves his desires behind him.

Even a mind that knows the path
Can be dragged from the path:
The senses are so unruly.
But he controls the senses
And recollects the mind.
And fixes it on me.
I call him illumined.

Thinking about sense-objects
Will attach you to sense-objects;
Grow attached, and you become addicted;
Thwart your addiction, it turns to anger;
Be angry, and you confuse your mind;
Confuse your mind, you forget the lesson of experience;
Forget experience, you lose discrimination;
Lose discrimination, and you miss life's only purpose.

When he has no lust, no hatred,
A man walks safely among the things of lust and hatred.
To obey the Atman
Is his peaceful joy:
Sorrow melts
Into that clear peace:
His quiet mind
Is soon established in peace.

The uncontrolled mind
Does not guess that the Atman is present:
How can it meditate?

Without meditation, where is peace?
Without peace, where is happiness?

The wind turns a ship
From its course upon the waters:
The wandering winds of the senses
Cast man's mind adrift
And turn his better judgment from its course.
When a man can still the senses
I call him illumined.
The recollected mind is awake
In the knowledge of the Atman
Which is dark night to the ignorant:
The ignorant are awake in their sense-life
Which they think is daylight:
To the seer it is darkness.

Water flows continually into the ocean
But the ocean is never disturbed:
Desire flows into the mind of the seer
But he is never disturbed.
The seer knows peace:
The man who stirs up his own lusts
Can never know peace.
He knows peace who has forgotten desire.
He lives without craving:
Free from ego, free from pride.

This is the state of enlightenment in Brahman:
A man does not fall back from it
Into delusion.
Even at the moment of death
He is alive in that enlightenment:
Brahman and he are one.

III. Karma Yoga

ARJUNA:

But, Krishna, if you consider knowledge of Brahman superior to any sort of action, why are you telling me to do these terrible deeds?

Your statements seem to contradict each other. They confuse my mind. Tell me one definite way of reaching the highest good.

SRI KRISHNA:

I have already told you that, in this world, aspirants may find enlightenment by two different paths. For the contemplative is the path of knowledge: for the active is the path of selfless action.

Freedom from activity is never achieved by abstaining from action. Nobody can become perfect by merely ceasing to act. In fact, nobody can ever rest from his activity* even for a moment. All are helplessly forced to act, by the gunas.

A man who renounces certain physical actions but still lets his mind dwell on the objects of his sensual desire, is deceiving himself. He can only be called a hypocrite. The truly admirable man controls his senses by the power of his will. All his actions are disinterested. All are directed along the path to union with Brahman.

Activity is better than inertia. Act, but with self-control. If you are lazy, you cannot even sustain your own body.

The world is imprisoned in its own activity, except when actions are performed as worship of God. Therefore

* Here 'activity' includes mental action, conscious and subconscious.

you must perform every action sacramentally, and be free
from all attachments to results.

> In the beginning
> The Lord of beings
> Created all men,
> To each his duty.
> 'Do this,' He said,
> 'And you shall prosper.
> Duty well done
> Fulfils desire
> Like Kamadhenu*
> The wish-fulfiller.'
>
> 'Doing of duty
> Honours the devas:†
> To you the devas
> In turn will be gracious:
> Each honouring other,
> Man reaches the Highest.
> Please the devas:
> Your prayer will be granted.'
> But he who enjoys the devas' bounty
> Showing no thanks,
> He thieves from the devas.
>
> Pious men eat
> What the gods leave over
> After the offering:
> Thus they are sinless.
> But those ungodly
> Cooking good food
> For the greed of their stomachs

* A legendary cow, mentioned in the Mahabharata.
† The inhabitants of heaven.

Sin as they eat it.
Food quickens the life-sperm:
Food grows from the rainfall
Called down out of heaven
By sacrifice offered:
Sacrifice speaks
Through the act of the ritual.
This is the ritual
Taught by the sacred
Scriptures that spring
From the lips of the Changeless:
Know therefore that Brahman
The all-pervading
Is dwelling for ever
Within this ritual.

If a man plays no part
In the acts thus appointed
His living is evil
His joy is in lusting.
Know this, O Prince:
His life is for nothing.

But when a man has found delight and satisfaction and
peace in the Atman, then he is no longer obliged to perform
any kind of action. He has nothing to gain in this world by
action, and nothing to lose by refraining from action. He
is independent of everybody and everything. Do your duty,
always; but without attachment. That is how a man reaches
the ultimate Truth; by working without anxiety about results. In fact, Janaka* and many others reached enlightenment, simply because they did their duty in this spirit.
Your motive in working should be to set others, by your
example, on the path of duty.

* A royal saint mentioned in the Upanishads.

Whatever a great man does, ordinary people will imitate; they follow his example. Consider me: I am not bound by any sort of duty. There is nothing, in all the three worlds, which I do not already possess; nothing I have yet to acquire. But I go on working, nevertheless. If I did not continue to work untiringly as I do, mankind would still follow me, no matter where I led them. Suppose I were to stop? They would all be lost. The result would be caste-mixture and universal destruction.

> The ignorant work
> For the fruit of their action:
> The wise must work also
> Without desire
> Pointing man's feet
> To the path of his duty.

> Let the wise beware
> Lest they bewilder
> The minds of the ignorant
> Hungry for action:
> Let them show by example
> How work is holy
> When the heart of the worker
> Is fixed on the Highest.

Every action is really performed by the gunas. Man, deluded by his egoism, thinks: 'I am the doer.' But he who has the true insight into the operations of the gunas and their various functions, knows that when senses attach themselves to objects, gunas are merely attaching themselves to gunas. Knowing this, he does not become attached to his actions.

The illumined soul must not create confusion in the minds of the ignorant by refraining from work. The ignorant, in their delusion, identify the Atman with the gunas.

They become tied to the senses and the action of the senses.

Shake off this fever of ignorance. Stop hoping for worldly rewards. Fix your mind on the Atman. Be free from the sense of ego. Dedicate all your actions to me. Then go forward and fight.

If a man keeps following my teaching with faith in his heart, and does not make mental reservations, he will be released from the bondage of his karma. But those who scorn my teaching, and do not follow it, are lost. They are without spiritual discrimination. All their knowledge is a delusion.

Even a wise man acts according to the tendencies of his own nature. All living creatures follow their tendencies. What use is any external restraint? The attraction and aversion which the senses feel for different objects are natural. But you must not give way to such feelings; they are obstacles.

It is better to do your own duty, however imperfectly, than to assume the duties of another person, however successfully. Prefer to die doing your own duty: the duty of another will bring you into great spiritual danger.

ARJUNA:

Krishna, what is it that makes a man do evil, even against his own will; under compulsion, as it were?

SRI KRISHNA:

The rajo-guna has two faces,
Rage and lust: the ravenous, the deadly:
Recognize these: they are your enemies.

Smoke hides fire,
Dust hides a mirror,
The womb hides the embryo:
By lust the Atman is hidden.

Lust hides the Atman in its hungry flames,
The wise man's faithful foe.
Intellect, senses and mind
Are fuel to its fire:
Thus it deludes
The dweller in the body,
Bewildering his judgment.

Therefore, Arjuna, you must first control your senses, then kill this evil thing which obstructs discriminative knowledge and realization of the Atman.

The senses are said to be higher than the sense-objects. The mind is higher than the senses. The intelligent will is higher than the mind. What is higher than the intelligent will? The Atman Itself.

You must know Him who is above the intelligent will. Get control of the mind through spiritual discrimination. Then destroy your elusive enemy, who wears the form of lust.

IV. Renunciation Through Knowledge

SRI KRISHNA:

Foe-consumer,
Now I have shown you
Yoga that leads
To the truth undying.
I taught this yoga
First to Vivaswat,
Vivaswat taught it
In turn to Manu,
Next Ikshaku
Learnt it from Manu,

And so the sages
In royal succession
Carried it onward
From teacher to teacher,
Till at length it was lost,
Throughout ages forgotten.

ARJUNA:

Vivaswat was born long before you. How am I to believe
that you were the first to teach this yoga?

SRI KRISHNA:

You and I, Arjuna,
Have lived many lives.
I remember them all:
You do not remember.

I am the birthless, the deathless,
Lord of all that breathes.
I seem to be born:
It is only seeming,
Only my Maya.*
I am still master
Of my Prakriti,*
The power that makes me.

When goodness grows weak,
When evil increases,
I make myself a body.

In every age I come back
To deliver the holy,
To destroy the sin of the sinner,

* The two words are interchangeable. They both refer to the
creative power of Brahman, and, hence, to the basic stuff of which
the universe is made.

To establish righteousness.

He who knows the nature
Of my task and my holy birth
Is not reborn
When he leaves this body:
He comes to me.

Flying from fear,
From lust and anger,
He hides in me
His refuge, his safety:
Burnt clean in the blaze of my being,

In me many find home.
Whatever wish men bring me in worship,
That wish I grant them.
Whatever path men travel
Is my path:
No matter where they walk
It leads to me.

Most men worship the gods because they want success in their worldly undertakings. This kind of material success can be gained very quickly, here on earth.

I established the four castes, which correspond to the different types of guna and karma. I am their author; nevertheless, you must realize that I am beyond action and changeless. Action does not contaminate me. I have no desire at all for the fruits of action. A man who understands my nature in this respect will never become the slave of his own activity. Because they understood this, the ancient seekers for liberation could safely engage in action. You, too, must do your work in the spirit of those early seers.

What is action? What is inaction? Even the wise are

puzzled by this question. Therefore, I will tell you what action is. When you know that, you will be free from all impurity. You must learn what kind of work to do, what kind of work to avoid, and how to reach a state of calm detachment from your work. The real nature of action is hard to understand.

He who sees the inaction that is in action, and the action that is in inaction, is wise indeed. Even when he is engaged in action he remains poised in the tranquillity of the Atman.

> The seers say truly
> That he is wise
> Who acts without lust or scheming
> For the fruit of the act:
> His act falls from him,
> Its chain is broken,
> Melted in the flame of my knowledge.
> Turning his face from the fruit,
> He needs nothing:
> The Atman is enough.
> He acts, and is beyond action.
>
> Not hoping, not lusting,
> Bridling body and mind,
> He calls nothing his own:
> He acts, and earns no evil.
>
> What God's Will gives
> He takes, and is contented.
> Pain follows pleasure,
> He is not troubled:
> Gain follows loss,
> He is indifferent:

Of whom should he be jealous?
He acts, and is not bound by his action.

When the bonds are broken
His illumined heart
Beats in Brahman:
His every action
Is worship of Brahman:
Can such acts bring evil?
Brahman is the ritual,
Brahman is the offering,
Brahman is he who offers
To the fire that is Brahman.
If a man sees Brahman
In every action,
He will find Brahman.*

Some yogis merely worship the devas. Others are able, by the grace of the Atman, to meditate on the identity of the Atman with Brahman. For these, the Atman is the offering, and Brahman the sacrificial fire into which It is offered.

Some withdraw all their senses from contact with exterior sense-objects. For these, hearing and other senses are the offering, and self-discipline the sacrificial fire. Others allow their minds and senses to wander unchecked, and try to see Brahman within all exterior sense-objects. For these, sound and the other sense-objects are the offering, and sense-enjoyment the sacrificial fire.

Some renounce all the actions of the senses, and all the functions of the vital force. For these, such actions and functions are the offering, and the practice of self-control

* This verse is chanted by all Hindu monks as a grace before meals. In this case 'the fire' is regarded as the fire of hunger.

is the sacrificial fire, kindled by knowledge of the Atman.

Then there are others whose way of worship is to renounce sense-objects and material possessions. Others set themselves austerities and spiritual disciplines: that is their way of worship. Others worship through the practice of Raja Yoga.* Others who are earnest seekers for perfection and men of strict vows, study and meditate on the truths of the scriptures. That is their way of worship.

Others are intent on controlling the vital energy; so they practise breathing-exercises—inhalation, exhalation, and the stoppage of the breath. Others mortify their flesh by fasting, to weaken their sensual desires, and thus achieve self-control.

All these understand the meaning of sacrificial worship. Through worship, their sins are consumed away. They eat the food which has been blessed in the sacrifice. Thus they obtain immortality and reach eternal Brahman. He who does not worship God cannot be happy even in this world. What, then, can he expect from any other?

All these, and many other forms of worship are prescribed by the scriptures.

All of them involve the doing of some kind of action. When you fully understand this, you will be made free in Brahman.

The form of worship which consists in contemplating Brahman is superior to ritualistic worship with material offerings.

* The path of Raja Yoga is said to have eight steps: (1) Practice of the moral virtues. (2) Regular habits of purity, contentment, study, austerity and self-surrender to God. (3) Posture. (4) Control of the vital energy by breathing-exercises. (5) Withdrawal of the mind from sense-objects. (6) Concentration. (7) Meditation. (8) Absorption in the consciousness of God.

The reward of all action is to be found in enlightenment.

Those illumined souls who have realized the Truth will instruct you in the knowledge of Brahman, if you will prostrate yourself before them, question them and serve them as a disciple.

When you have reached enlightenment, ignorance will delude you no longer. In the light of that knowledge you will see the entire creation within your own Atman and in me.

> And though you were the foulest of sinners,
> This knowledge alone would carry you
> Like a raft, over all your sin.
>
> The blazing fire turns wood to ashes:
> The fire of knowledge turns all karmas to ashes.
>
> On earth there is no purifier
> As great as this knowledge,
> When a man is made perfect in yoga,
> He knows its truth within his heart.
> The man of faith,
> Whose heart is devoted,
> Whose senses are mastered:
> He finds Brahman.
> Enlightened, he passes
> At once to the highest,
> The peace beyond passion.
>
> The ignorant, the faithless, the doubter
> Goes to his destruction.
> How shall he enjoy
> This world, or the next,
> Or any happiness?

When a man can act without desire,
Through practice of yoga;
When his doubts are torn to shreds,
Because he knows Brahman;
When his heart is poised
In the being of the Atman
No bonds can bind him.

Still I can see it:
A doubt that lingers
Deep in your heart
Brought forth by delusion.
You doubt the truth
Of the living Atman.

Where is your sword
Discrimination?
Draw it and slash
Delusion to pieces.
Then arise
O son of Bharata:
Take your stand
In Karma Yoga.

V. *The Yoga of Renunciation*

ARJUNA:

You speak so highly of the renunciation of action; yet you ask me to follow the yoga of action. Now tell me definitely: which of these is better?

SRI KRISHNA:

Action rightly renounced brings freedom:
Action rightly performed brings freedom:

Both are better
Than mere shunning of action.

When a man lacks lust and hatred,
His renunciation does not waver.
He neither longs for one thing
Nor loathes its opposite:
The chains of his delusion
Are soon cast off.

The yoga of action, say the ignorant,
Is different from the yoga of the knowledge of Brahman.

The wise see knowledge and action as one:
They see truly.
Take either path
And tread it to the end:
The end is the same.
There the followers of action
Meet the seekers after knowledge
In equal freedom.

It is hard to renounce action
Without following the yoga of action.
This yoga purifies
The man of meditation,
Bringing him soon to Brahman.

When the heart is made pure by that yoga,
When the body is obedient,
When the senses are mastered,
When man knows that his Atman
Is the Atman in all creatures,
Then let him act,
Untainted by action.

The illumined soul
Whose heart is Brahman's heart
Thinks always: 'I am doing nothing.'
No matter what he sees,
Hears, touches, smells, eats;
No matter whether he is moving,
Sleeping, breathing, speaking,
Excreting, or grasping something with his hand,
Or opening his eyes,
Or closing his eyes:
This he knows always:
'I am not seeing, I am not hearing:
It is the senses that see and hear
And touch the things of the senses.'

He puts aside desire,
Offering the act to Brahman.
The lotus leaf rests unwetted on water:
He rests on action, untouched by action.

To the follower of the yoga of action,
The body and the mind,
The sense-organs and the intellect
Are instruments only:
He knows himself other than the instrument
And thus his heart grows pure.

United with Brahman,
Cut free from the fruit of the act,
A man finds peace
In the work of the spirit.
Without Brahman,
Man is a prisoner,
Enslaved by action,
Dragged onward by desire.

Happy is that dweller
In the city of nine gates*
Whose discrimination
Has cut him free from his act:
He is not involved in action,
He does not involve others.

Do not say:
'God gave us this delusion.'
You dream you are the doer,
You dream that action is done,
You dream that action bears fruit.
It is your ignorance,
It is the world's delusion
That gives you these dreams.

The Lord is everywhere
And always perfect:
What does He care for man's sin
Or the righteousness of man?

The Atman is the light:
The light is covered by darkness:
This darkness is delusion:
That is why we dream.

When the light of the Atman
Drives out our darkness
That light shines forth from us,
A sun in splendour,
The revealed Brahman.

The devoted dwell with Him,
They know Him always
There in the heart,

* The human body.

Where action is not.
He is all their aim.
Made free by His Knowledge
From past uncleanness
Of deed or of thought,
They find the place of freedom,
The place of no return.*

Seeing all things equal,
The enlightened may look
On the Brahmin, learned and gentle,
On the cow, on the elephant,
On the dog, on the eater of dogs.

Absorbed in Brahman
He overcomes the world
Even here, alive in the world.
Brahman is one,
Changeless, untouched by evil:
What home have we but Him?

The enlightened, the Brahman-abiding,
Calm-hearted, unbewildered,
Is neither elated by the pleasant
Nor saddened by the unpleasant.

His mind is dead
To the touch of the external:
It is alive
To the bliss of the Atman,
Because his heart knows Brahman
His happiness is for ever.

* The state in which one is no longer subject to rebirth, because
illumination has been attained.

When senses touch objects
The pleasures therefrom
Are like wombs that bear sorrow.
They begin, they are ended:
They bring no delight to the wise.

Already, here on earth,
Before his departure,
Let man be the master
Of every impulse
Lust-begotten
Or fathered by anger:
Thus he finds Brahman,
Thus he is happy.

Only that yogi
Whose joy is inward,
Inward his peace,
And his vision inward
Shall come to Brahman
And know Nirvana.*

All consumed
Are their imperfections,
Doubts are dispelled,
Their senses mastered,
Their every action
Is wed to the welfare
Of fellow-creatures:
Such are the seers
Who enter Brahman
And know Nirvana.

Self-controlled,
Cut free from desire,

* The state of union with Brahman.

Curbing the heart
And knowing the Atman,
Man finds Nirvana
That is in Brahman,
Here and hereafter.

Shutting off sense
From what is outward,
Fixing the gaze
At the root of the eyebrows,*
Checking the breath-stream
In and outgoing
Within the nostrils,
Holding the senses,
Holding the intellect,
Holding the mind fast,
He who seeks freedom,
Thrusts fear aside,
Thrusts aside anger
And puts off desire:
Truly that man
Is made free for ever.

When thus he knows me
The end, the author
Of every offering
And all austerity,
Lord of the worlds
And the friend of all men:
O Son of Kunti
Shall he not enter
The peace of my presence?

* 'When the eyes are half closed in meditation, the eyeballs remain fixed and their gaze converges, as it were, between the eyebrows.' *Swami Swarupananda*

VI. The Yoga of Meditation

SRI KRISHNA:
He who does the task
Dictated by duty,
Caring nothing
For fruit of the action,
He is a yogi,
A true sannyasin.*
But he who follows
His vow to the letter
By mere refraining:
Lighting no fire
At the ritual offering,
Making excuse
For avoidance of labour,
He is no yogi,
No true sannyasin.

For you must understand that what has been called yoga is really sannyasa†; since nobody can practise the yoga of action who is anxious about his future, or the results of his actions.

Let him who would climb
In meditation
To heights of the highest
Union with Brahman
Take for his path

* Sannyasin: A monk.
† Sannyasa: The formal vow of renunciation taken by a monk. In taking this vow he gives up the performance of the Vedic sacrificial rites.

> The yoga of action:
> Then when he nears
> That height of oneness
> His acts will fall from him,
> His path will be tranquil.

For, when a man loses attachment to sense-objects and to action, when he renounces lustful anxiety and anxious lust, then he is said to have climbed to the height of union with Brahman.

> What is man's will
> And how shall he use it?
> Let him put forth its power
> To uncover the Atman
> Not hide the Atman:
> Man's will is the only
> Friend of the Atman:
> His will is also
> The Atman's enemy.

For when a man is self-controlled, his will is the Atman's friend. But the will of an uncontrolled man is hostile to the Atman, like an enemy.

> That serene one
> Absorbed in the Atman
> Masters his will,
> He knows no disquiet
> In heat or in cold,
> In pain or pleasure,
> In honour, dishonour.

For when a man's heart has reached fulfilment through knowledge and personal experience of the truth of Brahman, he is never again moved by the things of the senses. Earth, stone and gold seem all alike to one who has mastered his senses. Such a yogi is said to have achieved union with Brahman.

> He who regards
> With an eye that is equal
> Friends and comrades,
> The foe and the kinsman,
> The vile, the wicked,
> The men who judge him,
> And those who belong
> To neither faction:
> He is the greatest.

The yogi should retire into a solitary place, and live alone. He must exercise control over his mind and body. He must free himself from the hopes and possessions of this world. He should meditate on the Atman unceasingly.

The place where he sits should be firm, neither too high nor too low, and situated in a clean spot. He should first cover it with sacred grass, then with a deer skin; then lay a cloth over these.* As he sits there, he is to hold the senses and imagination in check, and keep the mind concentrated upon its object. If he practises meditation in this manner, his heart will become pure.

His posture will be motionless, with the body, head and neck held erect, and the vision indrawn, as if gazing at the tip of the nose. He must not look about him.

> So, with his heart serene and fearless,
> Firm in the vow of renunciation,

* The choice of materials is traditional, but not important for the spiritual aspirant of to-day. Any convenient seat will do.

Holding the mind from its restless roaming,
Now let him struggle to reach my oneness,
Ever-absorbed, his eyes on me always,
His prize, his purpose.

If a yogi has perfect control over his mind, and struggles continually in this way to unite himself with Brahman, he will come at last to the crowning peace of Nirvana, the peace that is in me.

Yoga is not for the man who overeats, or for him who fasts excessively. It is not for him who sleeps too much, or for the keeper of exaggerated vigils. Let a man be moderate in his eating and his recreation, moderately active, moderate in sleep and in wakefulness. He will find that yoga takes away all his unhappiness.

When can a man be said to have achieved union with Brahman? When his mind is under perfect control and freed from all desires, so that he becomes absorbed in the Atman, and nothing else. 'The light of a lamp does not flicker in a windless place': that is the simile which describes a yogi of one-pointed mind, who meditates upon the Atman. When, through the practice of yoga, the mind ceases its restless movements, and becomes still, he realizes the Atman. It satisfies him entirely. Then he knows that infinite happiness which can be realized by the purified heart but is beyond the grasp of the senses. He stands firm in this realization. Because of it, he can never again wander from the inmost truth of his being.

Now that he holds it
He knows this treasure
Above all others:
Faith so certain
Shall never be shaken
By heaviest sorrow.

To achieve this certainty is to know the real meaning of the word yoga. It is the breaking of contact with pain. You must practise this yoga resolutely, without losing heart. Renounce all your desires, for ever. They spring from wilfulness. Use your discrimination to restrain the whole pack of the scattering senses.

Patiently, little by little, a man must free himself from all mental distractions, with the aid of the intelligent will. He must fix his mind upon the Atman, and never think of anything else. No matter where the restless and unquiet mind wanders, it must be drawn back and made to submit to the Atman only.

> Utterly quiet,
> Made clean of passion,
> The mind of the yogi
> Knows that Brahman,
> His bliss is the highest.
>
> Released from evil
> His mind is constant
> In contemplation:
> The way is easy,
> Brahman has touched him,
> That bliss is boundless.
>
> His heart is with Brahman,
> His eye in all things
> Sees only Brahman
> Equally present,
> Knows his own Atman
> In every creature,
> And all creation
> Within that Atman.

That yogi sees me in all things, and all things within me. He never loses sight of me, nor I of him. He is established in union with me, and worships me devoutly in all beings. That yogi abides in me, no matter what his mode of life.

> Who burns with the bliss
> And suffers the sorrow
> Of every creature
> Within his own heart,
> Making his own
> Each bliss and each sorrow:
> Him I hold highest
> Of all the yogis.

ARJUNA:

Krishna, you describe this yoga as a life of union with Brahman. But I do not see how this can be permanent. The mind is so very restless.

> Restless man's mind is,
> So strongly shaken
> In the grip of the senses:
> Gross and grown hard
> With stubborn desire
> For what is worldly.
> How shall he tame it?
> Truly, I think
> The wind is no wilder.

SRI KRISHNA:

Yes, Arjuna, the mind is restless, no doubt, and hard to subdue. But it can be brought under control by constant practice, and by the exercise of dispassion. Certainly, if a man has no control over his ego, he will find this yoga difficult to master. But a self-controlled man can master it, if he struggles hard, and uses the right means.

Suppose a man has faith, but does not struggle hard enough? His mind wanders away from the practice of yoga and he fails to reach perfection. What will become of him then?

When a man goes astray from the path to Brahman, he has missed both lives, the worldly and the spiritual. He has no support anywhere. Is he not lost, as a broken cloud is lost in the sky?

This is the doubt that troubles me, Krishna; and only you can altogether remove it from my mind. Let me hear your answer.

No, my son. That man is not lost, either in this world or the next. No one who seeks Brahman ever comes to an evil end.

Even if a man falls away from the practice of yoga, he will still win the heaven of the doers of good deeds, and dwell there many long years. After that, he will be reborn into the home of pure and prosperous parents. He may even be born into a family of illumined yogis. But such a birth in this world is more difficult to obtain.

He will then regain that spiritual discernment which he acquired in his former body; and so will strive harder than ever for perfection. Because of his practices in the previous life, he will be driven on toward union with Brahman, even in spite of himself. For the man who has once asked the way to Brahman goes further than any mere fulfiller of the Vedic rituals. By struggling hard, and cleansing himself of all impurities, that yogi will move gradually toward perfection through many births, and reach the highest goal at last.

> Great is that yogi who seeks to be with Brahman,
> Greater than those who mortify the body,
> Greater than the learned,
> Greater than the doers of good works:
> Therefore, Arjuna, become a yogi.

> He gives me all his heart,
> He worships me in faith and love:
> That yogi, above every other,
> I call my very own.

VII. Knowledge and Experience

SRI KRISHNA:

Devote your whole mind to me, and practise yoga. Take me for your only refuge. I will tell you how, by doing this, you can know me in my total reality, without any shadow of doubt. I will give you all this knowledge, and direct spiritual experience, besides. When a man has that, nothing else in this world remains to be known.

> Who cares to seek
> For that perfect freedom?
> One man, perhaps,
> In many thousands.
> Then tell me how many
> Of those who seek freedom
> Shall know the total
> Truth of my being?
> Perhaps one only.

My Prakriti is of eightfold composition: earth, water, fire, air, ether, mind, intellect and ego. You must understand that behind this, and distinct from it, is That which is the principle of consciousness in all beings, and the source of life in all. It sustains the universe.

> Know this my Prakriti
> United with me:
> The womb of all beings.
> I am the birth of this cosmos:
> Its dissolution also.
> I am He who causes:
> No other beside me.
> Upon me, those worlds are held
> Like pearls strung on a thread.
>
> I am the essence of the waters,
> The shining of the sun and the moon:
> OM in all the Vedas,
> The word that is God.
> It is I who resound in the ether
> And am potent in man.
> I am the sacred smell of the earth,
> The light of the fire,
> Life of all lives,
> Austerity of ascetics.
>
> Know me, eternal seed
> Of everything that grows:
> The intelligence of those who understand,
> The vigour of the active.
> In the strong, I am strength
> Unhindered by lust
> And the objects of craving:

I am all that a man may desire
Without transgressing
The law of his nature.

You must know that whatever belongs to the states of sattwa, rajas and tamas, proceeds from me. They are contained in me, but I am not in them. The entire world is deluded by the moods and mental states which are the expression of these three gunas. That is why the world fails to recognize me as I really am. I stand apart from them all, supreme and deathless.

How hard to break through
Is this, my Maya,
Made of the gunas!
But he who takes refuge
Within me only
Shall pass beyond Maya:
He, and no other.

The evil-doers
Turn not toward me:
These are deluded,
Sunk low among mortals.
Their judgment is lost
In the maze of Maya,
Until the heart
Is human no longer:
Changed within
To the heart of a devil.

Among those who are purified by their good deeds, there are four kinds of men who worship me: the world-weary, the seeker for knowledge, the seeker for happiness and the man of spiritual discrimination. The man of discrimination is the highest of these. He is continually united with me. He

devotes himself to me always, and to no other. For I am
very dear to that man, and he is dear to me.

> Certainly, all these are noble:
> But the man of discrimination
> I see as my very Self.
> For he alone loves me
> Because I am myself:
> The last and only goal
> Of his devoted heart.

> Through many a long life
> His discrimination ripens:
> He makes me his refuge,
> Knows that Brahman is all.
> How rare are such great ones!

Men whose discrimination has been blunted by worldly
desires, establish this or that ritual or cult and resort to
various deities, according to the impulse of their inborn
natures. But it does not matter what deity a devotee chooses
to worship. If he has faith, I make his faith unwavering.
Endowed with the faith I give him, he worships that deity,
and gets from it everything he prays for. In reality, I alone
am the giver.

But these men of small understanding only pray for
what is transient and perishable. The worshippers of the
devas will go to the devas. So, also, my devotees will come
to me.

> Thus think the ignorant: that I, the unmanifest,
> Am become man. They do not know my nature
> That is one with Brahman, changeless, superhuman.

> Veiled in my Maya, I am not shown to many.
> How shall this world, bewildered by delusion,
> Recognize me, who am not born and change not?

I know all beings, Arjuna: past, present and to come. But no one knows me.

All living creatures are led astray as soon as they are born, by the delusion that this relative world is real. This delusion arises from their own desire and hatred. But the doers of good deeds, whose bad karma is exhausted, are freed from this delusion about the relative world. They hold firmly to their vows, and worship me.

Men take refuge in me, to escape from their fear of old age and death. Thus they come to know Brahman, and the entire nature of the Atman, and the creative energy which is in Brahman. Knowing me, they understand the nature of the relative world and the individual man, and of God who presides over all action. Even at the hour of death, they continue to know me thus. In that hour, their whole consciousness is made one with mine.

VIII. The Way to Eternal Brahman

ARJUNA:

Tell me, Krishna, what Brahman is. What is the Atman, and what is the creative energy of Brahman? Explain the nature of this relative world, and of the individual man.

Who is God who presides over action in this body, and how does He dwell here? How are you revealed at the hour of death to those whose consciousness is united with you?

SRI KRISHNA:

Brahman is that which is immutable, and independent of any cause but Itself. When we consider Brahman as lodged within the individual being, we call Him the Atman. The creative energy of Brahman is that which causes all existences to come into being.

The nature of the relative world is mutability. The nature of the individual man is his consciousness of ego. I alone am God who presides over action, here in this body.

At the hour of death, when a man leaves his body, he must depart with his consciousness absorbed in me. Then he will be united with me. Be certain of that. Whatever a man remembers at the last, when he is leaving the body, will be realized by him in the hereafter; because that will be what his mind has most constantly dwelt on, during this life.

Therefore you must remember me at all times, and do your duty. If your mind and heart are set upon me constantly, you will come to me. Never doubt this.

Make a habit of practising meditation, and do not let your mind be distracted. In this way you will come finally to the Lord, who is the light-giver, the highest of the high.

He is all-knowing God, lord of the emperors,
Ageless, subtler far than mind's inmost subtlety,
Universal sustainer,
Shining sunlike, self-luminous.

What fashion His form has, who shall conceive of it?
He dwells beyond delusion, the dark of Maya.
On Him let man meditate
Always, for then at the last hour
Of going hence from his body he will be strong
In the strength of this yoga, faithfully followed:
The mind is firm, and the heart
So full, it hardly holds its love.

Thus he will take his leave: and now, with the life-force
Indrawn utterly, held fast between the eyebrows,

He goes forth to find his Lord,
That light-giver, who is greatest.

Now I will tell you briefly about the nature of Him who
is called the deathless by those seers who truly understand
the Vedas. Devotees enter into Him when the bonds of
their desire are broken. To reach this goal, they practise
control of the passions.

When a man leaves his body and departs,* he must close
all the doors of the senses. Let him hold the mind firmly
within the shrine of the heart, and fix the life-force between
the eyebrows. Then let him take refuge in steady concentration, uttering the sacred syllable OM and meditating
upon me. Such a man reaches the highest goal. When a
yogi has meditated upon me unceasingly for many years,
with an undistracted mind, I am easy of access to him, because he is always absorbed in me.

Great souls who find me have found the highest perfection. They are no longer reborn into this condition of
transience and pain.

All the worlds, and even the heavenly realm of Brahma,†
are subject to the laws of rebirth. But, for the man who
comes to me, there is no returning.

There is day, also, and night in the universe:
The wise know this, declaring the day of Brahma

* According to yoga technique, the yogi must employ a special
method of leaving the body at death. First, the vital force is drawn
up the sushumna, the central spinal passage, and gathered in the
brain, 'between the eyebrows.' The yogi then leaves the body through
an aperture in the centre of the brain, called the sahashrara.

† Brahma (not to be confused with Brahman) is God in the
aspect of creator—one of the Hindu Trinity, with Vishnu, the pre-
server, and Shiva, the dissolver.

According to Hindu mythology, the worlds are variously classi-
fied as three, seven or fourteen. The Brahma-Loka (realm of Brahma) is said to be the highest.

A thousand ages in span
And the night a thousand ages.

Day dawns, and all those lives that lay hidden asleep
Come forth and show themselves, mortally manifest:
Night falls, and all are dissolved
Into the sleeping germ of life.

Thus they are seen, O Prince, and appear unceasingly,
Dissolving with the dark, and with day returning
Back to the new birth, new death:
All helpless. They do what they must.

But behind the manifest and the unmanifest, there is
another Existence, which is eternal and changeless. This is
not dissolved in the general cosmic dissolution. It has been
called the unmanifest, the imperishable. To reach It is said
to be the greatest of all achievements. It is my highest
state of being. Those who reach It are not reborn. That
highest state of being can only be achieved through devotion to Him in whom all creatures exist, and by whom
this universe is pervaded.

I show you two paths.*
Let a yogi choose either
When he leaves this body:
The path that leads back to birth,
The path of no return.

There is the path of light,
Of fire and day,
The path of the moon's bright fortnight

* The 'path of no return' is called in the Upanishads the Deva
Yana, 'the path of the bright ones,' who are liberated from rebirth.
The path that leads back to birth is the Pitri Yana, the 'path of the
fathers,' who reach the 'lunar light' (a paradise subject to the laws
of time) and must ultimately be reborn.

And the six months' journey
Of the sun to the north:
The knower of Brahman
Who takes this path
Goes to Brahman:
He does not return.

There is the path of night and smoke,
The path of the moon's dark fortnight
And the six months' journey
Of the sun to the south:
The yogi who takes this path
Will reach the lunar light:*
This path leads back
To human birth, at last.

These two paths, the bright and the dark, may be said to
have existed in this world of change from a time without
any beginning. By the one, a man goes to the place of no
return. By the other, he comes back to human birth. No
yogi who knows these two paths is ever misled. Therefore,
Arjuna, you must be steadfast in yoga, always.

The scriptures declare that merit can be acquired by
studying the Vedas, performing ritualistic sacrifices, practising austerities and giving alms. But the yogi who has
understood this teaching of mine will gain more than any
who do these things. He will reach that universal source,
which is the uttermost abode of God.

* Fire, light, smoke, night, etc., probably represent stages of the
soul's experience after death. Thus, light may symbolize knowledge;
and smoke, ignorance.

IX. *The Yoga of Mysticism*

SRI KRISHNA:
Since you accept me
And do not question,
Now I shall tell you
That innermost secret:
Knowledge of God
Which is nearer than knowing,
Open vision
Direct and instant.
Understand this
And be free for ever
From birth and dying
With all their evil.

This is the knowledge
Above all other:
Purifier
And king of secrets,
Only made plain
To the eye of the mystic.
Great is its virtue,
Its practice easy:
Thus man is brought
To truth eternal.

Those without faith
In this, my knowledge,
Shall fail to find me:
Back they must turn
To the mortal pathway,

> Subject still
> To birth and to dying.

This entire universe is pervaded by me, in that eternal form of mine which is not manifest to the senses. Although I am not within any creature, all creatures exist within me. I do not mean that they exist within me physically. That is my divine mystery. You must try to understand its nature. My Being sustains all creatures and brings them to birth, but has no physical contact with them.

> For, as the vast air, wandering world-wide,
> Remains within the ether always,
> So these, my wandering creatures,
> Are always within me.

> These, when the round of ages is accomplished,
> I gather back to the seed of their becoming:
> These I send forth again
> At the hour of creation.

> Helpless all, for Maya is their master,
> And I, their Lord, the master of this Maya:
> Ever and again, I send these multitudes
> Forth from my Being.

> How shall these acts bind me, who am indifferent
> To the fruit they bear? For my spirit
> Stands apart, watching over
> Maya, the maker.

> Maya makes all things: what moves, what is unmoving.
> O Son of Kunti, that is why the world spins,
> Turning its wheel through birth
> And through destruction.

Fools pass blindly by the place of my dwelling
Here in the human form, and of my majesty
They know nothing at all,
Who am the Lord, their soul.

Vain is their hope, and in vain their labour, their
    knowledge:
All their understanding is but bewilderment;
Their nature has fallen into the madness
Of the fiends and monsters.

Great in soul are they who become what is godlike:
They alone know me, the origin, the deathless:
They offer me the homage
Of an unwavering mind.

Praising my might with heart and lips for ever,
Striving for the virtue that wins me, and steadfast
In all their vows, they worship adoring,
One with me always.
Others worship me, knowing Brahman in all things:
Some see me one with themselves, or separate:
Some bow to the countless gods that are only
My million faces.

Rites that the Vedas ordain, and the rituals taught by
    the scriptures:
All these am I, and the offering made to the ghosts of
    the fathers,
Herbs of healing and food, the mantram,* the clarified
    butter:
I the oblation and I the flame into which it is offered.

* Name, or names, of God, which the devotee must repeat and
meditate upon. An individual mantram is given by the teacher to
each of his disciples at the time of initiation.

I am the sire of the world, and this world's mother and
    grandsire:

I am He who awards to each the fruit of his action:

I make all things clean, I am OM, I am absolute
    knowledge:

I am also the Vedas—the Sama, the Rik and the
    Yajus.

I am the end of the path, the witness, the Lord, the
    sustainer:

I am the place of abode, the beginning, the friend and
    the refuge:

I am the breaking-apart, and the storehouse of life's
    dissolution:

I lie under the seen, of all creatures the seed that is
    changeless.

I am the heat of the sun; and the heat of the fire am
    I also:

Life eternal and death. I let loose the rain, or withhold
    it.

Arjuna, I am the cosmos revealed, and its germ that
    lies hidden.

> They that are versed
> In the triple Veda,
> Worshipping me
> With the rites appointed,
> Drinking the wine
> Of the gods' communion,
> Cleansed from their sinning:
> These men pray
> For passage to heaven,
> Thus attaining
> The realm of Indra,

Home of the happy;
There they delight
In celestial pleasures.

Pleasures more spacious
Than any earthly
They taste awhile,
Till the merit that won them
Is all exhausted:
Then they return
To the world of mortals.

Thus go the righteous
Who follow the road
Of the triple Veda
In formal observance;
Hungry still
For the food of the senses,
Drawn by desire
To endless returning.

But if a man will worship me, and meditate upon me with an undistracted mind, devoting every moment to me, I shall supply all his needs, and protect his possessions from loss. Even those who worship other deities, and sacrifice to them with faith in their hearts, are really worshipping me, though with a mistaken approach. For I am the only enjoyer and the only God of all sacrifices. Nevertheless, such men must return to life on earth, because they do not recognize me in my true nature.

Those who sacrifice to the various deities, will go to those deities. The ancestor-worshippers will go to their ancestors. Those who worship elemental powers and spirits will go to them. So, also, my devotees will come to me.

Whatever man gives me
In true devotion:
Fruit or water,
A leaf, a flower:
I will accept it.
That gift is love,
His heart's dedication.

Whatever your action,
Food or worship;
Whatever the gift
That you give to another;
Whatever you vow
To the work of the spirit:
O son of Kunti,
Lay these also
As offerings before me.

Thus you will free yourself from both the good and the evil effects of your actions. Offer up everything to me. If your heart is united with me, you will be set free from karma even in this life, and come to me at the last.

My face is equal
To all creation,
Loving no one
Nor hating any.

Nevertheless,
My devotees dwell
Within me always:
I also show forth
And am seen within them.

Though a man be soiled
With the sins of a lifetime,
Let him but love me,
Rightly resolved,
In utter devotion:
I see no sinner,
That man is holy.
Holiness soon
Shall refashion his nature
To peace eternal;
O son of Kunti,
Of this be certain:
The man that loves me,
He shall not perish.

Even those who belong to the lower castes—women, Vaishyas,* and Sudras too—can reach the highest spiritual realization, if they will take refuge in me. Need I tell you, then, that this is also true of the holy Brahmins and pious philosopher-kings?

You find yourself in this transient, joyless world. Turn from it, and take your delight in me. Fill your heart and mind with me, adore me, make all your acts an offering to me, bow down to me in self-surrender. If you set your heart upon me thus, and take me for your ideal above all others, you will come into my Being.

* The four Hindu castes are: Brahmins (the priests), Kshatriyas (the warriors), Vaishyas (the merchants) and Sudras (the servants). Compare Chapter XVIII, page 97, where the caste-names are used with a more psychological significance, and have been translated accordingly.

X. *Divine Glory*

SRI KRISHNA:
Once more, warrior,
Hear this highest
Word of my wisdom:
Wishing your welfare,
To you I teach it
Since your heart
Delights in the telling.

How shall the mighty
Seers or the devas
Know my beginning?
I am the origin,
I the sustainer
Of seers and devas.

Who knows me birthless,
Never-beginning,
Lord of the worlds;
He alone among mortals
Is stainless of sin,
Unvexed by delusion.

All that makes Man
In his many natures:
Knowledge and power
Of understanding
Unclouded by error,
Truth, forbearance,
Calm of spirit,
Control of senses,
Happiness, sorrow,

Birth and destruction,
What fears, what is fearless,
What harms no creature,
The mind unshaken,
The heart contented,
The will austere,
The hand of the giver,
Fame and honour
And infamy also:
It is by me only
That these are allotted.
Forth from my thought
Came the seven Sages,
The Ancient Four
And at last the Manus:
Thus I gave birth
To the first begetters
Of all earth's children.

Who truly knows me,
In manifold Being
Everywhere present
And all-prevailing,
Dwells in my yoga
That shall not be shaken:
Of this be certain.

I am where all things began, the issuing-forth of the creatures,
Known to the wise in their love when they worship with hearts overflowing:

Mind and sense are absorbed, I alone am the theme of their discourse:

Thus delighting each other, they live in bliss and contentment.
Always aware of their Lord are they, and ever devoted:
Therefore the strength of their thought is illumined and
guided toward me.

There in the ignorant heart where I dwell, by the grace of
my mercy,
I am knowledge, that brilliant lamp, dispelling its darkness.

ARJUNA:

You are Brahman, the highest abode, the utterly holy:
All the sages proclaim you eternal, Lord of the devas:
Saintly Narada knew you the birthless, the everywhere
present:
Devala echoed your praise; Asita, too, and Vyasa:*
Now I also have heard, for to me your own lips have con-
firmed it,
Krishna, this is the truth that you tell: my heart bids me
believe you.

God of gods, Lord of the world, Life's Source, O King of
all creatures:
How shall deva or titan know all the extent of your glory?
You alone know what you are, by the light of your innermost nature.
Therefore teach me now, and hold back no word in the
telling,
All the sum of your shapes by which the three worlds are
pervaded;
Tell me how you will make yourself known to my meditation;
Show me beneath what form and disguise I must learn to
behold you;

* Ancient sages.

Number them all, your heavenly powers, your manifestations:

Speak, for each word is immortal nectar; I never grow
weary.

SRI KRISHNA:

O Arjuna, I will indeed make known to you my divine
manifestations; but I shall name the chief of these, only.
For, of the lesser variations in all their detail, there is no
end.

I am the Atman that dwells in the heart of every mortal
creature: I am the beginning, the life-span, and the end of
all.

I am Vishnu: I am the radiant sun among the light-givers:
I am Marichi, the wind-god: among the stars of night, I am
the moon.

I am the Sama Veda: I am Indra, king of heaven: of
sense-organs, I am the mind: I am consciousness in the
living.

I am Shiva: I am the Lord of all riches: I am the spirit
of fire: I am Meru, among the mountain peaks.

Know me as Brihaspati, leader of the high priests, and as
Skanda, the warrior-chief. I am the ocean among the waters.

I am Bhrigu, the great seer: among words, I am the
sacred syllable OM: I am the vow of japam:* I am Hima-
laya among the things that cannot be moved.

I am the holy fig tree: I am Narada, the godly sage,
Chitraratha, the celestial musician, and Kapila among the
perfected souls.

Among horses, you may know me as Uchchaishrava,
who was brought forth from the sea of nectar: I am Airavata
among royal elephants: I am king among men.

* The practice of repeating a mantram (name of God). See note
on Chapter IX, page 53.

Of weapons, I am God's thunderbolt: I am Kamadhenu, the heavenly cow: I am the love-god, begetter of children: I am Vasuki, god of snakes.

I am Ananta, the holy serpent: of water beings, I am Varuna: Aryaman among the Fathers: I am Death, who distributes the fruit of all action.

I am Prahlada, the giant: among those who measure, I am Time: I am the lion among beasts: Vishnu's eagle among the birds.

Among purifiers, I am the wind: I am Rama among the warriors: the shark among fish: Ganges among the rivers.

I am the beginning, the middle and the end in creation: I am the knowledge of things spiritual: I am the logic of those who debate.

In the alphabet, I am A: among compounds, the copulative: I am Time without end: I am the Sustainer: my face is everywhere.

I am death that snatches all: I, also, am the source of all that shall be born: I am glory, prosperity, beautiful speech, memory, intelligence, steadfastness and forgiveness.

I am the great Sama of the Vedic hymns, and the Gayatri among poetic metres: of the months, I am Margashirsha:* of seasons, the time of flowers.

I am the dice-play of the cunning: I am the strength of the strong: I am triumph and perseverance: I am the purity of the good.

I am Krishna among the Vrishnis, Arjuna among the Pandavas, Vyasa among the sages, Ushanas among the illumined poets.

I am the sceptre and the mastery of those who rule, the policy of those who seek to conquer: I am the silence of things secret: I am the knowledge of the knower.

* A month of the Hindu year, including parts of November and December.

O Arjuna, I am the divine seed of all lives. In this world, nothing animate or inanimate exists without me.

There is no limit to my divine manifestations, nor can they be numbered, O foe-consumer. What I have described to you are only a few of my countless forms.

Whatever in this world is powerful, beautiful or glorious, that you may know to have come forth from a fraction of my power and glory.

But what need have you, Arjuna, to know this huge variety? Know only that I exist, and that one atom of myself sustains the universe.

XI. The Vision of God in His Universal Form

ARJUNA:

By your grace, you have taught me the truth about the Atman. Your words are mystic and sublime. They have dispelled my ignorance.

From you, whose eyes are like the lotus-flowers, I have learnt in detail of the origin and dissolution of creatures, and of your own infinite glory.

O Supreme Lord, you are as you describe yourself to be: I do not doubt that. Nevertheless, I long to behold your divine Form.

If you find me worthy of that vision, then reveal to me, O Master of yogis, your changeless Atman.

SRI KRISHNA:

Behold, O Prince, my divine forms, hundreds upon thousands, various in kind, various in colour and in shape.

Behold the Adityas, and the Vasus, and the Rudras, and

the Aswins, and the Maruts.* Behold many wonders, O Descendant of Bharata, that no man has seen before.

O conqueror of sloth, this very day you shall behold the whole universe with all things animate and inert made one within this body of mine. And whatever else you desire to see, that you shall see also.

But you cannot see me thus with those human eyes. Therefore, I give you divine sight. Behold—this is my yoga power.

SANJAYA:

Then, O King, when he had spoken these words, Sri Krishna, Master of all yogis, revealed to Arjuna his transcendent, divine Form, speaking from innumerable mouths, seeing with a myriad eyes, of many marvellous aspects, adorned with countless divine ornaments, brandishing all kinds of heavenly weapons, wearing celestial garlands and the raiment of paradise, anointed with perfumes of heavenly fragrance, full of revelations, resplendent, boundless, of ubiquitous regard.

Suppose a thousand suns should rise together into the sky: such is the glory of the Shape of Infinite God.

Then the son of Pandu beheld the entire universe, in all its multitudinous diversity, lodged as one being within the body of the God of gods.

Then was Arjuna, that lord of mighty riches, overcome with wonder. His hair stood erect. He bowed low before God in adoration, and clasped his hands, and spoke:

ARJUNA:

Ah, my God, I see all gods within your body;
Each in his degree, the multitude of creatures;

* Various classes of celestial beings.

See Lord Brahma throned upon the lotus;
See all the sages, and the holy serpents.

Universal Form, I see you without limit,
Infinite of arms, eyes, mouths and bellies—
See, and find no end, midst, or beginning.

Crowned with diadems, you wield the mace and discus,
Shining every way—the eyes shrink from your splendour
Brilliant like the sun; like fire, blazing, boundless.

You are all we know, supreme, beyond man's measure,
This world's sure-set plinth and refuge never shaken,
Guardian of eternal law, life's Soul undying.

Birthless, deathless; yours the strength titanic,
Million-armed, the sun and moon your eyeballs,
Fiery-faced, you blast the world to ashes,

Fill the sky's four corners, span the chasm
Sundering heaven from earth. Superb and awful
Is your Form that makes the three worlds tremble.

Into you, the companies of devas
Enter with clasped hands, in dread and wonder.
Crying 'Peace,' the Rishis and the Siddhas
Sing your praise with hymns of adoration.

Adityas and Rudras, Sadhyas, Viswas, Aswins,
Maruts and Vasus, the hosts of the Gandharvas,
Yakshas, Asuras, Ushmapas and Siddhas—
All of them gaze upon you in amazement.

At the sight of this, your Shape stupendous
Full of mouths and eyes, feet, thighs and bellies,
Terrible with fangs, O mighty master,
All the worlds are fear-struck, even as I am.

When I see you, Vishnu, omnipresent,
Shouldering the sky, in hues of rainbow,
With your mouths agape and flame-eyes staring—
All my peace is gone; my heart is troubled.

Now with frightful tusks your mouths are gnashing,
Flaring like the fires of Doomsday morning—
North, south, east and west seem all confounded—
Lord of devas, world's abode, have mercy!

Dhritarashtra's offspring, many a monarch,
Bhisma, Drona, and the son of Karna,
There they go—with our own warriors also—
Hurrying to your jaws, wide-fanged and hideous—
See where mangled heads lie crushed between them!

Swift as many rivers streaming to the ocean,
Rush the heroes to your fiery gullets:
Mothlike, to meet the flame of their destruction,
Headlong these plunge into you, and perish.

Licking with your burning tongues, devouring
All the worlds, you probe the heights of heaven
With intolerable beams, O Vishnu.

Tell me who you are, and were from the beginning,
You of aspect grim, O God of gods, be gracious.
Take my homage, Lord. From me your ways are hidden.

SRI KRISHNA:

I am come as Time, the waster of the peoples,
Ready for that hour that ripens to their ruin.
All these hosts must die; strike, stay your hand—no matter.

Therefore, strike. Win kingdom, wealth and glory.
Arjuna, arise, O ambidextrous bowman.
Seem to slay. By me these men are slain already.

You but smite the dead, the doom-devoted heroes,
Jayadratha, Drona, Bhisma, Karna.
Fight, and have no fear. The foe is yours to conquer.

SANJAYA:

After Arjuna had heard these words of the Lord Krishna,
he folded his palms and bowed down, trembling. Prostrating
himself, with great fear, he addressed Krishna once
more, in a choking voice:

ARJUNA:

Well it is the world delights to do you honour!
At the sight of you, O master of the senses,
Demons scatter every way in terror,
And the hosts of Siddhas bow adoring.

Mightiest, how should they indeed withhold their homage?
O Prime Cause of all, even Brahma the Beginner—
Deathless, world's abode, the Lord of devas,
You are what is not, what is, and what transcends them.

You are first and highest in heaven, O ancient Spirit.
It is within you the cosmos rests in safety.
You are known and knower, goal of all our striving.
Endless in your change, you body forth creation.

Lord of fire and death, of wind and moon and waters,
Father of the born, and this world's father's Father.
Hail, all hail to you—a thousand salutations.

Take our salutations, Lord, from every quarter,
Infinite of might and boundless in your glory,
You are all that is, since everywhere we find you.

Carelessly I called you 'Krishna' and 'my comrade,'
Took undying God for friend and fellow-mortal,
Overbold with love, unconscious of your greatness.

Often I would jest, familiar, as we feasted
Midst the throng, or walked, or lay at rest together:
Did my words offend? Forgive me, Lord Eternal.

Author of this world, the unmoved and the moving,
You alone are fit for worship, you the highest.
Where in the three worlds shall any find your equal?

Therefore I bow down, prostrate and ask for pardon:
Now forgive me, God, as friend forgives his comrade,
Father forgives son, and man his dearest lover.

I have seen what no man ever saw before me:
Deep is my delight, but still my dread is greater.
Show me now your other Form, O Lord, be gracious.

Thousand-membered, Universal Being,
Show me now the Shape I knew of old, the four-armed,*
With your diadem and mace, the discus-bearer.

SRI KRISHNA:

This my Form of fire, world-wide, supreme, primeval,
Manifest by yoga power, alone of all men,
Arjuna, I showed to you because I love you.

Neither through sacrifice, nor study of the Vedas,
Nor strict austerities, nor alms, nor rituals,
Shall this my Shape be viewed by any mortal,
Other than you, O hero of the Pandus.

* The only explanation of this passage seems to be that Arjuna
is asking Sri Krishna to assume the shape of his chosen deity, Vishnu
—since it cannot mean that Krishna had four arms while in his human shape. If this interpretation is correct, we may assume that God
took on the four-armed shape of Vishnu for a moment, before reappearing as Krishna. As has been stated elsewhere, Krishna was
regarded as an incarnation of Vishnu.

Now you need fear no more, nor be bewildered,
Seeing me so terrible. Be glad, take courage.
Look, here am I, transformed, as first you knew me.

SANJAYA:

Having spoken thus to Arjuna, Krishna appeared in his
own shape. The Great-Souled One, assuming once more
his mild and pleasing form, brought peace to him in his
terror.

ARJUNA:

O Krishna, now I see your pleasant human form, I am
myself again.

SRI KRISHNA:

That Shape of mine which you have seen is very difficult
to behold. Even the devas themselves are always longing
to see it. Neither by study of the Vedas, nor by austerities,
nor by alms-giving, nor by rituals can I be seen as you have
seen me. But by single-minded and intense devotion, that
Form of mine may be completely known, and seen, and
entered into, O Consumer of the foe.

Whosoever works for me alone, makes me his only goal
and is devoted to me, free from attachment, and without
hatred toward any creature—that man, O Prince, shall
enter into me.

XII. The Yoga of Devotion

ARJUNA:

Some worship you with steadfast love. Others worship
God the unmanifest and changeless. Which kind of devotee has the greater understanding of yoga?

SRI KRISHNA:

Those whose minds are fixed on me in steadfast love, worshipping me with absolute faith. I consider them to have the greater understanding of yoga.

As for those others, the devotees of God the unmanifest, indefinable and changeless, they worship that which is omnipresent, constant, eternal, beyond thought's compass, never to be moved. They hold all the senses in check. They are tranquil-minded, and devoted to the welfare of humanity. They see the Atman in every creature. They also will certainly come to me.

But the devotees of the unmanifest have a harder task, because the unmanifest is very difficult for embodied souls to realize.

> Quickly I come
> To those who offer me
> Every action,
> Worship me only,
> Their dearest delight,
> With devotion undaunted.
>
> Because they love me
> These are my bondsmen
> And I shall save them
> From mortal sorrow
> And all the waves
> Of Life's deathly ocean.
>
> Be absorbed in me,
> Lodge your mind in me:
> Thus you shall dwell in me,
> Do not doubt it,
> Here and hereafter.

If you cannot become absorbed in me, then try to reach me by repeated concentration. If you lack the strength to concentrate, then devote yourself to works which will please me. For, by working for my sake only, you will achieve perfection. If you cannot even do this, then surrender yourself to me altogether. Control the lusts of your heart, and renounce the fruits of every action.

Concentration which is practised with discernment is certainly better than the mechanical repetition of a ritual or a prayer. Absorption in God—to live with Him and be one with Him always—is even better than concentration. But renunciation brings instant peace to the spirit.

A man should not hate any living creature. Let him be friendly and compassionate to all. He must free himself from the delusion of 'I' and 'mine.' He must accept pleasure and pain with equal tranquillity. He must be forgiving, ever-contented, self-controlled, united constantly with me in his meditation. His resolve must be unshakable. He must be dedicated to me in intellect and in mind. Such a devotee is dear to me.

He neither molests his fellow men, nor allows himself to become disturbed by the world. He is no longer swayed by joy and envy, anxiety and fear. Therefore he is dear to me.

He is pure, and independent of the body's desire. He is able to deal with the unexpected: prepared for everything, unperturbed by anything. He is neither vain nor anxious about the results of his actions. Such a devotee is dear to me.

He does not desire or rejoice in what is pleasant. He does not dread what is unpleasant, or grieve over it. He remains unmoved by good or evil fortune. Such a devotee is dear to me.

His attitude is the same toward friend and foe. He is indifferent to honour and insult, heat and cold, pleasure and pain. He is free from attachment. He values praise and blame equally. He can control his speech. He is content with whatever he gets. His home is everywhere and nowhere. His mind is fixed upon me, and his heart is full of devotion. He is dear to me.

This true wisdom I have taught will lead you to immortality. The faithful practise it with devotion, taking me for their highest aim. To me they surrender heart and mind. They are exceedingly dear to me.

XIII. *The Field and Its Knower*

ARJUNA:

And now, Krishna, I wish to learn about Prakriti and Brahman, the Field and the Knower of the Field. What is knowledge? What is it that has to be known?

SRI KRISHNA:

This body is called the Field, because a man sows seeds of action in it, and reaps their fruit. Wise men say that the Knower of the Field is he who watches what takes place within this body.

Recognize me as the Knower of the Field in every body. I regard discrimination between Field and Knower as the highest kind of knowledge.

Now listen, and I will tell you briefly what the Field is; its nature, modifications and origin. I will tell you also who the Knower is, and what are his powers.

The sages have expressed these truths variously, in many hymns, and in aphorisms on the nature of Brahman, subtly reasoned and convincing in their arguments.

Briefly I name them:
First, Prakriti
Which is the cosmos
In cause unseen
And visible feature;
Intellect, ego;
Earth, water and ether,
Air and fire;
Man's ten organs
Of knowing and doing,
Man's mind also;
The five sense-objects—
Sound in its essence,
Essence of aspect,
Essence of odour,
Of touch and of tasting;
Hate and desire,
And pain and pleasure;
Consciousness, lastly,
And resolution;
These, with their sum
Which is blent in the body:
These make the Field
With its limits and changes.

Therefore I tell you:
Be humble, be harmless,
Have no pretension,
Be upright, forbearing,
Serve your teacher
In true obedience,
Keeping the mind
And the body in cleanness,

Tranquil, steadfast,
Master of ego,
Standing apart
From the things of the senses,
Free from self;
Aware of the weakness
In mortal nature,
Its bondage to birth,
Age, suffering, dying;
To nothing be slave,
Nor desire possession
Of man-child or wife,
Of home or of household;
Calmly encounter
The painful, the pleasant;
Adore me only
With heart undistracted;
Turn all your thought
Toward solitude, spurning
The noise of the crowd,
Its fruitless commotion;
Strive without ceasing
To know the Atman,
Seek this knowledge
And comprehend clearly
Why you should seek it:
Such, it is said,
Are the roots of true wisdom:
Ignorance, merely,
Is all that denies them.

Now I shall describe That which has to be known, in order that its knower may gain immortality. That Brahman is beginningless, transcendent, eternal. He is said to be equally beyond what is, and what is not.

Everywhere are His hands, eyes, feet; His heads and His faces:
This whole world is His ear; He exists, encompassing all things;
Doing the tasks of each sense, yet Himself devoid of the senses:
Standing apart, He sustains: He is free from the gunas but feels them.
He is within and without: He lives in the live and the life-less:
Subtle beyond mind's grasp; so near us, so utterly distant:
Undivided, He seems to divide into objects and creatures;
Sending creation forth from Himself, He upholds and with-draws it;
Light of all lights, He abides beyond our ignorant darkness;
Knowledge, the one thing real we may study or know, the heart's dweller.

Now I have told you briefly what the Field is, what knowledge is, and what is that one Reality which must be known. When my devotee knows these things, he becomes fit to reach union with me.

You must understand that both Prakriti and Brahman are without beginning. All evolution and all the gunas proceed from Prakriti. From Prakriti the evolution of body and senses is said to originate. The sense of individuality in us is said to cause our experience of pleasure and pain. The individual self, which is Brahman mistakenly identified with Prakriti, experiences the gunas which proceed from Prakriti. It is born of pure or impure parents, according to that kind of guna to which it is most attached.

The supreme Brahman in this body is also known as the Witness. It makes all our actions possible, and, as it were, sanctions them, experiencing all our experiences. It is the infinite Being, the supreme Atman. He who has experienced Brahman directly and known it to be other than Prakriti and the gunas, will not be reborn, no matter how he has lived his life.

Some, whose hearts are purified, realize the Atman within themselves through contemplation. Some realize the Atman philosophically, by meditating upon its independence of Prakriti. Others realize it by following the yoga of right action. Others, who do not know these paths, worship God as their teachers have taught them. If these faithfully practise what they have learned, they also will pass beyond death's power.

> Know this, O Prince:
> Of things created
> All are come forth
> From the seeming union
> Of Field and Knower,
> Prakriti with Brahman.
>
> Who sees his Lord
> Within every creature,
> Deathlessly dwelling
> Amidst the mortal:
> That man sees truly.
>
> Thus ever aware
> Of the Omnipresent
> Always about him,
> He offers no outrage
> To his own Atman,

Hides the face of God
Beneath ego no longer:
Therefore he reaches
That bliss which is highest.

Who sees all action
Ever performed
Alone by Prakriti,
That man sees truly:
The Atman is actless.

Who sees the separate
Lives of all creatures
United in Brahman
Brought forth from Brahman,
Himself finds Brahman.

Not subject to change
Is the infinite Atman,
Without beginning,
Beyond the gunas:
Therefore, O Prince,
Though It dwells in the body,
It acts not, nor feels
The fruits of our action.

For, like the ether,
Pervading all things,
Too subtle for taint,
This Atman also
Inhabits all bodies
But never is tainted.

By the single sun
This whole world is illumined:

By its one Knower
The Field is illumined.

Who thus perceives
With the eye of wisdom
In what manner the Field
Is distinct from its Knower,
How men are made free
From the toils of Prakriti:
His aim is accomplished,
He enters the Highest.

XIV. *The Three Gunas*

SRI KRISHNA:
Once more I shall teach you
That uttermost wisdom:
The sages who found it
Were all made perfect,
Escaping the bonds of the body.

In that wisdom they lived,
Made one with my holy nature:
Now they are not reborn
When a new age begins,
Nor have they any part
In its dissolution.

Prakriti, this vast womb,
I quicken into birth
With the seed of all life:
Thence, O son of Bharata,
The many creatures spring.

Many are the forms of the living,
Many the wombs that bear them;
Prakriti, the womb of all wombs
And I the seed-giving Father.

From Prakriti the gunas come forth,
Sattwa, rajas, tamas:
These are the bonds that bind
The undying dweller
Imprisoned in the body.

Sattwa the shining
Can show the Atman
By its pure light:
Yet sattwa will bind you
To search for happiness,
Longing for knowledge.

Rajas the passionate
Will make you thirsty
For pleasure and possession:
Rajas will bind you
To hunger for action.

Tamas the ignorant
Bewilders all men:
Tamas will bind you
With bonds of delusion,
Sluggishness, stupor.

The power of sattwa
Enslaves the happy,
The power of rajas
Enslaves the doers,
The power of tamas

Enslaves the deluded
And darkens their judgment.

When sattwa prevails
Over rajas, tamas,
Man feels that sattwa:
When rajas prevails
Over sattwa, tamas,
Man is seized by that rajas:
When tamas prevails
Over rajas, sattwa,
Man yields to that tamas.

When understanding
Shines in through the senses,
The doors of the body:
Know sattwa is present.
In greed, in the heat of action,
In eager enterprise,
In restlessness, in all desire,
Know rajas the ruler.

When the mind is dark,
Bewildered, slothful
And lost in delusion:
Know tamas prevailing.

That man who meets death
In the hour of sattwa
Goes to a sinless home
Among the saints of God.

He who dies in rajas
Will be reborn
Among those whose bondage is action:
He who dies in tamas will return
To the womb of a dullard.

Fruit of the righteous act
Is sattwa, purest joy:
As for the deeds of rajas,
Pain is their fruit:
Truly, ignorance is all
The fruit of tamas.

Of sattwa, knowledge is born;
Of rajas, greed;
Tamas brings forth bewilderment,
Delusion, darkness.

Abiding in sattwa,
Man goes to higher realms;
Remaining in rajas,
In this world he remains;
Sunk in tamas,
His lowest nature,
He sinks to the underworld.

Let the wise man know
These gunas alone as the doers
Of every action;
Let him learn to know That
Which is beyond them, also:
Thus he will reach my oneness.

When the dweller in the body
Has overcome the gunas
That cause this body,
Then he is made free
From birth and death,
From pain and decay:
He becomes immortal.

A man is said to have transcended the gunas when he
does not hate the light of sattwa, or the activity of rajas,

or even the delusion of tamas, while these prevail; and yet does not long for them after they have ceased. He is like one who sits unconcerned, and is not disturbed by the gunas. He knows that they are the doers of all action, and never loses this power of discrimination. He rests in the inner calm of the Atman, regarding happiness and suffering as one. Gold, mud and stone are of equal value to him. The pleasant and the unpleasant are alike. He has true discernment. He pays no attention to praise or to blame. His behaviour is the same when he is honoured and when he is insulted. When men go to war, he does not regard either side as his enemies or his partisans. He feels no lack of anything; therefore he never initiates any action.

He who worships me with unfaltering love transcends these gunas. He becomes fit to reach union with Brahman.

> For I am Brahman
> Within this body,
> Life immortal
> That shall not perish:
> I am the Truth
> And the Joy for ever.

XV. *Devotion to the Supreme Spirit*

SRI KRISHNA:

> There is a fig tree
> In ancient story,
> The giant Aswattha,
> The everlasting,
> Rooted in heaven,
> Its branches earthward:

Each of its leaves
Is a song of the Vedas,
And he who knows it
Knows all the Vedas.

Downward and upward
Its branches bending
Are fed by the gunas,
The buds it puts forth
Are the things of the senses,
Roots it has also
Reaching downward
Into this world,
The roots of man's action.

What its form is,
Its end and beginning,
Its very nature,
Can never be known here.

Therefore, a man should contemplate Brahman until he has sharpened the axe of his non-attachment. With this axe, he must cut through the firmly-rooted Aswattha tree. Then he must try to realize that state from which there is no return to future births. Let him take refuge in that Primal Being, from whom all this seeming activity streams forth for ever.

When men have thrown off their ignorance, they are free from pride and delusion. They have conquered the evil of worldly attachment. They live in constant union with the Atman. All craving has left them. They are no longer at the mercy of opposing sense-reactions. Thus they reach that state which is beyond all change.

This is my Infinite Being; shall the sun lend it
Any light—or the moon, or fire? For it shines
Self-luminous always: and he who attains me
Will never be reborn.

Part of myself is the God within every creature,
Keeps that nature eternal, yet seems to be separate,
Putting on mind and senses five, the garment
Made of Prakriti.

When the Lord puts on a body, or casts it from him,
He enters or departs, taking the mind and senses
Away with him, as the wind steals perfume
Out of the flowers.

Watching over the ear and the eye, and presiding
There behind touch, and taste, and smell, he is also
Within the mind: he enjoys and suffers
The things of the senses.

Dwelling in flesh, or departing, or one with the gunas,
Knowing their moods and motions, he is invisible
Always to the ignorant, but his sages see him
With the eye of wisdom.

Yogis who have gained tranquillity through the practice
of spiritual disciplines, behold him in their own consciousness. But those who lack tranquillity and discernment will
not find him, even though they may try hard to do so.

> The light that lives in the sun.
> Lighting all the world,
> The light of the moon,
> The light that is in fire:
> Know that light to be mine.

My energy enters the earth,
Sustaining all that lives:
I become the moon,
Giver of water and sap,
To feed the plants and the trees.

Flame of life in all,
I consume the many foods,
Turning them into strength
That upholds the body.

I am in all hearts,
I give and take away
Knowledge and memory:
I am all that the Vedas tell,
I am the teacher,
The knower of Vedanta.

There are two kinds of personality in this world, the mortal and the immortal. The personality of all creatures is mortal. The personality of God is said to be immortal. It is the same for ever. But there is one other than these; the Impersonal Being who is called the supreme Atman. He is the unchanging Lord who pervades and supports the three worlds. And since I, the Atman, transcend the mortal and even the immortal, I am known in this world and in the Vedas as the supreme Reality.

He who is free from delusion, and knows me as the supreme Reality, knows all that can be known. Therefore he adores me with his whole heart.

This is the most sacred of all the truths I have taught you. He who has realized it becomes truly wise. The purpose of his life is fulfilled.

XVI. *Divine and Demonic Tendencies*

SRI KRISHNA:

A man who is born with tendencies toward the Divine, is fearless and pure in heart. He perseveres in that path to union with Brahman which the scriptures and his teacher have taught him. He is charitable. He can control his passions. He studies the scriptures regularly, and obeys their directions. He practises spiritual disciplines. He is straightforward, truthful, and of an even temper. He harms no one. He renounces the things of this world. He has a tranquil mind and an unmalicious tongue. He is compassionate toward all. He is not greedy. He is gentle and modest. He abstains from useless activity. He has faith in the strength of his higher nature. He can forgive and endure. He is clean in thought and act. He is free from hatred and from pride. Such qualities are his birthright.

When a man is born with demonic tendencies, his birthright is hypocrisy, arrogance, conceit, anger, cruelty and ignorance.

The birthright of the divine nature leads to liberation. The birthright of the demonic nature leads to greater bondage. But you need not fear, Arjuna: your birthright is divine.

In this world there are two kinds of beings: those whose nature tends toward the Divine, and those who have the demonic tendencies. I have already described the divine nature to you in some detail. Now you shall learn more about the demonic nature.

Men of demonic nature know neither what they ought to do, nor what they should refrain from doing. There is no truth in them, or purity, or right conduct. They maintain that the scriptures are a lie, and that the universe is not based upon a moral law, but godless, conceived in lust and created by copulation, without any other cause. Because they believe this in the darkness of their little minds, these degraded creatures do horrible deeds, attempting to destroy the world. They are enemies of mankind.

Their lust can never be appeased. They are arrogant, and vain, and drunk with pride. They run blindly after what is evil. The ends they work for are unclean. They are sure that life has only one purpose: gratification of the senses. And so they are plagued by innumerable cares, from which death alone can release them. Anxiety binds them with a hundred chains, delivering them over to lust and wrath. They are ceaselessly busy, piling up dishonest gains to satisfy their cravings.

'I wanted this and to-day I got it. I want that: I shall get it to-morrow. All these riches are now mine: soon I shall have more. I have killed this enemy. I will kill all the rest. I am a ruler of men. I enjoy the things of this world. I am successful, strong and happy. Who is my equal? I am so wealthy and so nobly born. I will sacrifice to the gods. I will give alms. I will make merry.' That is what they say to themselves, in the blindness of their ignorance.

They are addicts of sensual pleasure, made restless by their many desires, and caught in the net of delusion. They fall into the filthy hell of their own evil minds. Conceited, haughty, foolishly proud, and intoxicated by their wealth, they offer sacrifice to God in name only, for outward show, without following the sacred rituals. These malignant creatures are full of egoism, vanity, lust, wrath, and consciousness of power. They loathe me, and deny my presence both in themselves and in others. They are enemies of all men and of myself; cruel, despicable and vile. I cast them back, again and again, into the wombs of degraded parents, subjecting them to the wheel of birth and death. And so they are constantly reborn, in degradation and delusion. They do not reach me, but sink down to the lowest possible condition of the soul.

Hell has three doors: lust, rage and greed. These lead to man's ruin. Therefore he must avoid them all. He who passes by these three dark doors has achieved his own salvation. He will reach the highest goal at last.

But he who flouts the commandments of the scriptures, and acts on the impulse of his desires, cannot reach perfection, or happiness, or the highest goal.

Let the scriptures be your guide, therefore, in deciding what you must do, and what you must abstain from. First learn the path of action, as the scriptures teach it. Then act accordingly.

XVII. *Three Kinds of Faith*

ARJUNA:

There are men who sacrifice to God with faith in their hearts, although they do not follow the instructions of the scriptures. What is the nature of that faith? Does it belong to sattwa, or to rajas, or to tamas?

SRI KRISHNA:

Faith, among human beings, is of three kinds. It is characterized by sattwa, or by rajas, or by tamas, according to a man's dominant tendencies. Now listen. The faith of each individual corresponds to his temperament. A man consists of the faith that is in him. Whatever his faith is, he is.

Men whose temperament is dominated by sattwa, worship God, in His various aspects. Men of rajas worship power and wealth. As for the rest—the men of tamas—they worship the spirits of the dead, and make gods of the ghosts of their ancestors.

You may know these men to be of demonic nature who mortify the body excessively, in ways not prescribed by the scriptures. They do this because their lust and attachment to sense-objects has filled them with egotism and vanity. In their foolishness, they weaken all their sense-organs, and outrage me, the dweller within the body.

The food which is agreeable to different men is also of three sorts. So, too, are the kinds of sacrifice, austerity and alms-giving. Listen; this is how they may be distinguished.

Men of sattwa like foods which increase their vital force, energy, strength and health. Such foods add to the pleasure of physical and mental life. They are juicy, soothing, fresh and agreeable. But men of rajas prefer foods which are violently bitter, sour, salty, hot, pungent, acid and burning. These cause ill-health, and distemper of the mind and body. And men of tamas take a perverse pleasure in foods which are stale, tasteless, rotten and impure. They like to eat the leavings of others.

When men offer sacrifice in accordance with scriptural instructions, and do not desire any advantage for themselves, they are inspired by sattwa. Their hearts are set upon the sacrifice, for its own sake. An inner sense of duty impels them. But you may be sure that the performance of sacrifice for outward show, and in the hope of divine reward, is inspired by rajas. When the givers of the sacrifice are inspired by tamas, they disregard the scriptural instructions: there is no food-offering, no prayer of dedication, no gift to the chief priest, and no faith at all.

Reverence for the devas, the seers, the teachers and the sages; straightforwardness, harmlessness, physical cleanliness and sexual purity; these are the virtues whose practice is called austerity of the body. To speak without ever causing pain to another, to be truthful, to say always what is kind and beneficial, and to study the scriptures regularly: this practice is called austerity of speech. The practice of serenity, sympathy, meditation upon the Atman, withdrawal of the mind from sense-objects, and integrity of motive, is called austerity of the mind. When men practise this threefold austerity devotedly, with enlightened faith and no desire for reward, it is said to have the nature of sattwa.

Austerity which is practised out of selfish pride, or to gain notoriety, honour and worship, is said to have the nature of rajas. Its effect is not lasting, because it lacks resolution. Austerity is said to have the nature of tamas when it is practised for some foolish purpose, or for the excitement of self-torture, or in order to harm another person.*

A gift may be regarded as proceeding from sattwa when it is given to a deserving person, at a suitable time, and in a fit place; not because of past benefits, or in the hope of a future reward, but simply because the giver knows that it is right for him to give. Whatever is given in the hope of a like return, or with any other selfish motive, or reluctantly, may be known to proceed from rajas. From tamas comes the gift which is given to an unworthy person, at the wrong time and in the wrong place, disdainfully, without regard for the feelings of him who receives it.

OM TAT SAT: these three words designate Brahman, by whom the seers, the Vedas and the sacrificial rites were

* *i.e.* 'Black Magic.'

created in ancient times. Therefore OM is always uttered by the devotees of Brahman, as the scriptures direct, before undertaking any act of sacrifice, almsgiving or austerity. TAT, meaning the Absolute, is uttered by seekers after liberation who desire no reward for their deed, when they are about to make sacrifice, or give alms, or practise some austerity. SAT means goodness, and existence. It also means an auspicious act. All perseverance in sacrifice, austerity or almsgiving is SAT. All actions dedicated to Brahman are SAT.

If a man performs any act of sacrifice, or gives any gift, or practises any austerity without directing his faith and will toward Brahman, then what he does is *asat,* unreal. It cannot produce any good result, either in this world or the next.

XVIII. The Yoga of Renunciation

ARJUNA:

I want to learn the truth about renunciation and non-attachment. What is the difference between these two principles?

SRI KRISHNA:

The sages tell us that renunciation means the complete giving-up of all actions which are motivated by desire. And they say that non-attachment means abandonment of the fruits of action.

Some philosophers declare that all kinds of action should be given up, because action always contains a certain measure of evil. Others say that acts of sacrifice, almsgiving and austerity should not be given up. Now you shall hear the truth of this matter.

Acts of sacrifice, almsgiving and austerity should not

be given up: their performance is necessary. For sacrifice, almsgiving and austerity are a means of purification to those who rightly understand them. But even these acts must be performed without attachment or regard for their fruits. Such is my final and considered judgment.

Renunciation is said to be of three kinds. If a man, in his ignorance, renounces those actions which the scriptures ordain, his renunciation is inspired by tamas. If he abstains from any action merely because it is disagreeable, or because he fears it will cause him bodily pain, his renunciation is inspired by rajas. He will not obtain any spiritual benefit from such renunciation. But when a man performs an action which is sanctioned by the scriptures, and does it for duty's sake only, renouncing all attachment and desire for its fruits, then his renunciation is inspired by sattwa.

When a man is endowed with spiritual discrimination and illumined by knowledge of the Atman, all his doubts are dispelled. He does not shrink from doing what is disagreeable to him, nor does he long to do what is agreeable. No human being can give up action altogether, but he who gives up the fruits of action is said to be non-attached.

To those who have not yet renounced the ego and its desires, action bears three kinds of fruit—pleasant, unpleasant, and a mixture of both. They will be reaped in due season. But those who have renounced ego and desire will reap no fruit at all, either in this world or in the next.

> All our action
> Has five partakers:
> So say the scriptures
> That teach us wisdom
> To break the bondage
> Earned by our action:
> Listen and learn them.

First, this body;
Then ego, the doer;
The organs of sense
And the many motions
Of Life in the body;
Lastly, the devas
In spirit presiding.*

Whatever the action,
Excellent, evil;
Whether of speech,
Of mind, or of body:
These are its causers.

Falsely he sees,
And with small discernment,
Who sees this Atman
The doer of action:
His mind is not purged
In the work of the spirit.

But he whose mind dwells
Beyond attachment,
Untainted by ego,
No act shall bind him
With any bond:
Though he slay these thousands
He is no slayer.

There are three things which motivate action: knowledge, the knower and that which is known. There are three
constituents of action: the instrument, the purpose and
the doer, Sankhya† philosophy declares that knowledge,

* According to Hindu mythology, each sense-organ has a presiding deity.
† The system of philosophy compiled by Kapila.

action and doer are of three kinds only, according to the guna which predominates in each. Listen, this is their nature.

There is that knowledge
From sattwa proceeding
Which knows one Being
Deathless in every creature,
Entire amidst all division.

The knowledge that is rajas
Knows nothing but difference:
Many souls in many creatures,
All various, each
Apart from his fellow.

The knowledge that is tamas
Knows no reason:
Its sight distorted
Takes the part for the whole,
Misreading Nature.

The act of sacred duty,
Done without attachment,
Not as pleasure desired,
Not as hated compulsion,
By him who has no care
For the fruit of his action:
That act is of sattwa.

The act of weary toil
Done in despite of nature
Under the whip of lust
And the will of the ego:
That act is of rajas.

The act undertaken
In the hour of delusion
Without count of cost,
Squandering strength and treasure,
Heedless of harm to another,
By him who does not question
His power to perform it:
That act is of tamas.

The doer without desire,
Who does not boast of his deed,
Who is ardent, enduring,
Untouched by triumph,
In failure untroubled:
He is a man of sattwa.

The doer with desire,
Hot for the prize of vainglory,
Brutal, greedy and foul,
In triumph too quick to rejoice,
In failure despairing:
He is a man of rajas.

The indifferent doer
Whose heart is not in his deed,
Stupid and stubborn,
A cheat, and malicious,
The idle lover of delay,
Easily dejected:
He is a man of tamas.

There are three kinds of conscience and three kinds of determination, according to the predominance of each guna. Now listen: I will explain them fully, one by one.

A man's conscience has the nature of sattwa when it can

distinguish between the paths of renunciation and worldly desire. Then it knows what actions are right or wrong, what is safe and what is dangerous, what binds the embodied spirit and what sets it free. But when the conscience cannot distinguish truly between right and wrong, or know what should and what should not be done, then it has the nature of rajas. And when the conscience is so thickly wrapped in ignorance that it mistakes wrong for right and sees everything distorted, then it has the nature of tamas.

Determination inspired by sattwa never wavers. It is strengthened by the practice of yoga. A man who has this kind of determination gains absolute control over his mind, vital energy and senses. Rajas, on the other hand, inspires that kind of determination with which a man follows the object of his desire, or seeks wealth, or does a duty, looking for reward and personal advantage. As for the determination inspired by tamas, it is nothing but obstinacy. It makes a man stubbornly refuse to shake off his dullness, fear, grief, low spirits or vanity.

And now, Arjuna, I will tell you about the three kinds of happiness:

> Who knows the Atman
> Knows that happiness
> Born of pure knowledge:
> The joy of sattwa.
> Deep his delight
> After strict self-schooling:
> Sour toil at first
> But at last what sweetness,
> The end of sorrow.
>
> Senses also
> Have joy in their marriage

With things of the senses,
Sweet at first
But at last how bitter:
Steeped in rajas,
That pleasure is poison.
Bred of tamas
Is brutish contentment
In stupor and sloth
And obstinate error:
Its end, its beginning
Alike are delusion.

There is no creature, either on earth or among the devas in heaven, who is free from these three gunas which come forth from Prakriti.

Seer and leader,
Provider and server:*
Each has the duty
Ordained by his nature
Born of the gunas.
The seer's duty,
Ordained by his nature,
Is to be tranquil
In mind and in spirit,
Self-controlled,
Austere and stainless,
Upright, forbearing;
To follow wisdom,
To know the Atman,
Firm of faith
In the truth that is Brahman.

* See note on Chapter IX, page 57.

The leader's duty,
Ordained by his nature,
Is to be bold,
Unflinching and fearless,
Subtle of skill
And open-handed,
Great-hearted in battle,
A resolute ruler.

Others are born
To the tasks of providing:
These are the traders,
The cultivators,
The breeders of cattle.

To work for all men,
Such is the duty
Ordained for the servers:
This is their nature.
All mankind
Is born for perfection
And each shall attain it
Will he but follow
His nature's duty.

Now you shall hear how a man may become perfect, if he devotes himself to the work which is natural to him. A man will reach perfection if he does his duty as an act of worship to the Lord, who is the source of the universe, prompting all action, everywhere present.

A man's own natural duty, even if it seems imperfectly done, is better than work not naturally his own even if this is well performed. When a man acts according to the law of his nature, he cannot be sinning. Therefore, no one should give up his natural work, even though he does it imperfectly. For all action is involved in imperfection, like fire in smoke.

When a man has achieved non-attachment, self-mastery and freedom from desire through renunciation, he reaches union with Brahman, who is beyond all action.

> Learn from me now,
> O son of Kunti,
> How man made perfect
> Is one with Brahman,
> The goal of wisdom.
> When the mind and the heart
> Are freed from delusion,
> United with Brahman,
> When steady will
> Has subdued the senses,
> When sight and taste
> And sound are abandoned
> Without regretting,
> Without aversion;
> When man seeks solitude,
> Eats but little,
> Curbing his speech,
> His mind and his body,
> Ever engaged
> In his meditation
> On Brahman the truth,
> And full of compassion;
> When he casts from him
> Vanity, violence,
> Pride, lust, anger
> And all his possessions,

Totally free
From the sense of ego
And tranquil of heart:
That man is ready
For oneness with Brahman.
And he who dwells
United with Brahman,
Calm in mind,
Not grieving, not craving,
Regarding all men
With equal acceptance:
He loves me most dearly.

To love is to know me,
My innermost nature,
The truth that I am:
Through this knowledge he enters
At once to my Being.

All that he does
Is offered before me
In utter surrender:
My grace is upon him,
He finds the eternal,
The place unchanging.

Mentally resign all your action to me. Regard me as
your dearest loved one. Know me to be your only refuge.
Be united always in heart and consciousness with me.

United with me, you shall overcome all difficulties by my
grace. But if your heart is full of conceit, and you do not
heed me, you are lost. If, in your vanity, you say: 'I will
not fight,' your resolve is vain. Your own nature will drive
you to the act. For you yourself have created the karma

that binds you. You are helpless in its power. And you will do that very thing which your ignorance seeks to avoid.

The Lord lives in the heart of every creature. He turns them round and round upon the wheel of his Maya. Take refuge utterly in him. By his grace you will find supreme peace, and the state which is beyond all change.

Now I have taught you that wisdom which is the secret of secrets. Ponder it carefully. Then act as you think best. These are the last words that I shall say to you, the deepest of all truths. I speak for your own good. You are the friend I chose and love.

> Give me your whole heart,
> Love and adore me,
> Worship me always,
> Bow to me only,
> And you shall find me:
> This is my promise
> Who love you dearly.
>
> Lay down all duties
> In me, your refuge.
> Fear no longer,
> For I will save you
> From sin and from bondage.

You must never tell this holy truth to anyone who lacks self-control and devotion, or who despises his teacher and mocks at me. But the man who loves me, and teaches my devotees this supreme truth of the Gita, will certainly come to me. No one can do me a higher service than this. No one on earth can be dearer to me.

And if any man meditates upon this sacred discourse of ours, I shall consider that he has worshipped me in spirit.

Even if a man simply listens to these words with faith, and does not doubt them, he will be freed from his sins and reach the heaven of the righteous.

Have you listened carefully, Arjuna, to everything I have told you? Have I dispelled the delusions of your ignorance?

ARJUNA:

By your grace, O Lord, my delusions have been dispelled. My mind stands firm. Its doubts are ended. I will do your bidding.

SANJAYA:

Such were the words that thrilled my heart, that marvellous discourse,
Heard from the lips of the high-souled Prince and the great Lord Krishna,
Not with these earthly ears, but by mystic grace of Vyasa,
Thus I learned that yoga supreme from the Master of yogis.
Ever and ever again I rejoice, O King, and remember
Sacred and wonderful truths that Krishna told to his comrade.
Ever again, O King, I am glad and remember rejoicing
That most splendid of forms put on by Krishna, the Sweet One.
Where Lord Krishna is, and Arjuna, great among archers,
There, I know, is goodness and peace, and triumph and glory.

OM. Peace. Peace. Peace.

WILLIAM SHAKESPEARE *is a person whose identity and activities are the subject of much controversy, although his plays are the best known in the English language. His date of birth is uncertain, but it is known that he was baptized at Stratford-on-Avon, England in 1564. About twenty years later he drifted to London where he found menial work in the theater. He became an actor and a playwright, although his acting was probably confined to minor roles. His earliest play may be dated 1591 and his latest 1613. The two parts of* Henry the Fourth *are dated around 1597. That Shakespeare had some financial success is indicated by the fact that he purchased a large house in Stratford and made some investments. He died in 1616.*

DRAMATIS PERSONAE

KING HENRY *the Fourth.*
HENRY, PRINCE OF WALES,
JOHN OF LANCASTER, } *sons to the King.*
EARL OF WESTMORELAND.
SIR WALTER BLUNT.
THOMAS PERCY, *Earl of Worcester.*
HENRY PERCY, *Earl of Northumberland.*
HENRY PERCY, *surnamed* HOTSPUR, *his son.*
EDMUND MORTIMER, *Earl of March.*
RICHARD SCROOP, *Archbishop of York.*
ARCHIBALD, *Earl of Douglas.*
OWEN GLENDOWER.
SIR RICHARD VERNON.
SIR JOHN FALSTAFF.
SIR MICHAEL, *a friend to the Archbishop of York.*

POINS.
GADSHILL.
PETO.
BARDOLPH.

LADY PERCY, *wife to Hotspur, and sister to Mortimer.*
LADY MORTIMER, *daughter to Glendower, and wife to Mortimer.*
MISTRESS QUICKLY, *hostess of a tavern in Eastcheap.*

LORDS, OFFICERS, SHERIFF, VINTNER, CHAMBERLAIN, DRAWERS, *two* CARRIERS, TRAVELLERS, *and* ATTENDANTS.

Scene: ENGLAND *and* WALES.

THE HISTORY OF
KING HENRY THE FOURTH
PART ONE

ACT I

SCENE I — LONDON. *The palace.*

Enter KING HENRY, LORD JOHN OF LANCASTER, *the* EARL
OF WESTMORELAND, SIR WALTER BLUNT, *and others.*]

KING. So shaken as we are, so wan with care,
    Find we a time for frighted peace to pant,
    And breathe short-winded accents of new broils
    To be commenced in stronds afar remote.
    No more the thirsty entrance of this soil
    Shall daub her lips with her own children's blood;
    No more shall trenching war channel her fields,
    Nor bruise her flowerets with the armed hoofs
    Of hostile paces: those opposed eyes,
    Which, like the meteors of a troubled heaven,
    All of one nature, of one substance bred,
    Did lately meet in the intestine shock
    And furious close of civil butchery,
    Shall now, in mutual well-beseeming ranks,
    March all one way, and be no more opposed
    Against acquaintance, kindred and allies:
    The edge of war, like an ill-sheathed knife,
    No more shall cut his master. Therefore, friends,
    As far as to the sepulchre of Christ,
    Whose soldier now, under whose blessèd cross

1

We are impressed and engaged to fight,
Forthwith a power of English shall we levy;
Whose arms were moulded in their mothers' womb
To chase these pagans in those holy fields
Over whose acres walk'd those blessed feet,
Which fourteen hundred years ago were nail'd
For our advantage on the bitter cross.
But this our purpose now is twelve month old,
And bootless 'tis to tell you we will go:
Therefore we meet not now. Then let me hear
Of you, my gentle cousin Westmoreland,
What yesternight our council did decree
In forwarding this dear expedience.

WESTMORELAND. My liege, this haste was hot in question,
And many limits of the charge set down
But yesternight: when all athwart there came
A post from Wales loaden with heavy news;
Whose worst was, that the noble Mortimer,
Leading the men of Herefordshire to fight
Against the irregular and wild Glendower,
Was by the rude hands of that Welshman taken,
A thousand of his people butchered;
Upon whose dead corpse there was such misuse,
Such beastly shameless transformation,
By those Welshwomen done, as may not be
Without much shame retold or spoken of.

KING. It seems then that the tidings of this broil
Brake off our business for the Holy Land.

WEST. This match'd with other did, my gracious lord;
For more uneven and unwelcome news
Came from the north and thus it did import:
On Holy-rood day, the gallant Hotspur there,
Young Harry Percy, and brave Archibald,

That ever-valiant and approved Scot,
At Holmedon met,
Where they did spend a sad and bloody hour;
As by discharge of their artillery,
And shape of likelihood, the news was told;
For he that brought them, in the very heat
And pride of their contention did take horse,
Uncertain of the issue any way.

KING. Here is a dear, a true industrious friend,
Sir Walter Blunt, new lighted from his horse,
Stain'd with the variation of each soil
Betwixt that Holmedon and this seat of ours;
And he hath brought us smooth and welcome news.
The Earl of Douglas is discomfited:
Ten thousand bold Scots, two and twenty knights,
Balk'd in their own blood did Sir Walter see
On Holmedon's plains. Of prisoners, Hotspur took
Mordake the Earl of Fife, and eldest son
To beaten Douglas; and the Earl of Athol,
Of Murray, Angus, and Menteith:
And is not this an honourable spoil?
A gallant prize? ha, cousin, is it not?

WEST. In faith,
It is a conquest for a prince to boast of.

KING. Yea, there thou makest me sad and makest me sin
In envy that my Lord Northumberland
Should be the father to so blest a son,
A son who is the theme of honour's tongue;
Amongst a grove, the very straightest plant;
Who is sweet Fortune's minion and her pride:
Whilst I, by looking on the praise of him,
See riot and dishonour stain the brow
Of my young Harry. O that it could be proved

That some night-tripping fairy had exchanged
In cradle-clothes our children where they lay,
And call'd mine Percy, his Plantagenet!
Then would I have his Harry, and he mine.
But let him from my thoughts. What think you, coz,
Of this young Percy's pride? the prisoners,
Which he in this adventure hath surprised,
To his own use he keeps; and sends me word,
I shall have none but Mordake Earl of Fife.

WEST. This is his uncle's teaching: this is Worcester,
Malevolent to you in all aspects;
Which makes him prune himself, and bristle up
The crest of youth against your dignity.

KING. But I have sent for him to answer this;
And for this cause awhile we must neglect
Our holy purpose to Jerusalem.
Cousin, on Wednesday next our council we
Will hold at Windsor; so inform the lords:
But come yourself with speed to us again;
For more is to be said and to be done
Than out of anger can be uttered.

WEST. I will, my liege. [*Exeunt.*

SCENE II — LONDON. *An apartment of the* PRINCE'S

Enter the PRINCE OF WALES *and* FALSTAFF.]

FALSTAFF. Now, Hal, what time of day is it, lad?

PRINCE. Thou art so fat-witted, with drinking of old sack
and unbuttoning thee after supper and sleeping upon
benches after noon, that thou hast forgotten to demand
that truly which thou wouldst truly know. What a devil
hast thou to do with the time of the day? Unless hours
were cups of sack, and minutes capons, and clocks the
tongues of bawds, and dials the signs of leaping-houses,

and the blessed sun himself a fair hot wench in flame-
coloured taffeta, I see no reason why thou shouldst be so
superfluous to demand the time of the day.

FALSTAFF. Indeed, you come near me now, Hal; for we
that take purses go by the moon and the seven stars, and
not by Phœbus, he, 'that wandering knight so fair.' And,
I prithee, sweet wag, when thou art king, as, God save
thy grace,—majesty I should say, for grace thou wilt have
none,—

PRINCE. What, none?

FALSTAFF. No, by my troth, not so much as will serve to be
prologue to an egg and butter.

PRINCE. Well, how then? come, roundly, roundly.

FALSTAFF. Marry, then, sweet wag, when thou art king, let
not us that are squires of the night's body be called
thieves of the day's beauty: let us be Diana's foresters,
gentlemen of the shade, minions of the moon; and let
men say we be men of good government, being governed,
as the sea is, by our noble and chaste mistress the moon,
under whose countenance we steal.

PRINCE. Thou sayest well, and it holds well too; for the fortune of us that are the moon's men doth ebb and flow like
the sea, being governed, as the sea is, by the moon. As,
for proof, now: a purse of gold most resolutely snatched
on Monday night and most dissolutely spent on Tues-
day morning; got with swearing 'Lay by' and spent with
crying 'Bring in;' now in as low an ebb as the foot of the
ladder, and by and by in as high a flow as the ridge of the
gallows.

FALSTAFF. By the Lord, thou sayest true, lad. And is not
my hostess of the tavern a most sweet wench?

PRINCE. As the honey of Hybla, my old lad of the castle.
And is not a buff jerkin a most sweet robe of durance?

FALSTAFF. How now, how now, mad wag! what, in thy

quips and thy quiddities? what a plague have I to do with a buff jerkin?

PRINCE. Why, what a pox have I to do with my hostess of the tavern?

FALSTAFF. Well, thou hast called her to a reckoning many a time and oft.

PRINCE. Did I ever call for thee to pay thy part?

FALSTAFF. No; I'll give thee thy due, thou hast paid all there.

PRINCE. Yea, and elsewhere, so far as my coin would stretch; and where it would not, I have used my credit.

FALSTAFF. Yea, and so used it that, were it not here apparent that thou art heir apparent—But, I prithee, sweet wag, shall there be gallows standing in England when thou art king? and resolution thus fobbed as it is with the rusty curb of old father antic the law? Do not thou, when thou art king, hang a thief.

PRINCE. No; thou shalt.

FALSTAFF. Shall I? O rare! By the Lord, I'll be a brave judge.

PRINCE. Thou judgest false already: I mean, thou shalt have the hanging of the thieves and so become a rare hangman.

FALSTAFF. Well, Hal, well; and in some sort it jumps with my humour as well as waiting in the court, I can tell you.

PRINCE. For obtaining of suits?

FALSTAFF. Yea, for obtaining of suits, whereof the hangman hath no lean wardrobe. 'Sblood, I am as melancholy as a gib cat or a lugged bear.

PRINCE. Or an old lion, or a lover's lute.

FALSTAFF. Yea, or the drone of a Lincolnshire bagpipe.

PRINCE. What sayest thou to a hare, or the melancholy of Moor-ditch?

FALSTAFF. Thou hast the most unsavoury similes, and art indeed the most comparative, rascalliest, sweet young prince. But, Hal, I prithee, trouble me no more with vanity. I would to God thou and I knew where a commodity of good names were to be bought. An old lord of the council rated me the other day in the street about you, sir, but I marked him not; and yet he talked very wisely, but I regarded him not; and yet he talked wisely, and in the street too.

PRINCE. Thou didst well, for wisdom cries out in the streets, and no man regards it.

FALSTAFF. O, thou hast damnable iteration, and art indeed able to corrupt a saint. Thou hast done much harm upon me, Hal; God forgive thee for it! Before I knew thee, Hal, I knew nothing; and now am I, if a man should speak truly, little better than one of the wicked. I must give over this life, and I will give it over: by the Lord, an I do not, I am a villain: I'll be damned for never a king's son in Christendom.

PRINCE. Where shall we take a purse to-morrow, Jack?

FALSTAFF. 'Zounds, where thou wilt, lad; I'll make one; an I do not, call me villain and baffle me.

PRINCE. I see a good amendment of life in thee; from praying to purse-taking.

FALSTAFF. Why, Hal, 'tis my vocation, Hal; 'tis no sin for a man to labour in his vocation.

Enter POINS.]

Poins! Now shall we know if Gadshill have set a match. O, if men were to be saved by merit, what hole in hell were hot enough for him? This is the most omnipotent villain that ever cried 'Stand' to a true man.

PRINCE. Good morrow, Ned.

POINS. Good morrow, sweet Hal. What says Monsieur Re-

morse? what says Sir John Sack and Sugar? Jack! how
agrees the devil and thee about thy soul, that thou soldest
him on Good Friday last for a cup of Madeira and a cold
capon's leg?

PRINCE. Sir John stands to his word, the devil shall have his
bargain; for he was never yet a breaker of proverbs: he
will give the devil his due.

POINS. Then art thou damned for keeping thy word with
the devil.

PRINCE. Else he had been damned for cozening the devil.

POINS. But, my lads, my lads, to-morrow morning, by four
o'clock, early at Gadshill! there are pilgrims going to
Canterbury with rich offerings, and traders riding to
London with fat purses: I have vizards for you all; you
have horses for yourselves: Gadshill lies to-night in
Rochester: I have bespoke supper to-morrow night in
Eastcheap: we may do it as secure as sleep. If you will go,
I will stuff your purses full of crowns; if you will not,
tarry at home and be hanged.

FALSTAFF. Hear ye, Yedward; if I tarry at home and go
not, I'll hang you for going.

POINS. You will, chops?

FALSTAFF. Hal, wilt thou make one?

PRINCE. Who, I rob? I a thief? not I, by my faith.

FALSTAFF. There's neither honesty, manhood, nor good
fellowship in thee, nor thou camest not of the blood
royal, if thou darest not stand for ten shillings.

PRINCE. Well then, once in my days I'll be a madcap.

FALSTAFF. Why, that's well said.

PRINCE. Well, come what will, I'll tarry at home.

FALSTAFF. By the Lord, I'll be a traitor then, when thou
art king.

PRINCE. I care not.

POINS. Sir John, I prithee, leave the prince and me alone: I
   will lay him down such reasons for this adventure that he
   shall go.

FALSTAFF. Well, God give thee the spirit of persuasion and
   him the ears of profiting, that what thou speakest may
   move and what he hears may be believed, that the true
   prince may, for recreation sake, prove a false thief; for
   the poor abuses of the time want countenance. Farewell:
   you shall find me in Eastcheap.

PRINCE. Farewell, thou latter spring! farewell, All-hallown
   summer!   [*Exit* FALSTAFF.

POINS. Now, my good sweet honey lord, ride with us to-
   morrow: I have a jest to execute that I cannot manage
   alone. Falstaff, Bardolph, Peto and Gadshill shall rob
   those men that we have already waylaid; yourself and I
   will not be there; and when they have the booty, if you
   and I do not rob them, cut this head off from my
   shoulders.

PRINCE. How shall we part with them in setting forth?

POINS. Why, we will set forth before or after them, and ap-
   point them a place of meeting, wherein it is at our pleasure to fail, and then will they adventure upon the exploit
   themselves; which they shall have no sooner achieved,
   but we'll set upon them.

PRINCE. Yea, but 'tis like that they will know us by our
   horses, by our habits, and by every other appointment,
   to be ourselves.

POINS. Tut! our horses they shall not see; I'll tie them in the
   wood; our vizards we will change after we leave them:
   and, sirrah, I have cases of buckram for the nonce, to
   immask our noted outward garments.

PRINCE. Yea, but I doubt they will be too hard for us.

POINS. Well, for two of them, I know them to be as true-bred cowards as ever turned back; and for the third, if he fight longer than he sees reason, I'll forswear arms. The virtue of this jest will be, the incomprehensible lies that this same fat rogue will tell us when we meet at supper: how thirty, at least, he fought with; what wards, what blows, what extremities he endured; and in the reproof of this lies the jest.

PRINCE. Well, I'll go with thee: provide us all things necessary and meet me to-morrow night in Eastcheap; there I'll sup. Farewell.

POINS. Farewell, my lord. [*Exit.*

PRINCE. I know you all, and will a while uphold
The unyoked humour of your idleness:
Yet herein will I imitate the sun,
Who doth permit the base contagious clouds
To smother up his beauty from the world,
That, when he please again to be himself,
Being wanted, he may be more wonder'd at,
By breaking through the foul and ugly mists
Of vapours that did seem to strangle him.
If all the year were playing holidays,
To sport would be as tedious as to work;
But when they seldom come, they wish'd for come,
And nothing pleaseth but rare accidents.
So, when this loose behaviour I throw off
And pay the debt I never promised,
By how much better than my word I am,
By so much shall I falsify men's hopes;
And like bright metal on a sullen ground,
My reformation, glittering o'er my fault,
Shall show more goodly and attract more eyes
Than that which hath no foil to set it off.

I'll so offend, to make offence a skill;
Redeeming time when men think least I will.   [*Exit.*

SCENE III — LONDON. *The palace.*

Enter the KING, NORTHUMBERLAND, WORCESTER,
        HOTSPUR, SIR WALTER BLUNT, *with others.*]
KING. My blood hath been too cold and temperate,
    Unapt to stir at these indignities,
    And you have found me; for accordingly
    You tread upon my patience: but be sure
    I will from henceforth rather be myself,
    Mighty and to be fear'd, than my condition;
    Which hath been smooth as oil, soft as young down,
    And therefore lost that title of respect
    Which the proud soul ne'er pays but to the proud.
WORCESTER. Our house, my sovereign liege, little deserves
    The scourge of greatness to be used on it;
    And that same greatness too which our own hands
    Have holp to make so portly.
NORTHUMBERLAND. My lord,—
KING. Worcester, get thee gone; for I do see
    Danger and disobedience in thine eye:
    O, sir, your presence is too bold and peremptory,
    And majesty might never yet endure
    The moody frontier of a servant brow.
    You have good leave to leave us: when we need
    Your use and counsel, we shall send for you.
                                    [*Exit* WORCESTER.
    You were about to speak.   [*To* NORTHUMBERLAND.
NORTH.   Yea, my good lord.
    Those prisoners in your highness' name demanded,

Which Harry Percy here at Holmedon took,
Were, as he says, not with such strength denied
As is deliver'd to your majesty:
Either envy, therefore, or misprision
Is guilty of this fault and not my son.

HOTSPUR. My liege, I did deny no prisoners.
But I remember, when the fight was done,
When I was dry with rage and extreme toil,
Breathless and faint, leaning upon my sword,
Came there a certain lord, neat, and trimly dress'd,
Fresh as a bridegroom; and his chin new reap'd
Show'd like a stubble-land at harvest-home;
He was perfumed like a milliner;
And 'twixt his finger and his thumb he held
A pouncet-box, which ever and anon
He gave his nose and took 't away again;
Who therewith angry, when it next came there,
Took it in snuff; and still he smiled and talk'd,
And as the soldiers bore dead bodies by,
He call'd them untaught knaves, unmannerly,
To bring a slovenly unhandsome corse
Betwixt the wind and his nobility.
With many holiday and lady terms
He question'd me; amongst the rest, demanded
My prisoners in your majesty's behalf.
I then, all smarting with my wounds being cold,
To be so pester'd with a popinjay,
Out of my grief and my impatience,
Answer'd neglectingly I know not what,
He should, or he should not; for he made me mad
To see him shine so brisk, and smell so sweet,
And talk so like a waiting-gentlewoman
Of guns and drums and wounds,—God save the mark!—

And telling me the sovereign'st thing on earth
Was parmaceti for an inward bruise;
And that it was great pity, so it was,
This villanous salt-petre should be digg'd
Out of the bowels of the harmless earth,
Which many a good tall fellow had destroy'd
So cowardly; and but for these vile guns,
He would himself have been a soldier.
This bald unjointed chat of his, my lord,
I answer'd indirectly, as I said;
And I beseech you, let not his report
Come current for an accusation
Betwixt my love and your high majesty.

BLUNT. The circumstance consider'd, good my lord,
Whate'er Lord Harry Percy then had said
To such a person and in such a place,
At such a time, with all the rest re-told,
May reasonably die and never rise
To do him wrong, or any way impeach
What then he said, so he unsay it now.

KING. Why, yet he doth deny his prisoners,
But with proviso and exception,
That we at our own charge shall ransom straight
His brother-in-law, the foolish Mortimer;
Who, on my soul, hath wilfully betray'd
The lives of those that he did lead to fight
Against that great magician, damn'd Glendower,
Whose daughter, as we hear, the Earl of March
Hath lately married. Shall our coffers, then,
Be emptied to redeem a traitor home?
Shall we buy treason? and indent with fears,
When they have lost and forfeited themselves?
No, on the barren mountains let him starve;

For I shall never hold that man my friend
Whose tongue shall ask me for one penny cost
To ransom home revolted Mortimer.

HOTSPUR. Revolted Mortimer!
He never did fall off, my sovereign liege,
But by the chance of war: to prove that true
Needs no more but one tongue for all those wounds,
Those mouthed wounds, which valiantly he took,
When on the gentle Severn's sedgy bank,
In single opposition, hand to hand,
He did confound the best part of an hour
In changing hardiment with great Glendower:
Three times they breathed and three times did they drink,
Upon agreement, of swift Severn's flood;
Who then, affrighted with their bloody looks,
Ran fearfully among the trembling reeds,
And hid his crisp head in the hollow bank
Bloodstained with these valiant combatants.
Never did base and rotten policy
Colour her working with such deadly wounds;
Nor never could the noble Mortimer
Receive so many, and all willingly:
Then let not him be slander'd with revolt.

KING. Thou dost belie him, Percy, thou dost belie him;
He never did encounter with Glendower:
I tell thee,
He durst as well have met the devil alone
As Owen Glendower for an enemy.
Art thou not ashamed? But, sirrah, henceforth
Let me not hear you speak of Mortimer:
Send me your prisoners with the speediest means,
Or you shall hear in such a kind from me
As will displease you. My Lord Northumberland,

We license your departure with your son.
Send us your prisoners, or you will hear of it.

        [*Exeunt* KING HENRY, BLUNT, *and train.*

HOTSPUR. An if the devil come and roar for them,
  I will not send them: I will after straight
  And tell him so; for I will ease my heart,
  Albeit I make a hazard of my head.

NORTH. What, drunk with choler? stay and pause a while:
  Here comes your uncle.

Re-enter WORCESTER.]

HOTSPUR.   Speak of Mortimer!
  'Zounds, I will speak of him; and let my soul
  Want mercy, if I do not join with him:
  Yea, on his part I'll empty all these veins,
  And shed my dear blood drop by drop in the dust,
  But I will lift the down-trod Mortimer
  As high in the air as this unthankful king,
  As this ingrate and canker'd Bolingbroke.

NORTH. Brother, the king hath made your nephew mad.

WORCESTER. Who struck this heat up after I was gone?

HOTSPUR. He will, forsooth, have all my prisoners;
  And when I urged the ransom once again
  Of my wife's brother, then his cheek look'd pale,
  And on my face he turn'd an eye of death,
  Trembling even at the name of Mortimer.

WORCESTER. I cannot blame him: was not he proclaim'd
  By Richard that dead is the next of blood?

NORTH. He was; I heard the proclamation:
  And then it was when the unhappy king,—
  Whose wrongs in us God pardon!—did set forth
  Upon his Irish expedition;
  From whence he intercepted did return
  To be deposed and shortly murdered.

WORCESTER. And for whose death we in the world's wide
    mouth
Live scandalized and foully spoken of.
HOTSPUR. But, soft, I pray you; did King Richard then
    Proclaim my brother Edmund Mortimer
    Heir to the crown?
NORTH. He did; myself did hear it.
HOTSPUR. Nay, then I cannot blame his cousin king,
    That wish'd him on the barren mountains starve.
    But shall it be, that you, that set the crown
    Upon the head of this forgetful man,
    And for his sake wear the detested blot
    Of murderous subornation, shall it be,
    That you a world of curses undergo,
    Being the agents, or base second means,
    The cords, the ladder, or the hangman rather?
    O, pardon me that I descend so low,
    To show the line and the predicament
    Wherein you range under this subtle king;
    Shall it for shame be spoken in these days,
    Or fill up chronicles in time to come,
    That men of your nobility and power
    Did gage them both in an unjust behalf,
    As both of you—God pardon it!—have done,
    To put down Richard, that sweet lovely rose,
    And plant this thorn, this canker, Bolingbroke?
    And shall it in more shame be further spoken,
    That you are fool'd, discarded and shook off
    By him for whom these shames ye underwent?
    No; yet time serves wherein you may redeem
    Your banish'd honours, and restore yourselves
    Into the good thoughts of the world again,
    Revenge the jeering and disdain'd contempt

Of this proud king, who studies day and night
To answer all the debt he owes to you
Even with the bloody payment of your deaths:
Therefore, I say,—

WORCESTER.   Peace, cousin, say no more:
And now I will unclasp a secret book,
And to your quick-conceiving discontents
I'll read you matter deep and dangerous,
As full of peril and adventurous spirit
As to o'er-walk a current roaring loud
On the unsteadfast footing of a spear.

HOTSPUR. If he fall in, good night! or sink or swim:
Send danger from the east unto the west,
So honour cross it from the north to south,
And let them grapple: O, the blood more stirs
To rouse a lion than to start a hare!

NORTH. Imagination of some great exploit
Drives him beyond the bounds of patience.

HOTSPUR. By heaven, methinks it were an easy leap,
To pluck bright honour from the pale-faced moon,
Or dive into the bottom of the deep,
Where fathom-line could never touch the ground,
And pluck up drowned honour by the locks;
So he that doth redeem her thence might wear
Without corrival all her dignities:
But out upon this half-faced fellowship!

WORCESTER. He apprehends a world of figures here,
But not the form of what he should attend.
Good cousin, give me audience for a while.

HOTSPUR. I cry you mercy.

WORCESTER.   Those same noble Scots
That are your prisoners,—

HOTSPUR.   I'll keep them all;

By God, he shall not have a Scot of them;
No, if a Scot would save his soul, he shall not:
I'll keep them, by this hand.

WORCESTER.   You start away
And lend no ear unto my purposes.
Those prisoners you shall keep.

HOTSPUR.   Nay, I will; that's flat:
He said he would not ransom Mortimer;
Forbad my tongue to speak of Mortimer;
But I will find him when he lies asleep,
And in his ear I'll holla 'Mortimer!'
Nay,
I'll have a starling shall be taught to speak
Nothing but 'Mortimer,' and give it him,
To keep his anger still in motion.

WORCESTER. Hear you, cousin; a word.

HOTSPUR. All studies here I solemnly defy,
Save how to gall and pinch this Bolingbroke:
And that same sword-and-buckler Prince of Wales,
But that I think his father loves him not
And would be glad he met with some mischance,
I would have him poison'd with a pot of ale.

WORCESTER. Farewell, kinsman: I'll talk to you
When you are better temper'd to attend.

NORTH. Why, what a wasp-stung and impatient fool
Art thou to break into this woman's mood,
Tying thine ear to no tongue but thine own!

HOTSPUR. Why, look you, I am whipp'd and scourged with
rods,
Nettled, and stung with pismires, when I hear
Of this vile politician, Bolingbroke.
In Richard's time,—what do you call the place?—
A plague upon it, it is in Gloucestershire;

'Twas where the madcap duke his uncle kept,
His uncle York; where I first bow'd my knee
Unto this king of smiles, this Bolingbroke,—
'Sblood!—
When you and he came back from Ravenspurgh.
NORTH. At Berkley-castle.
HOTSPUR. You say true:
Why, what a candy deal of courtesy
This fawning greyhound then did proffer me!
Look, 'when his infant fortune came to age,'
And 'gentle Harry Percy,' and 'kind cousin;'
O, the devil take such cozeners! God forgive me!
Good uncle, tell your tale; I have done.
WORCESTER. Nay, if you have not, to it again;
We will stay your leisure.
HOTSPUR.   I have done, i' faith.
WORCESTER. Then once more to your Scottish prisoners.
Deliver them up without their ransom straight,
And make the Douglas' son your only mean
For powers in Scotland; which, for divers reasons
Which I shall send you written, be assured,
Will easily be granted. You, my lord,
                          [*To* NORTHUMBERLAND.
Your son in Scotland being thus employ'd,
Shall secretly into the bosom creep
Of that same noble prelate, well beloved,
The archbishop.
HOTSPUR. Of York, is it not?
WORCESTER. True; who bears hard
His brother's death at Bristol, the Lord Scroop.
I speak not this in estimation,
As what I think might be, but what I know
Is ruminated, plotted and set down,

    And only stays but to behold the face
    Of that occasion that shall bring it on.
HOTSPUR. I smell it: upon my life, it will do well.
NORTH. Before the game is a-foot, thou still let'st slip.
HOTSPUR. Why, it cannot choose but be a noble plot:
    And then the power of Scotland and of York,
    To join with Mortimer, ha?
WORCESTER.   And so they shall.
HOTSPUR. In faith, it is exceedingly well aim'd.
WORCESTER. And 'tis no little reason bids us speed,
    To save our heads by raising of a head;
    For, bear ourselves as even as we can,
    The king will always think him in our debt,
    And think we think ourselves unsatisfied,
    Till he hath found a time to pay us home:
    And see already how he doth begin
    To make us strangers to his looks of love.
HOTSPUR. He does, he does: we'll be revenged on him.
WORCESTER. Cousin, farewell: no further go in this
    Than I by letters shall direct your course.
    When time is ripe, which will be suddenly,
    I'll steal to Glendower and Lord Mortimer;
    Where you and Douglas and our powers at once,
    As I will fashion it, shall happily meet,
    To bear our fortunes in our own strong arms,
    Which now we hold at much uncertainty.
NORTH. Farewell, good brother: we shall thrive, I trust.
HOTSPUR. Uncle, adieu: O, let the hours be short
    Till fields and blows and groans applaud our sport!
                               [Exeunt.

ACT II

SCENE I — ROCHESTER. *An inn yard.*

Enter a CARRIER *with a lantern in his hand.*]

FIRST CARRIER. Heigh-ho! an it be not four by the day, I'll
be hanged: Charles' wain is over the new chimney, and
yet our horse not packed. What, ostler!

OSTLER [*Within*] Anon, anon.

FIRST CARRIER. I prithee, Tom, beat Cut's saddle, put a few
flocks in the point; poor jade, is wrung in the withers out
of all cess.

Enter another CARRIER.]

SECOND CARRIER. Peas and beans are as dank here as a dog,
and that is the next way to give poor jades the bots: this
house is turned upside down since Robin Ostler died.

FIRST CARRIER. Poor fellow, never joyed since the price of
oats rose; it was the death of him.

SECOND CARRIER. I think this be the most villanous house
in all London road for fleas: I am stung like a tench.

FIRST CARRIER. Like a tench! by the mass, there is ne'er a
king christen could be better bit than I have been since
the first cock.

SECOND CARRIER. Why, they will allow us ne'er a jordan,
and then we leak in your chimney; and your chamber-lie
breeds fleas like a loach.

FIRST CARRIER. What, ostler! come away and be hanged!
come away.

SECOND CARRIER. I have a gammon of bacon and two razes
of ginger, to be delivered as far as Charing-cross.

FIRST CARRIER. God's body! the turkeys in my pannier are

21

quite starved. What, ostler! A plague on thee! hast thou never an eye in thy head? canst not hear? An 'twere not as good deed as drink, to break the pate on thee, I am a very villain. Come, and be hanged! hast no faith in thee?

Enter GADSHILL.]

GADSHILL. Good morrow, carriers. What's o'clock?

FIRST CARRIER. I think it be two o'clock.

GADSHILL. I prithee, lend me thy lantern, to see my gelding in the stable.

FIRST CARRIER. Nay, by God, soft; I know a trick worth two of that, i' faith.

GADSHILL. I pray thee, lend me thine.

SECOND CARRIER. Ay, when? canst tell? Lend me thy lantern, quoth he? marry, I'll see thee hanged first.

GADSHILL. Sirrah carrier, what time do you mean to come to London?

SECOND CARRIER. Time enough to go to bed with a candle, I warrant thee. Come, neighbour Mugs, we'll call up the gentlemen: they will along with company, for they have great charge.   [*Exeunt* CARRIERS.

GADSHILL. What, ho! chamberlain!

CHAMBERLAIN. [*Within*] At hand, quoth pick-purse.

GADSHILL. That's even as fair as—at hand, quoth the chamberlain; for thou variest no more from picking of purses than giving direction doth from labouring; thou layest the plot how.

Enter CHAMBERLAIN.]

CHAMBERLAIN. Good morrow, Master Gadshill. It holds current that I told you yesternight: there's a franklin in the wild of Kent hath brought three hundred marks with him in gold: I heard him tell it to one of his company last night at supper; a kind of auditor; one that hath abundance of charge too, God knows what. They are up

already, and call for eggs and butter: they will away
presently.

GADSHILL. Sirrah, if they meet not with Saint Nicholas'
clerks, I'll give thee this neck.

CHAMBERLAIN. No, I'll none of it: I pray thee, keep that
for the hangman; for I know thou worshippest Saint
Nicholas as truly as a man of falsehood may.

GADSHILL. What talkest thou to me of the hangman? if I
hang, I'll make a fat pair of gallows; for if I hang, old Sir
John hangs with me, and thou knowest he is no starveling.
Tut! there are other Trojans that thou dreamest not of,
the which for sport sake are content to do the profession
some grace; that would, if matters should be looked into,
for their own credit sake, make all whole. I am joined
with no foot landrakers, no long-staff sixpenny strikers,
none of these mad mustachio purple-hued malt-worms;
but with nobility and tranquillity, burgomasters and great
oneyers, such as can hold in, such as will strike sooner
than speak, and speak sooner than drink, and drink
sooner than pray: and yet, 'zounds, I lie; for they pray
continually to their saint, the commonwealth; or rather,
not pray to her, but prey on her, for they ride up and
down on her and make her their boots.

CHAMBERLAIN. What, the commonwealth their boots? will
she hold out water in foul way?

GADSHILL. She will, she will; justice hath liquored her. We
steal as in a castle, cock-sure; we have the receipt of fern-
seed, we walk invisible.

CHAMBERLAIN. Nay, by my faith, I think you are more be-
holding to the night than to fern-seed for your walking invisible.

GADSHILL. Give me thy hand: thou shalt have a share in our
purchase, as I am a true man.

CHAMBERLAIN. Nay, rather let me have it, as you are a false thief.

GADSHILL. Go to; 'homo' is a common name to all men. Bid the ostler bring my gelding out of the stable. Farewell, you muddy knave. [*Exeunt.*

SCENE II — *The highway, near* GADSHILL.

Enter PRINCE HENRY *and* POINS.]

POINS. Come, shelter, shelter: I have removed Falstaff's horse, and he frets like a gummed velvet.

PRINCE. Stand close.

Enter FALSTAFF.]

FALSTAFF. Poins! Poins, and be hanged! Poins!

PRINCE. Peace, ye fat-kidneyed rascal! what a brawling dost thou keep!

FALSTAFF. Where's Poins, Hal?

PRINCE. He is walked up to the top of the hill: I'll go seek him.

FALSTAFF. I am accursed to rob in that thief's company: the rascal hath removed my horse, and tied him I know not where. If I travel but four foot by the squier further afoot, I shall break my wind. Well, I doubt not but to die a fair death for all this, if I 'scape hanging for killing that rogue. I have forsworn his company hourly any time this two and twenty years, and yet I am bewitched with the rogue's company. If the rascal have not given me medicines to make me love him, I'll be hanged; it could not be else; I have drunk medicines. Poins! Ha! a plague upon you both! Bardolph! Peto! I'll starve ere I'll rob a foot further. An 'twere not as good a deed as drink, to turn true man and to leave these rogues, I am the veriest varlet that ever chewed with a tooth. Eight yards of uneven

ground is threescore and ten miles afoot with me; and the
stony-hearted villains know it well enough: a plague upon
it when thieves cannot be true one to another! [*They
whistle*] Whew! A plague upon you all! Give me my
horse, you rogues; give me my horse, and be hanged!

PRINCE. Peace, ye fat-guts! lie down; lay thine ear close to
the ground and list if thou canst hear the tread of travellers.

FALSTAFF. Have you any levers to lift me up again, being
down? 'Sblood, I'll not bear mine own flesh so far afoot
again for all the coin in thy father's exchequer. What a
plague mean ye to colt me thus?

PRINCE. Thou liest; thou art not colted, thou art uncolted.

FALSTAFF. I prithee, good Prince Hal, help me to my horse,
good king's son.

PRINCE. Out, ye rogue! shall I be your ostler?

FALSTAFF. Go hang thyself in thine own heir-apparent gar-
ters! If I be ta'en, I'll peach for this. An I have not bal-
lads made on you all and sung to filthy tunes, let a cup
of sack be my poison: when a jest is so forward, and afoot
too! I hate it.

Enter GADSHILL, BARDOLPH *and* PETO *with him*.]

GADSHILL. Stand.

FALSTAFF. So I do, against my will.

POINS. O, 'tis our setter: I know his voice. Bardolph, what
news?

BARDOLPH. Case ye, case ye; on with your vizards: there's
money of the king's coming down the hill; 'tis going to the
king's exchequer.

FALSTAFF. You lie, ye rogue; 'tis going to the king's tavern.

GADSHILL. There's enough to make us all.

FALSTAFF. To be hanged.

PRINCE. Sirs, you four shall front them in the narrow lane;

Ned Poins and I will walk lower: if they 'scape from your encounter, then they light on us.

PETO. How many be there of them?

GADSHILL. Some eight or ten.

FALSTAFF. 'Zounds, will they not rob us?

PRINCE. What, a coward, Sir John Paunch?

FALSTAFF. Indeed, I am not John of Gaunt, your grandfather; but yet no coward, Hal.

PRINCE. Well, we leave that to the proof.

POINS. Sirrah Jack, thy horse stands behind the hedge: when thou needest him, there thou shalt find him. Farewell, and stand fast.

FALSTAFF. Now cannot I strike him, if I should be hanged.

PRINCE. Ned, where are our disguises?

POINS. Here, hard by: stand close.

[*Exeunt* PRINCE *and* POINS.

FALSTAFF. Now, my masters, happy man be his dole, say I: every man to his business.

Enter the TRAVELLERS.]

FIRST TRAVELLER. Come, neighbour: the boy shall lead our horses down the hill; we'll walk afoot awhile, and ease our legs.

THIEVES. Stand!

TRAVELLERS. Jesus bless us!

FALSTAFF. Strike; down with them; cut the villains' throats: ah! whoreson caterpillars! bacon-fed knaves! they hate us youth: down with them; fleece them.

TRAVELLERS. O, we are undone, both we and ours for ever!

FALSTAFF. Hang ye, gorbellied knaves, are ye undone? No, ye fat chuffs; I would your store were here! On, bacons, on! What, ye knaves! young men must live. You are grand-jurors, are ye? we'll jure ye, 'faith.

[*Here they rob them and bind them. Exeunt.*

Re-enter PRINCE HENRY *and* POINS *disguised.*]

PRINCE. The thieves have bound the true men. Now could
thou and I rob the thieves and go merrily to London, it
would be argument for a week, laughter for a month and
a good jest for ever.

POINS. Stand close; I hear them coming.

Enter the THIEVES *again.*]

FALSTAFF. Come, my masters, let us share, and then to
horse before day. An the Prince and Poins be not two
arrant cowards, there's no equity stirring: there's no more
valour in that Poins than in a wild-duck.

PRINCE. Your money!

POINS. Villains! [*As they are sharing, the* PRINCE *and*
POINS *set upon them; they all run away; and* FALSTAFF,
*after a blow or two, runs away too, leaving the booty
behind them.*]

PRINCE. Got with much ease. Now merrily to horse:
The thieves are all scatter'd and possess'd with fear
So strongly that they dare not meet each other;
Each takes his fellow for an officer.
Away, good Ned. Falstaff sweats to death,
And lards the lean earth as he walks along:
Were't not for laughing, I should pity him.

POINS. How the rogue roar'd!   [*Exeunt.*

SCENE III—WARKWORTH CASTLE.

Enter HOTSPUR *solus, reading a letter.*]

HOTSPUR. 'But, for mine own part, my lord, I could be well
contented to be there, in respect of the love I bear your
house.' He could be contented: why is he not, then? In
respect of the love he bears our house: he shows in this,
he loves his own barn better than he loves our house. Let

me see some more. 'The purpose you undertake is dangerous;'—why, that's certain: 'tis dangerous to take a cold,
to sleep, to drink; but I tell you, my lord fool, out of this
nettle, danger, we pluck this flower, safety. 'The purpose
you undertake is dangerous; the friends you have named
uncertain; the time itself unsorted; and your whole plot
too light for the counterpoise of so great an opposition.'
Say you so, say you so? I say unto you again, you are
a shallow cowardly hind, and you lie. What a lack-brain
is this! By the Lord, our plot is a good plot as ever was
laid; our friends true and constant: a good plot, good
friends, and full of expectation; an excellent plot, very
good friends. What a frosty-spirited rogue is this! Why,
my lord of York commends the plot and the general
course of the action. 'Zounds, an I were now by this rascal,
I could brain him with his lady's fan. Is there not my
father, my uncle, and myself? lord Edmund Mortimer,
my lord of York, and Owen Glendower? is there not
besides the Douglas? have I not all their letters to meet
me in arms by the ninth of the next month? and are they
not some of them set forward already? What a pagan
rascal is this! an infidel! Ha! you shall see now in very
sincerity of fear and cold heart, will he to the king, and
lay open all our proceedings. O, I could divide myself,
and go to buffets, for moving such a dish of skim milk
with so honourable an action! Hang him! let him tell the
king: we are prepared. I will set forward to-night.
Enter LADY PERCY.]
How now, Kate! I must leave you within these two hours.
LADY PERCY. O, my good lord, why are you thus alone?
For what offence have I this fortnight been
A banish'd woman from my Harry's bed?
Tell me, sweet lord, what is't that takes from thee

Thy stomach, pleasure, and thy golden sleep?
Why dost thou bend thine eyes upon the earth,
And start so often when thou sit'st alone?
Why hast thou lost the fresh blood in thy cheeks,
And given my treasures and my rights of thee
To thick-eyed musing and cursed melancholy?
In thy faint slumbers I by thee have watch'd,
And heard thee murmur tales of iron wars;
Speak terms of manage to thy bounding steed;
Cry 'Courage! to the field!' And thou hast talk'd
Of sallies and retires, of trenches, tents,
Of palisadoes, frontiers, parapets,
Of basilisks, of cannon, culverin,
Of prisoners' ransom, and of soldiers slain,
And all the currents of a heady fight.
Thy spirit within thee hath been so at war
And thus hath so bestirr'd thee in thy sleep,
That beads of sweat have stood upon thy brow,
Like bubbles in a late-disturbed stream;
And in thy face strange motions have appear'd,
Such as we see when men restrain their breath
On some great sudden hest. O, what portents are these?
Some heavy business hath my lord in hand,
And I must know it, else he loves me not.

HOTSPUR. What, ho!

Enter SERVANT.]

                    Is Gilliams with the packet gone?

SERVANT. He is, my lord, an hour ago.

HOTSPUR. Hath Butler brought those horses from the
  sheriff?

SERVANT. One horse, my lord, he brought even now.

HOTSPUR. What horse? a roan, a crop-ear, is it not?

SERVANT. It is, my lord.

HOTSPUR.That roan shall be my throne.
Well, I will back him straight: O *esperance!*
Bid Butler lead him forth into the park. [*Exit* SERVANT.
LADY P. But hear you, my lord.
HOTSPUR. What say'st thou, my lady?
LADY P. What is it carries you away?
HOTSPUR. Why, my horse, my love, my horse.
LADY P. Out, you mad-headed ape!
A weasel hath not such a deal of spleen
As you are toss'd with. In faith,
I'll know your business, Harry, that I will.
I fear my brother Mortimer doth stir
About his title, and hath sent for you
To line his enterprize: but if you go—
HOTSPUR. So far afoot, I shall be weary, love.
LADY P. Come, come, you paraquito, answer me
Directly unto this question that I ask:
In faith, I'll break thy little finger, Harry,
And if thou wilt not tell me all things true.
HOTSPUR. Away,
Away, you trifler! Love! I love thee not,
I care not for thee, Kate: this is no world
To play with mammets and to tilt with lips:
We must have bloody noses and crack'd crowns,
And pass them current too. God's me, my horse!
What say'st thou, Kate? what wouldst thou have with me?
LADY P. Do you not love me? do you not, indeed?
Well, do not then; for since you love me not,
I will not love myself. Do you not love me?
Nay, tell me if you speak in jest or no.
HOTSPUR. Come, wilt thou see me ride?
And when I am o' horseback, I will swear
I love thee infinitely. But hark you, Kate;

I must not have you henceforth question me
Whither I go, nor reason whereabout:
Whither I must, I must; and, to conclude,
This evening must I leave you, gentle Kate.
I know you wise, but yet no farther wise
Than Harry Percy's wife: constant you are,
But yet a woman: and for secrecy,
No lady closer; for I well believe
Thou wilt not utter what thou dost not know;
And so far will I trust thee, gentle Kate.

LADY P. How! so far?

HOTSPUR. Not an inch further. But hark you, Kate:
Whither I go, thither shall you go too;
To-day will I set forth, to-morrow you.
Will this content you, Kate?

LADY P.   It must of force.   [*Exeunt.*

SCENE IV—*The* BOAR'S-HEAD TAVERN *in Eastcheap.*

Enter the PRINCE, *and* POINS.]

PRINCE. Ned, prithee, come out of that fat room, and lend
me thy hand to laugh a little.

POINS. Where hast been, Hal?

PRINCE. With three or four loggerheads amongst three or
fourscore hogsheads. I have sounded the very base-string
of humility. Sirrah, I am sworn brother to a leash of drawers; and can call them all by their christen names, as Tom,
Dick, and Francis. They take it already upon their salvation, that though I be but Prince of Wales, yet I am the
king of courtesy; and tell me flatly I am no proud Jack,
like Falstaff, but a Corinthian, a lad of mettle, a good boy,
by the Lord, so they call me, and when I am king of England, I shall command all the good lads in Eastcheap.

They call drinking deep, dyeing scarlet; and when you
breathe in your watering, they cry 'hem!' and bid you
play it off. To conclude, I am so good a proficient in one
quarter of an hour, that I can drink with any tinker in
his own language during my life. I tell thee, Ned, thou
hast lost much honour, that thou wert not with me in
this action. But, sweet Ned,—to sweeten which name of
Ned, I give thee this pennyworth of sugar, clapped even
now into my hand by an under-skinker, one that never
spake other English in his life than 'Eight shillings and
sixpence,' and 'You are welcome,' with this shrill addi-
tion, 'Anon, anon, sir! Score a pint of bastard in the Half-
moon,' or so. But, Ned, to drive away the time till Falstaff
come, I prithee, do thou stand in some by-room, while I
question my puny drawer to what end he gave me the
sugar; and do thou never leave calling 'Francis,' that his
tale to me may be nothing but 'Anon.' Step aside, and I'll
show thee a precedent.

POINS. Francis!

PRINCE. Thou art perfect.

POINS. Francis!   [*Exit* POINS.
Enter FRANCIS.]

FRANCIS. Anon, anon, sir. Look down into the Pomgarnet,
Ralph.

PRINCE. Come hither, Francis.

FRANCIS. My lord?

PRINCE. How long hast thou to serve, Francis?

FRANCIS. Forsooth, five years, and as much as to—

POINS. [*Within*] Francis!

FRANCIS. Anon, anon, sir.

PRINCE. Five year! by'r lady, a long lease for the clinking
of pewter. But, Francis, darest thou be so valiant as to
play the coward with thy indenture and show it a fair pair
of heels and run from it?

FRANCIS. O Lord, sir, I'll be sworn upon all the books in
England, I could find in my heart.

POINS [*Within*] Francis!

FRANCIS. Anon, sir.

PRINCE. How old art thou, Francis?

FRANCIS. Let me see—about Michaelmas next I shall be—

POINS. [*Within*] Francis!

FRANCIS. Anon, sir. Pray stay a little, my lord.

PRINCE. Nay, but hark you, Francis: for the sugar thou
gavest me, 'twas a pennyworth, was't not?

FRANCIS. O Lord I would it had been two!

PRINCE. I will give thee for it a thousand pound: ask me
when thou wilt, and thou shalt have it.

POINS. [*Within*] Francis!

FRANCIS. Anon, anon.

PRINCE. Anon, Francis? No, Francis; but to-morrow, Francis; or Francis, o' Thursday; or indeed, Francis, when
thou wilt. But, Francis!

FRANCIS. My lord?

PRINCE. Wilt thou rob this leathern jerkin, crystal-button,
not-pated, agate-ring, puke-stocking, caddis-garter,
smooth-tongue, Spanish-pouch,—

FRANCIS. O lord, sir, who do you mean?

PRINCE. Why, then, your brown bastard is your only drink,
for look you, Francis, your white canvas doublet will
sully: in Barbary, sir, it cannot come to so much.

FRANCIS. What, sir?

POINS. [*Within*] Francis!

PRINCE. Away, you rogue! dost thou not hear them call?
    [*Here they both call him; the* DRAWER *stands amazed,
                        not knowing which way to go.*

Enter VINTNER.]

VINTNER. What, standest thou still, and hearest such a calling? Look to the guests within. [*Exit* FRANCIS.] My lord,

old Sir John, with half-a-dozen more, are at the door:
shall I let them in?

PRINCE. Let them alone awhile, and then open the door.
[*Exit* VINTNER.] Poins!

Re-enter POINS.]

POINS. Anon, anon, sir.

PRINCE. Sirrah, Falstaff and the rest of the thieves are at
the door: shall we be merry?

POINS. As merry as crickets, my lad. But hark ye; what
cunning match have you made with this jest of the drawer? come, what's the issue?

PRINCE. I am now of all humours that have showed themselves humours since the old days of goodman Adam to
the pupil age of this present twelve o'clock at midnight.

Re-enter FRANCIS.]

What's o'clock, Francis?

FRANCIS. Anon, anon, sir.   [*Exit.*

PRINCE. That ever this fellow should have fewer words than
a parrot, and yet the son of a woman! His industry is up-
stairs and down-stairs; his eloquence the parcel of a
reckoning. I am not yet of Percy's mind, the Hotspur of
the north; he that kills me some six or seven dozen of
Scots at a breakfast, washes his hands, and says to his
wife 'Fie upon this quiet life! I want work.' 'O my sweet
Harry,' says she, 'how many hast thou killed to-day?'
'Give my roan horse a drench,' says he; and answers
'Some fourteen,' an hour after; 'a trifle, a trifle.' I prithee,
call in Falstaff: I'll play Percy, and that damned brawn
shall play Dame Mortimer his wife. 'Rivo!' says the
drunkard. Call in ribs, call in tallow.

Enter FALSTAFF, GADSHILL, BARDOLPH, *and*
        PETO; FRANCIS *following with wine*.]

POINS. Welcome, Jack; where hast thou been?

FALSTAFF. A plague of all cowards, I say, and a vengeance
too! marry, and amen! Give me a cup of sack, boy. Ere I
lead this life long, I'll sew nether stocks and mend them
and foot them too. A plague of all cowards! Give me a
cup of sack, rogue. Is there no virtue extant? [*He drinks.*

PRINCE. Didst thou never see Titan kiss a dish of butter?
pitiful-hearted Titan, that melted at the sweet tale of the
sun's! if thou didst, then behold that compound.

FALSTAFF. You rogue, here's lime in this sack too: there is
nothing but roguery to be found in villanous man: yet a
coward is worse than a cup of sack with lime in it. A villanous coward! Go thy ways, old Jack; die when thou
wilt, if manhood, good manhood, be not forgot upon the
face of the earth, then am I a shotten herring. There lives
not three good men unhanged in England; and one of
them is fat, and grows old: God help the while! a bad
world, I say. I would I were a weaver; I could sing psalms
or any thing. A plague of all cowards, I say still.

PRINCE. How now, wool-sack! what mutter you?

FALSTAFF. A king's son! If I do not beat thee out of thy
kingdom with a dagger of lath, and drive all thy subjects
afore thee like a flock of wild-geese, I'll never wear hair
on my face more. You Prince of Wales!

PRINCE. Why, you whoreson round man, what's the matter?

FALSTAFF. Are not you a coward? answer me to that: and
Poins there?

POINS. 'Zounds, ye fat paunch, an ye call me coward, by the
Lord, I'll stab thee.

FALSTAFF. I call thee coward! I'll see thee damned ere I call
thee coward: but I would give a thousand pound I could
run as fast as thou canst. You are straight enough in the
shoulders, you care not who sees your back: call you that
backing of your friends? A plague upon such backing!

give me them that will face me. Give me a cup of sack: I am a rogue, if I drunk to-day.

PRINCE. O villain! thy lips are scarce wiped since thou drunkest last.

FALSTAFF. All's one for that. [*He drinks*.] A plague of all cowards, still say I.

PRINCE. What's the matter?

FALSTAFF. What's the matter! there be four of us here have ta'en a thousand pound this day morning.

PRINCE. Where is it, Jack? where is it?

FALSTAFF. Where is it! taken from us it is: a hundred upon poor four of us.

PRINCE. What, a hundred, man?

FALSTAFF. I am a rogue, if I were not at half-sword with a dozen of them two hours together. I have 'scaped by miracle. I am eight times thrust through the doublet, four through the hose; my buckler cut through and through; my sword hacked like a hand-saw—*ecce signum!* I never dealt better since I was a man: all would not do. A plague of all cowards! Let them speak: if they speak more or less than truth, they are villains and the sons of darkness.

PRINCE. Speak, sirs; how was it?

GADSHILL. We four set upon some dozen—

FALSTAFF. Sixteen at least, my lord.

GADSHILL. And bound them.

PETO. No, no, they were not bound.

FALSTAFF. You rogue, they were bound, every man of them; or I am a Jew else, an Ebrew Jew.

GADSHILL. As we were sharing, some six or seven fresh men set upon us—

FALSTAFF. And unbound the rest, and then come in the other.

PRINCE. What, fought you with them all?

FALSTAFF. All! I know not what you call all; but if I fought

not with fifty of them, I am a bunch of radish: if there
were not two or three and fifty upon poor old Jack, then
am I no two-legged creature.

PRINCE. Pray God you have not murdered some of them.

FALSTAFF. Nay, that's past praying for: I have peppered
two of them; two I am sure I have paid, two rogues in
buckram suits. I tell thee what, Hal, if I tell thee a lie,
spit in my face, call me horse. Thou knowest my old
ward; here I lay, and thus I bore my point. Four rogues
in buckram let drive at me—

PRINCE. What, four? thou saidst but two even now.

FALSTAFF. Four, Hal; I told thee four.

POINS. Ay, ay, he said four.

FALSTAFF. These four came all a-front, and mainly thrust
at me. I made me no more ado but took all their seven
points in my target, thus.

PRINCE. Seven? why, there were but four even now.

FALSTAFF. In buckram?

POINS. Ay, four, in buckram suits.

FALSTAFF. Seven, by these hilts, or I am a villain else.

PRINCE. Prithee, let him alone; we shall have more anon.

FALSTAFF. Dost thou hear me, Hal?

PRINCE. Ay, and mark thee too, Jack.

FALSTAFF. Do so, for it is worth the listening to. These
nine in buckram that I told thee of,—

PRINCE. So, two more already.

FALSTAFF. Their points being broken,—

POINS. Down fell their hose.

FALSTAFF. Began to give me ground: but I followed me
close, came in foot and hand; and with a thought seven
of the eleven I paid.

PRINCE. O monstrous! eleven buckram men grown out of
two!

FALSTAFF. But, as the devil would have it, three misbegotten knaves in Kendal green came at my back and let drive at me; for it was so dark, Hal, that thou couldst not see thy hand.

PRINCE. These lies are like their father that begets them; gross as a mountain, open, palpable. Why, thou clay-brained guts, thou knotty-pated fool, thou whoreson, obscene, greasy tallow-catch,—

FALSTAFF. What, art thou mad? art thou mad? is not the truth the truth?

PRINCE. Why, how couldst thou know these men in Kendal green, when it was so dark thou couldst not see thy hand? come, tell us your reason: what sayest thou to this?

POINS. Come, your reason, Jack, your reason.

FALSTAFF. What, upon compulsion? 'Zounds, an I were at the strappado, or all the racks in the world, I would not tell you on compulsion. Give you a reason on compulsion! if reasons were as plentiful as blackberries, I would give no man a reason upon compulsion, I.

PRINCE. I'll be no longer guilty of this sin; this sanguine coward, this bed-presser, this horse-back-breaker, this huge hill of flesh,—

FALSTAFF. 'Sblood, you starveling, you elf-skin, you dried neat's tongue, you bull's pizzle, you stock-fish! O for breath to utter what is like thee! you tailor's-yard, you sheath, you bow-case, you vile standing tuck,—

PRINCE. Well, breathe a while, and then to it again: and when thou hast tired thyself in base comparisons, hear me speak but this.

POINS. Mark, Jack.

PRINCE. We two saw you four set on four and bound them, and were masters of their wealth. Mark now, how a plain tale shall put you down. Then did we two set on you four; and, with a word, out-faced you from your prize, and

have it; yea, and can show it you here in the house: and,
Falstaff, you carried your guts away as nimbly, with as
quick dexterity, and roared for mercy, and still run and
roared, as ever I heard bull-calf. What a slave art thou,
to hack thy sword as thou hast done, and then say it was
in fight! What trick, what device, what starting-hole,
canst thou now find out to hide thee from this open and
apparent shame?

POINS. Come, let's hear, Jack; what trick hast thou now?

FALSTAFF. By the Lord, I knew ye as well as he that made
ye. Why, hear you, my masters: was it for me to kill the
heir-apparent? should I turn upon the true prince? why,
thou knowest I am as valiant as Hercules: but beware
instinct; the lion will not touch the true prince. Instinct is
a great matter; I was now a coward on instinct. I shall
think the better of myself and thee during my life; I for
a valiant lion, and thou for a true prince. But, by the
Lord, lads, I am glad you have the money. Hostess, clap
to the doors: watch to-night, pray to-morrow. Gallants,
lads, boys, hearts of gold, all the titles of good fellowship
come to you! What, shall we be merry? shall we have a
play extempore?

PRINCE. Content; and the argument shall be thy running
away.

FALSTAFF. Ah, no more of that, Hal, an thou lovest me!

Enter HOSTESS.]

HOSTESS. O Jesu, my lord the prince!

PRINCE. How now, my lady the hostess! what sayest thou
to me?

HOSTESS. Marry, my lord, there is a nobleman of the court
at door would speak with you: he says he comes from
your father.

PRINCE. Give him as much as will make him a royal man, and send him back again to my mother.

FALSTAFF. What manner of man is he?

HOSTESS. An old man.

FALSTAFF. What doth gravity out of his bed at midnight? Shall I give him his answer?

PRINCE. Prithee, do, Jack.

FALSTAFF. Faith, and I'll send him packing. [*Exit.*

PRINCE. Now, sirs: by'r lady, you fought fair; so did you, Peto; so did you, Bardolph: you are lions too, you ran away upon instinct, you will not touch the true prince; no, fie!

BARDOLPH. Faith, I ran when I saw others run.

PRINCE. Faith, tell me now in earnest, how came Falstaff's sword so hacked?

PETO. Why, he hacked it with his dagger, and said he would swear truth out of England but he would make you believe it was done in fight, and persuaded us to do the like.

BARDOLPH. Yea, and to tickle our noses with spear-grass to make them bleed, and then to beslubber our garments with it and swear it was the blood of true men. I did that I did not this seven year before, I blushed to hear his monstrous devices.

PRINCE. O villain, thou stolest a cup of sack eighteen years ago, and wert taken with the manner, and ever since thou hast blushed extempore. Thou hadst fire and sword on thy side, and yet thou rannest away: what instinct hadst thou for it?

BARDOLPH. My lord, do you see these meteors? do you behold these exhalations?

PRINCE. I do.

BARDOLPH. What think you they portend?

PRINCE. Hot livers and cold purses.

BARDOLPH. Choler, my lord, if rightly taken.

PRINCE. No, if rightly taken, halter.

Re-enter FALSTAFF.]

Here comes lean Jack, here comes bare-bone. How now,
my sweet creature of bombast! How long is't ago, Jack,
since thou sawest thine own knee?

FALSTAFF. My own knee! when I was about thy years, Hal,
I was not an eagle's talon in the waist; I could have crept
into any alderman's thumb-ring: a plague of sighing and
grief! it blows a man up like a bladder. There's villanous
news abroad: here was Sir John Bracy from your father;
you must to the court in the morning. That same mad
fellow of the north, Percy, and he of Wales, that gave
Amamon the bastinado, and made Lucifer cuckold, and
swore the devil his true liegeman upon the cross of a
Welsh hook—what a plague call you him?

POINS. O, Glendower.

FALSTAFF. Owen, Owen, the same; and his son-in-law Mortimer, and old Northumberland, and that sprightly Scot
of Scots, Douglas, that runs o' horseback up a hill per-
pendicular,—

PRINCE. He that rides at high speed and with his pistol kills
a sparrow flying.

FALSTAFF. You have hit it.

PRINCE. So did he never the sparrow.

FALSTAFF. Well, that rascal hath good mettle in him; he
will not run.

PRINCE. Why, what a rascal art thou then, to praise him so
for running!

FALSTAFF. O' horseback, ye cuckoo; but afoot he will not
budge a foot.

PRINCE. Yes, Jack, upon instinct.

FALSTAFF. I grant ye, upon instinct. Well, he is there too, and one Mordake, and a thousand blue-caps more: Worcester is stolen away to-night; thy father's beard is turned white with the news: you may buy land now as cheap as stinking mackerel.

PRINCE. Why, then, it is like, if there come a hot June and this civil buffeting hold, we shall buy maidenheads as they buy hob-nails, by the hundreds.

FALSTAFF. By the mass, lad, thou sayest true; it is like we shall have good trading that way. But tell me, Hal, art not thou horrible afeard? thou being heir-apparent, could the world pick thee out three such enemies again as that fiend Douglas, that spirit Percy, and that devil Glendower? art thou not horribly afraid? doth not thy blood thrill at it?

PRINCE. Not a whit, i' faith; I lack some of thy instinct.

FALSTAFF. Well, thou wilt be horribly chid to-morrow when thou comest to thy father: if thou love me, practise an answer.

PRINCE. Do thou stand for my father, and examine me upon the particulars of my life.

FALSTAFF. Shall I? content: this chair shall be my state, this dagger my sceptre, and this cushion my crown.

PRINCE. Thy state is taken for a joined-stool, thy golden sceptre for a leaden dagger, and thy precious rich crown for a pitiful bald crown!

FALSTAFF. Well, an the fire of grace be not quite out of thee, now shalt thou be moved. Give me a cup of sack to make my eyes look red, that it may be thought I have wept; for I must speak in passion, and I will do it in King Cambyses' vein.

PRINCE. Well, here is my leg.

FALSTAFF. And here is my speech. Stand aside, nobility.

HOSTESS. O Jesu, this is excellent sport, i' faith!

FALSTAFF. Weep not, sweet queen; for trickling tears are vain.

HOSTESS. O, the father, how he holds his countenance!

FALSTAFF. For God's sake, lords, convey my tristful queen; For tears do stop the flood-gates of her eyes.

HOSTESS. O Jesu, he doth it as like one of these harlotry players as ever I see!

FALSTAFF. Peace, good pint-pot; peace, good tickle-brain. Harry, I do not only marvel where thou spendest thy time, but also how thou art accompanied: for though the camomile, the more it is trodden on the faster it grows, yet youth, the more it is wasted the sooner it wears. That thou art my son, I have partly thy mother's word, partly my own opinion, but chiefly a villanous trick of thine eye, and a foolish hanging of thy nether lip, that doth warrant me. If then thou be son to me, here lies the point; why, being son to me, art thou so pointed at? Shall the blessed sun of heaven prove a micher and eat blackberries? a question not to be asked. Shall the son of England prove a thief and take purses? a question to be asked. There is a thing, Harry, which thou hast often heard of, and it is known to many in our land by the name of pitch: this pitch, as ancient writers do report, doth defile; so doth the company thou keepest: for, Harry, now I do not speak to thee in drink but in tears, not in pleasure but in passion, not in words only, but in woes also: and yet there is a virtuous man whom I have often noted in thy company, but I know not his name.

PRINCE. What manner of man, an it like your majesty?

FALSTAFF. A goodly portly man, i' faith, and a corpulent; of a cheerful look, a pleasing eye, and a most noble carriage; and, as I think, his age some fifty, or, by'r lady, inclining to three score; and now I remember me, his name is Falstaff: if that man should be lewdly given, he deceiveth me; for, Harry, I see virtue in his looks. If then the tree may be known by the fruit, as the fruit by the tree, then, peremptorily I speak it, there is virtue in that Falstaff: him keep with, the rest banish. And tell me now, thou naughty varlet, tell me, where hast thou been this month?

PRINCE. Dost thou speak like a king? Do thou stand for me, and I'll play my father.

FLSTAFF. Depose me? if thou dost it half so gravely, so majestically, both in word and matter, hang me up by the heels for a rabbit-sucker or a poulter's hare.

PRINCE. Well, here I am set.

FALSTAFF. And here I stand: judge, my masters.

PRINCE. Now, Harry, whence come you?

FALSTAFF. My noble lord, from Eastcheap.

PRINCE. The complaints I hear of thee are grievous.

FALSTAFF. 'Sblood, my lord, they are false: nay, I'll tickle ye for a young prince, i' faith.

PRINCE. Swearest thou, ungracious boy? henceforth ne'er look on me. Thou art violently carried away from grace: there is a devil haunts thee in the likeness of an old fat man; a tun of man is thy companion. Why dost thou converse with that trunk of humours, that bolting-hutch of beastliness, that swollen parcel of dropsies, that huge bombard of sack, that stuffed cloak-bag of guts, that roasted Manningtree ox with the pudding in his belly, that reverend vice, that grey iniquity, that father ruffian, that vanity in years? Wherein is he good, but to taste sack and drink it? wherein neat and cleanly, but to carve a capon and eat it? wherein cunning, but in craft? wherein crafty, but in villany? wherein villanous, but in all things? wherein worthy, but in nothing?

FALSTAFF. I would your grace would take me with you: whom means your grace?

PRINCE. That villanous abominable misleader of youth, Falstaff, that old white-bearded Satan.

FALSTAFF. My lord, the man I know.

PRINCE. I know thou dost.

FALSTAFF. But to say I know more harm in him than in myself, were to say more than I know. That he is old, the more the pity, his white hairs do witness it; but that he is, saving your reverence, a whoremaster, that I utterly deny. If sack and sugar be a fault, God help the wicked! if to be old and merry be a sin, then many an old host that I know is damned: if to be fat be to be hated, then Pharaoh's lean kine are to be loved. No, my good lord; banish Peto, banish Bardolph, banish Poins: but for sweet Jack Falstaff, kind Jack Falstaff, true Jack Falstaff, valiant Jack Falstaff, and therefore more valiant, being, as he is, old Jack Falstaff, banish not him thy Harry's company, banish not him thy Harry's company: banish plump Jack, and banish all the world.

PRINCE. I do, I will.   [*A knocking heard.*

[*Exeunt* HOSTESS, FRANCIS, *and* BARDOLPH.

Re-enter BARDOLPH, *running.*]

BARDOLPH. O, my lord, my lord! the sheriff with a most monstrous watch is at the door.

FALSTAFF. Out, ye rogue! Play out the play: I have much to say in the behalf of that Falstaff.

Re-enter the HOSTESS.]

HOSTESS. O Jesu, my lord, my lord!—

PRINCE. Heigh, heigh! the devil rides upon a fiddlestick: what's the matter?

HOSTESS. The sheriff and all the watch are at the door: they are come to search the house. Shall I let them in?

FALSTAFF. Dost thou hear, Hal? never call a true piece of
gold a counterfeit: thou art essentially mad, without
seeming so.

PRINCE. And thou a natural coward, without instinct.

FALSTAFF. I deny your major: if you will deny the sheriff,
so; if not, let him enter: if I become not a cart as well as
another man, a plague on my bringing up! I hope I shall
as soon be strangled with a halter as another.

PRINCE. Go, hide thee behind the arras: the rest walk up
above. Now, my masters, for a true face and good conscience.

FALSTAFF. Both which I have had: but their date is out,
and therefore I'll hide me.

PRINCE. Call in the sheriff.

[*Exeunt all except the* PRINCE *and* PETO.
Enter SHERIFF *and the* CARRIER.]

Now, master sheriff, what is your will with me?

SHERIFF. First, pardon me, my lord. A hue and cry
Hath follow'd certain men unto this house.

PRINCE. What men?

SHERIFF. One of them is well known, my gracious lord,
A gross fat man.

CARRIER.　　　　As fat as butter.

PRINCE. The man, I do assure you, is not here;
For I myself at this time have employ'd him.
And, sheriff, I will engage my word to thee
That I will, by to-morrow dinner-time,
Send him to answer thee, or any man,
For any thing he shall be charged withal:
And so let me entreat you leave the house.

SHERIFF. I will, my lord. There are two gentlemen
Have in this robbery lost three hundred marks.

PRINCE. It may be so: if he have robb'd these men,
He shall be answerable; and so farewell.

SHERIFF. Good night, my noble lord.

PRINCE. I think it is good morrow, is it not?

SHERIFF. Indeed, my lord, I think it be two o'clock.

[*Exeunt* SHERIFF *and* CARRIER.

PRINCE. This oily rascal is known as well as Paul's.
Go, call him forth.

PETO. Falstaff!—Fast asleep behind the arras, and snorting
like a horse.

PRINCE. Hark, how hard he fetches breath. Search his
pockets. [*He searcheth his pockets, and findeth certain
papers*.] What hast thou found?

PETO. Nothing but papers, my lord.

PRINCE. Let's see what they be: read them.

PETO. [*Reads*.] Item, A capon, ... 2s. 2d.
　　　　　　　　Item, Sauce, ...   4d.
　　　　　　　　Item, Sack, two gallons, . . . 5s. 8d.
　　　　　　　　Item, Anchovies and sack
　　　　　　　　　　after supper, ... 2s. 6d.
　　　　　　　　Item, Bread, ...   ob.

PRINCE. O monstrous! but one half-pennyworth of bread to
this intolerable deal of sack! What there is else, keep
close; we'll read it at more advantage: there let him sleep
till day. I'll to the court in the morning. We must all to the
wars, and thy place shall be honourable. I'll procure this
fat rogue a charge of foot; and I know his death will be a
march of twelve-score. The money shall be paid back
again with advantage. Be with me betimes in the morning; and so, good morrow, Peto.

PETO. Good morrow, good my lord.   [*Exeunt*.

ACT III

Scene I—Bangor. *The* Archdeacon's *house.*

Enter Hotspur, Worcester, Mortimer, *and* Glendower.]

MORTIMER. These promises are fair, the parties sure.
   And our induction full of prosperous hope.

HOTSPUR. Lord Mortimer, and cousin Glendower,
   Will you sit down?
   And uncle Worcester: a plague upon it!
   I have forgot the map.

GLENDOWER.   No, here it is.
   Sit, cousin Percy; sit, good cousin Hotspur,
   For by that name as oft as Lancaster
   Doth speak of you, his cheek looks pale, and with
   A rising sigh he wisheth you in heaven.

HOTSPUR. And you in hell, as oft as he hears Owen Glendower spoke of.

GLENDOWER. I cannot blame him: at my nativity
   The front of heaven was full of fiery shapes,
   Of burning cressets; and at my birth
   The frame and huge foundation of the earth
   Shaked like a coward.

HOTSPUR. Why, so it would have done at the same season,
   if your mother's cat had but kittened, though yourself
   had never been born.

GLENDOWER. I say the earth did shake when I was born.

HOTSPUR. And I say the earth was not of my mind,
   If you suppose as fearing you it shook.

GLENDOWER. The heavens were all on fire, the earth did
   tremble.

HOTSPUR. O, then the earth shook to see the heavens on fire,

48

And not in fear of your nativity.
Diseased nature oftentimes breaks forth
In strange eruptions; oft the teeming earth
Is with a kind of colic pinch'd and vex'd
By the imprisoning of unruly wind
Within her womb; which, for enlargement striving,
Shakes the old beldam earth and topples down
Steeples and moss-grown towers. At your birth
Our grandam earth, having this distemperature,
In passion shook.

GLENDOWER.   Cousin, of many men
I do not bear these crossings. Give me leave
To tell you once again that at my birth
The front of heaven was full of fiery shapes,
The goats ran from the mountains, and the herds
Were strangely clamorous to the frighted fields.
These signs have mark'd me extraordinary;
And all the courses of my life do show
I am not in the roll of common men.
Where is he living, clipp'd in with the sea
That chides the banks of England, Scotland, Wales,
Which calls me pupil, or hath read to me?
And bring him out that is but woman's son
Can trace me in the tedious ways of art,
And hold me pace in deep experiments.

HOTSPUR. I think there's no man speaks better Welsh.
I'll to dinner.

MORTIMER. Peace, cousin Percy; you will make him mad.

GLENDOWER. I can call spirits from the vasty deep.

HOTSPUR. Why, so can I, or so can any man;
But will they come when you do call for them?

GLENDOWER. Why, I can teach you, cousin, to command
The devil.

HOTSPUR. And I can teach thee, coz, to shame the devil
    By telling truth: tell truth, and shame the devil.
    If thou have power to raise him, bring him hither,
    And I'll be sworn I have power to shame him hence.
    O, while you live, tell truth, and shame the devil!
MORTIMER. Come, come, no more of this unprofitable chat.
GLENDOWER. Three times hath Henry Bolingbroke made
    head
    Against my power; thrice from the banks of Wye
    And sandy-bottom'd Severn have I sent him
    Bootless home and weather-beaten back.
HOTSPUR. Home without boots, and in foul weather too!
    How 'scapes he agues, in the devil's name?
GLENDOWER. Come, here's the map: shall we divide our
    right
    According to our threefold order ta'en?
MORTIMER. The Archdeacon hath divided it
    Into three limits very equally:
    England, from Trent and Severn hitherto,
    By south and east is to my part assign'd:
    All westward, Wales beyond the Severn shore,
    And all the fertile land within that bound,
    To Owen Glendower: and, dear coz, to you
    The remnant northward, lying off from Trent.
    And our indentures tripartite are drawn;
    Which being sealed interchangeably,
    A business that this night may execute,
    To-morrow, cousin Percy, you and I
    And my good Lord of Worcester will set forth
    To meet your father and the Scottish power,
    As is appointed us, at Shrewsbury.
    My father Glendower is not ready yet,
    Nor shall we need his help these fourteen days.

Within that space you may have drawn together
Your tenants, friends, and neighbouring gentlemen.

GLENDOWER. A shorter time shall send me to you, lords:
And in my conduct shall your ladies come;
From whom you now must steal and take no leave,
For there will be a world of water shed
Upon the parting of your wives and you.

HOTSPUR. Methinks my moiety, north from Burton here,
In quantity equals not one of yours:
See how this river comes me cranking in,
And cuts me from the best of all my land
A huge half-moon, a monstrous cantle out.
I'll have the current in this place damn'd up;
And here the smug and silver Trent shall run
In a new channel, fair and evenly;
It shall not wind with such a deep indent,
To rob me of so rich a bottom here.

GLENDOWER. Not wind? it shall, it must; you see it doth.

MORTIMER. Yea, but
Mark how he bears his course, and runs me up
With like advantage on the other side;
Gelding the opposed continent as much
As on the other side it takes from you.

WORCESTER. Yea, but a little charge will trench him here,
And on this north side win this cape of land;
And then he runs straight and even.

HOTSPUR. I'll have it so: a little charge will do it.

GLENDOWER. I'll not have it alter'd.

HOTSPUR.   Will not you?

GLENDOWER. No, nor you shall not.

HOTSPUR.   Who shall say me nay?

GLENDOWER. Why, that will I.

HOTSPUR. Let me not understand you, then; speak it in
    Welsh.
GLENDOWER. I can speak English, lord, as well as you;
    For I was train'd up in the English court;
    Where, being but young, I framed to the harp
    Many an English ditty lovely well,
    And gave the tongue a helpful ornament,
    A virtue that was never seen in you.
HOTSPUR. Marry,
    And I am glad of it with all my heart:
    I had rather be a kitten and cry mew
    Than one of these same metre ballad-mongers;
    I had rather hear a brazen canstick turn'd,
    Or a dry wheel grate on the axle-tree;
    And that would set my teeth nothing on edge,
    Nothing so much as mincing poetry:
    'Tis like the forced gait of a shuffling nag.
GLENDOWER. Come, you shall have Trent turn'd.
HOTSPUR. I do not care: I'll give thrice so much land
    To any well-deserving friend;
    But in the way of bargain, mark ye me,
    I'll cavil on the ninth part of a hair.
    Are the indentures drawn? shall we be gone?
GLENDOWER. The moon shines fair; you may away by night:
    I'll haste the writer, and withal
    Break with your wives of your departure hence:
    I am afraid my daughter will run mad,
    So much she doteth on her Mortimer.   [*Exit.*
MORTIMER. Fie, cousin Percy! how you cross my father!
HOTSPUR. I cannot choose: sometime he angers me
    With telling me of the moldwarp and the ant,
    Of the dreamer Merlin and his prophecies,
    And of a dragon and a finless fish,

A clip-wing'd griffin and a moulten raven,
A couching lion and a ramping cat,
And such a deal of skimble-skamble stuff
As puts me from my faith. I tell you what,—
He held me last night at least nine hours
In reckoning up the several devils' names
That were his lackeys: I cried 'hum,' and 'well, go to,'
But mark'd him not a word. O, he is as tedious
As a tired horse, a railing wife;
Worse than a smoky house: I had rather live
With cheese and garlic in a windmill, far,
Than feed on cates and have him talk to me
In any summer-house in Christendom.

MORTIMER. In faith, he is a worthy gentleman,
Exceedingly well read, and profited
In strange concealments; valiant as a lion,
And wondrous affable, and as bountiful
As mines of India. Shall I tell you, cousin?
He holds your temper in a high respect,
And curbs himself even of his natural scope
When you come 'cross his humour; faith, he does:
I warrant you, that man is not alive
Might so have tempted him as you have done,
Without the taste of danger and reproof:
But do not use it oft, let me entreat you.

WORCESTER. In faith, my lord, you are too wilful-blame;
And since your coming hither have done enough
To put him quite beside his patience.
You must needs learn, lord, to amend this fault:
Though sometimes it show greatness, courage, blood,—
And that's the dearest grace it renders you,—
Yet oftentimes it doth present harsh rage,
Defect of manners, want of government,

Pride, haughtiness, opinion and disdain:
The least of which haunting a nobleman
Loseth men's hearts, and leaves behind a stain
Upon the beauty of all parts besides,
Beguiling them of commendation.

HOTSPUR. Well, I am school'd: good manners be your
    speed!
Here come our wives, and let us take our leave.

Re-enter GLENDOWER *with the* LADIES.]

MORTIMER. This is the deadly spite that angers me;
  My wife can speak no English, I no Welsh.

GLENDOWER. My daughter weeps: she will not part with
  you;
  She'll be a soldier too, she'll to the wars.

MORTIMER. Good father, tell her that she and my aunt
  Percy
Shall follow in your conduct speedily.   [GLENDOWER
speaks to her in Welsh, and she answers him in the same.]

GLENDOWER. She is desperate here; a peevish self-will'd
  harlotry, one that no persuasion can do good upon.
                      [*The* LADY *speaks in Welsh.*

MORTIMER. I understand thy looks: that pretty Welsh
  Which thou pour'st down from these swelling heavens
  I am too perfect in; and, but for shame,
  In such a parley should I answer thee.
                 [*The* LADY *speaks again in Welsh.*
  I understand thy kisses and thou mine,
  And that's a feeling disputation:
  But I will never be a truant, love,
  Till I have learn'd thy language; for thy tongue
  Makes Welsh as sweet as ditties highly penn'd,
  Sung by a fair queen in a summer's bower,
  With ravishing division, to her lute.

GLENDOWER. Nay, if you melt, then will she run mad.

[*The* LADY *speaks again in Welsh.*

MORTIMER. O, I am ignorance itself in this!

GLENDOWER. She bids you on the wanton rushes lay you
    down
  And rest your gentle head upon her lap,
  And she will sing the song that pleaseth you,
  And on your eyelids crown the god of sleep,
  Charming your blood with pleasing heaviness,
  Making such difference 'twixt wake and sleep
  As is the difference betwixt day and night
  The hour before the heavenly-harness'd team
  Begins his golden progress in the east.

MORTIMER. With all my heart I'll sit and hear her sing:
  By that time will our book, I think, be drawn.

GLENDOWER. Do so;
  And those musicians that shall play to you
  Hang in the air a thousand leagues from hence,
  And straight they shall be here: sit, and attend.

HOTSPUR. Come, Kate, thou art perfect in lying down:
  come, quick, quick, that I may lay my head in thy lap.

LADY P. Go, ye giddy goose.   [*The music plays.*

HOTSPUR. Now I perceive the devil understands Welsh;
  And 'tis no marvel he is so humorous.
  By'r lady, he is a good musician.

LADY P. Then should you be nothing but musical, for you
  are altogether governed by humours. Lie still, ye thief,
  and hear the lady sing in Welsh.

HOTSPUR. I had rather hear Lady, my brach, howl in Irish.

LADY P. Wouldst thou have thy head broken?

HOTSPUR. No.

LADY P. Then be still.

HOTSPUR. Neither; 'tis a woman's fault.

LADY P. Now God help thee!

HOTSPUR. To the Welsh lady's bed.

LADY P. What's that?

HOTSPUR. Peace! she sings.

> [*Here the* LADY *sings a Welsh song.*

HOTSPUR. Come, Kate, I'll have your song too.

LADY P. Not mine, in good sooth.

HOTSPUR. Not yours, in good sooth! Heart! you swear like
a comfit-maker's wife. 'Not you, in good sooth,' and 'as
true as I live,' and 'as God shall mend me,' and 'as sure
as day,'

And givest such sarcenet surety for thy oaths,
As if thou never walk'st further than Finsbury.
Swear me, Kate, like a lady as thou art,
A good mouth-filling oath, and leave 'in sooth,'
And such protest of pepper-gingerbread,
To velvet-guards and Sunday-citizens.
Come, sing.

LADY P. I will not sing.

HOTSPUR. 'Tis the next way to turn tailor, or be red-breast
teacher. An the indentures be drawn, I'll away within
these two hours; and so, come in when ye will.   [*Exit.*

GLENDOWER. Come, come, Lord Mortimer; you are as slow
As hot Lord Percy is on fire to go.
But this our book is drawn; we'll but seal,
And then to horse immediately.

MORTIMER.   With all my heart.

>   [*Exeunt.*

SCENE II — LONDON. *The palace.*

Enter the KING, PRINCE OF WALES, *and others.*]

KING. Lords, give us leave; the Prince of Wales and I

Must have some private conference: but be near at hand,
For we shall presently have need of you. [*Exeunt* LORDS.
I know not whether God will have it so,
For some displeasing service I have done,
That, in his secret doom, out of my blood
He'll breed revengement and a scourge for me;
But thou dost in thy passages of life
Make me believe that thou art only mark'd
For the hot vengeance and the rod of heaven
To punish my mistreadings. Tell me else,
Could such inordinate and low desires,
Such poor, such bare, such lewd, such mean attempts,
Such barren pleasures, rude society,
As thou art match'd withal and grafted to,
Accompany the greatness of thy blood,
And hold their level with thy princely heart?

PRINCE. So please your majesty, I would I could
Quit all offences with as clear excuse
As well as I am doubtless I can purge
Myself of many I am charged withal:
Yet such extenuation let me beg,
As, in reproof of many tales devised,
Which oft the ear of greatness needs must hear,
By smiling pick-thanks and base newsmongers,
I may, for some things true, wherein my youth
Hath faulty wander'd and irregular,
Find pardon on my true submission.

KING. God pardon thee! yet let me wonder, Harry,
At thy affections, which do hold a wing
Quite from the flight of all thy ancestors.
Thy place in council thou hast rudely lost,
Which by thy younger brother is supplied,
And art almost an alien to the hearts

Of all the court and princes of my blood:
The hope and expectation of thy time
Is ruin'd, and the soul of every man
Prophetically doth forethink thy fall.
Had I so lavish of my presence been,
So common-hackney'd in the eyes of men,
So stale and cheap to vulgar company,
Opinion, that did help me to the crown,
Had still kept loyal to possession,
And left me in reputeless banishment,
A fellow of no mark nor likelihood.
By being seldom seen, I could not stir
But like a comet I was wonder'd at;
That men would tell their children 'This is he;'
Others would say 'Where, which is Bolingbroke?'
And then I stole all courtesy from heaven,
And dress'd myself in such humility
That I did pluck allegiance from men's hearts,
Loud shouts and salutations from their mouths,
Even in the presence of the crowned king.
Thus did I keep my person fresh and new;
My presence, like a robe pontifical,
Ne'er seen but wonder'd at: and so my state,
Seldom but sumptuous, showed like a feast,
And wan by rareness such solemnity.
The skipping king, he ambled up and down,
With shallow jesters and rash bavin wits,
Soon kindled and soon burnt; carded his state,
Mingled his royalty with capering fools,
Had his great name profaned with their scorns,
And gave his countenance, against his name,
To laugh at gibing boys, and stand the push
Of every beardless vain comparative;

Grew a companion to the common streets,
Enfeoff'd himself to popularity;
That, being daily swallow'd by men's eyes,
They surfeited with honey and began
To loathe the taste of sweetness, whereof a little
More than a little is by much too much.
So when he had occasion to be seen,
He was but as the cuckoo is in June,
Heard, not regarded; seen, but with such eyes
As, sick and blunted with community,
Afford no extraordinary gaze,
Such as is bent on sun-like majesty
When it shines seldom in admiring eyes;
But rather drowzed and hung their eyelids down,
Slept in his face and render'd such aspect
As cloudy men use to their adversaries,
Being with his presence glutted, gorged and full.
And in that very line, Harry, standest thou;
For thou hast lost thy princely privilege
With vile participation: not an eye
But is a-weary of thy common sight,
Save mine, which hath desired to see thee more;
Which now doth that I would not have it do,
Make blind itself with foolish tenderness.

PRINCE. I shall hereafter, my thrice gracious lord,
Be more myself.

KING.   For all the world
As thou art to this hour was Richard then
When I from France set foot at Ravenspurgh,
And even as I was then is Percy now.
Now, by my sceptre and my soul to boot,
He hath more worthy interest to the state
Than thou the shadow of succession;

For of no right, nor colour like to right,
He doth fill fields with harness in the realm,
Turns head against the lion's armed jaws,
And, being no more in debt to years than thou,
Leads ancient lords and reverend bishops on
To bloody battles and to bruising arms.
What never-dying honour hath he got
Against renowned Douglas! whose high deeds,
Whose hot incursions and great name in arms
Holds from all soldiers chief majority
And military title capital
Through all the kingdoms that acknowledge Christ:
Thrice hath this Hotspur, Mars in swathling clothes,
This infant warrior, in his enterprizes
Discomfited great Douglas, ta'en him once,
Enlarged him and made a friend of him,
To fill the mouth of deep defiance up,
And shake the peace and safety of our throne.
And what say you to this? Percy, Northumberland,
The Archbishop's grace of York, Douglas, Mortimer,
Capitulate against us and are up.
But wherefore do I tell these news to thee?
Why, Harry, do I tell thee of my foes,
Which art my near'st and dearest enemy?
Thou that art like enough, through vassal fear,
Base inclination and the start of spleen,
To fight against me under Percy's pay,
To dog his heels and curtsy at his frowns,
To show how much thou art degenerate.

PRINCE. Do not think so; you shall not find it so:
And God forgive them that so much have sway'd
Your majesty's good thoughts away from me!
I will redeem all this on Percy's head,

And in the closing of some glorious day
Be bold to tell you that I am your son;
When I will wear a garment all of blood,
And stain my favours in a bloody mask,
Which, wash'd away, shall scour my shame with it:
And that shall be the day, whene'er it lights,
That this same child of honour and renown,
This gallant Hotspur, this all-praised knight,
And your unthought-of Harry chance to meet.
For every honour sitting on his helm,
Would they were multitudes, and on my head
My shames redoubled! for the time will come,
That I shall make this northern youth exchange
His glorious deeds for my indignities.
Percy is but my factor, good my lord,
To engross up glorious deeds on my behalf;
And I will call him to so strict account,
That he shall render every glory up,
Yea, even the slightest worship of his time,
Or I will tear the reckoning from his heart.
This, in the name of God, I promise here:
The which if He be pleased I shall perform,
I do beseech your majesty may salve
The long-grown wounds of my intemperance:
If not, the end of life cancels all bands;
And I will die a hundred thousand deaths
Ere break the smallest parcel of this vow.
KING. A hundred thousand rebels die in this:
    Thou shalt have charge and sovereign trust herein.
Enter BLUNT.]
    How now, good Blunt? thy looks are full of speed.
BLUNT. So hath the business that I come to speak of.
    Lord Mortimer of Scotland hath sent word

That Douglas and the English rebels met
The eleventh of this month at Shrewsbury:
A mighty and a fearful head they are,
If promises be kept on every hand,
As ever offer'd foul play in a state.

KING. The Earl of Westmoreland set forth to-day;
With him my son, Lord John of Lancaster;
For this advertisement is five days old:
On Wednesday next, Harry, you shall set forward;
On Thursday we ourselves will march: our meeting
Is Bridgenorth: and, Harry, you shall march
Through Gloucestershire; by which account,
Our business valued, some twelve days hence
Our general forces at Bridgenorth shall meet.
Our hands are full of business: let's away;
Advantage feeds him fat, while men delay.   [*Exeunt.*

SCENE III — BOAR'S-HEAD TAVERN *in Eastcheap.*

Enter FALSTAFF *and* BARDOLPH.]

FALSTAFF. Bardolph, am I not fallen away vilely since this
last action? do I not bate? do I not dwindle? Why, my
skin hangs about me like an old lady's loose gown; I am
withered like an old apple-john. Well, I'll repent, and
that suddenly, while I am in some liking; I shall be out
of heart shortly, and then I shall have no strength to repent. An I have not forgotten what the inside of a church
is made of, I am a pepper-corn, a brew's horse: the inside
of a church! Company, villanous company, hath been
the spoil of me.

BARDOLPH. Sir John, you are so fretful, you cannot live
long.

FALSTAFF. Why, there is it: come sing me a bawdy song;

make me merry. I was as virtuously given as a gentleman
need to be; virtuous enough; swore little; diced not above
seven times a week; went to a bawdy-house not above
once in a quarter—of an hour; paid money that I borrowed, three or four times; lived well, and in good compass: and now I live out of all order, out of all compass.

BARDOLPH. Why, you are so fat, Sir John, that you must
needs be out of all compass, out of all reasonable compass, Sir John.

FALSTAFF. Do thou amend thy face, and I'll amend my life:
thou art our admiral, thou bearest the lantern in the poop,
but 'tis in the nose of thee; thou art the Knight of the
Burning Lamp.

BARDOLPH. Why, Sir John, my face does you no harm.

FALSTAFF. No, I'll be sworn; I make as good use of it as
many a man doth of a Death's-head or a *memento mori:*
I never see thy face but I think upon hell-fire, and Dives
that lived in purple; for there he is in his robes, burning,
burning. If thou wert any way given to virtue, I would
swear by thy face; my oath should be, 'By this fire, that's
God's angel:' but thou art altogether given over; and wert
indeed, but for the light in thy face, the son of utter darkness. When thou rannest up Gadshill in the night to catch
my horse, if I did not think thou hadst been an *ignis
fatuus* or a ball of wildfire, there's no purchase in money.
O, thou art a perpetual triumph, an everlasting bonfire-
light! Thou hast saved me a thousand marks in links and
torches, walking with thee in the night betwixt tavern and
tavern: but the sack that thou hast drunk me would have
bought me lights as good cheap at the dearest chandler's
in Europe. I have maintained that salamander of yours
with fire any time this two and thirty years; God reward
me for it!

BARDOLPH. 'Sblood, I would my face were in your belly!

FALSTAFF. God-a-mercy! so should I be sure to be heart burned.

Enter HOSTESS.]

How now, Dame Partlet the hen! have you inquired yet who picked my pocket?

HOSTESS. Why, Sir John, what do you think, Sir John? do you think I keep thieves in my house? I have searched, I have inquired, so has my husband, man by man, boy by boy, servant by servant: the tithe of a hair was never lost in my house before.

FALSTAFF. Ye lie, hostess: Bardolph was shaved, and lost many a hair; and I'll be sworn my pocket was picked. Go to, you are a woman, go.

HOSTESS. Who, I? no; I defy thee: God's light, I was never called so in mine own house before.

FALSTAFF. Go to, I know you well enough.

HOSTESS. No, Sir John; you do not know me, Sir John. I know you, Sir John: you owe me money, Sir John; and now you pick a quarrel to beguile me of it: I bought you a dozen of shirts to your back.

FALSTAFF. Dowlas, filthy dowlas: I have given them away to bakers' wives, and they have made bolters of them.

HOSTESS. Now, as I am a true woman, holland of eight shillings an ell. You owe money here besides, Sir John, for your diet and by-drinkings, and money lent you, four and twenty pound.

FALSTAFF. He had his part of it; let him pay.

HOSTESS. He? alas, he is poor; he hath nothing.

FALSTAFF. How! poor? look upon his face; what call you rich? let them coin his nose, let them coin his cheeks: I'll not pay a denier. What, will you make a younker of me? shall I not take mine ease in mine inn but I shall have

my pocket picked? I have lost a seal-ring of my grandfather's worth forty mark.

HOSTESS. O Jesu, I have heard the prince tell him, I know
not how oft, that that ring was copper!

FALSTAFF. How! the prince is a Jack, a sneak-cup: 'sblood,
an he were here, I would cudgel him like a dog, if he
would say so.

Enter the PRINCE *and* PETO, *marching, and* FALSTAFF *meets
them playing on his truncheon like a fife.*]

How now, lad! is the wind in that door, i' faith? must we
all march?

BARDOLPH. Yea, two and two, Newgate fashion.

HOSTESS. My lord, I pray you, hear me.

PRINCE. What sayest thou, Mistress Quickly? How doth thy
husband? I love him well; he is an honest man.

HOSTESS. Good my lord, hear me.

FALSTAFF. Prithee, let her alone, and list to me.

PRINCE. What sayest thou, Jack?

FALSTAFF. The other night I fell asleep here behind the
arras, and had my pocket picked: this house is turned
bawdy-house; they pick pockets.

PRINCE. What didst thou lose, Jack?

FALSTAFF. Wilt thou believe me, Hal? three or four bonds
of forty pound a-piece, and a seal-ring of my grandfather's.

PRINCE. A trifle, some eight-penny matter.

HOSTESS. So I told him, my lord; and I said I heard your
grace say so: and, my lord, he speaks most vilely of you,
like a foul-mouthed man as he is; and said he would
cudgel you.

PRINCE. What! he did not?

HOSTESS. There's neither faith, truth, nor womanhood in
me else.

FALSTAFF. There's no more faith in thee than in a stewed
    prune; nor no more truth in thee than in a drawn fox;
    and for womanhood, Maid Marian may be the deputy's
    wife of the ward to thee. Go, you thing, go.

HOSTESS. Say, what thing? what thing?

FALSTAFF. What thing! why, a thing to thank God on.

HOSTESS. I am no thing to thank God on, I would thou
    shouldst know it; I am an honest man's wife: and, setting
    thy knighthood aside, thou art a knave to call me so.

FALSTAFF. Setting thy womanhood aside, thou art a beast
    to say otherwise.

HOSTESS. Say, what beast, thou knave, thou?

FALSTAFF. What beast! why, an otter.

PRINCE. An otter, Sir John! why an otter?

FALSTAFF. Why, she's neither fish nor flesh; a man knows
    not where to have her.

HOSTESS. Thou art an unjust man in saying so: thou or any
    man knows where to have me, thou knave, thou!

PRINCE. Thou sayest true, hostess; and he slanders thee
    most grossly.

HOSTESS. So he doth you, my lord; and said this other day
    you ought him a thousand pound.

PRINCE. Sirrah, do I owe you a thousand pound?

FALSTAFF. A thousand pound, Hal! a million: thy love is
    worth a million: thou owest me thy love.

HOSTESS. Nay, my lord, he called you Jack, and said he
    would cudgel you.

FALSTAFF. Did I, Bardolph?

BARDOLPH. Indeed, Sir John, you said so.

FALSTAFF. Yea, if he said my ring was copper.

PRINCE. I say 'tis copper: darest thou be as good as thy
    word now?

FALSTAFF. Why, Hal, thou knowest, as thou art but man, I

dare: but as thou art prince, I fear thee as I fear the roaring of the lion's whelp.

PRINCE. And why not as the lion?

FALSTAFF. The king himself is to be feared as the lion: dost thou think I'll fear thee as I fear thy father? nay, an I do, I pray God my girdle break.

PRINCE. O, if it should, how would thy guts fall about thy knees! But, sirrah, there's no room for faith, truth, nor honesty in this bosom of thine; it is all filled up with guts and midriff. Charge an honest woman with picking thy pocket! why, thou whoreson, impudent, embossed rascal, if there were anything in thy pocket but tavern-reckonings, memorandums of bawdy-houses, and one poor pennyworth of sugar-candy to make thee long-winded, if thy pocket were enriched with any other injuries but these, I am a villain: and yet you will stand to it; you will not pocket up wrong: art thou not ashamed?

FALSTAFF. Dost thou hear, Hal? thou knowest in the state of innocency Adam fell; and what should poor Jack Falstaff do in the days of villany? Thou seest I have more flesh than another man; and therefore more frailty. You confess then, you picked my pocket?

PRINCE. It appears so by the story.

FALSTAFF. Hostess, I forgive thee: go, make ready breakfast; love thy husband, look to thy servants, cherish thy guests: thou shalt find me tractable to any honest reason: thou seest I am pacified still. Nay, prithee, be gone. [*Exit* HOSTESS.] Now, Hal, to the news at court: for the robbery, lad, how is that answered?

PRINCE. O, my sweet beef, I must still be good angel to thee: the money is paid back again.

FALSTAFF. O, I do not like that paying back; 'tis a double labour.

PRINCE. I am good friends with my father, and may do any thing.

FALSTAFF. Rob me the exchequer the first thing thou doest, and do it with unwashed hands too.

BARDOLPH. Do, my lord.

PRINCE. I have procured thee, Jack, a charge of foot.

FALSTAFF. I would it had been of horse. Where shall I find one that can steal well? O for a fine thief, of the age of two and twenty or thereabouts! I am heinously unprovided. Well, God be thanked for these rebels, they offend none but the virtuous: I laud them, I praise them.

PRINCE. Bardolph!

BARDOLPH. My lord?

PRINCE. Go bear this letter to Lord John of Lancaster, to my brother John; this to my Lord of Westmoreland. [*Exit* BARDOLPH.] Go, Peto, to horse, to horse; for thou and I have thirty miles to ride yet ere dinner time. [*Exit* PETO.] Jack, meet me to-morrow in the Temple hall at two o'clock in the afternoon.

There shalt thou know thy charge, and there receive
Money and order for their furniture.
The land is burning; Percy stands on high;
And either we or they must lower lie. [*Exit.*

FALSTAFF. Rare words! brave world! Hostess, my breakfast, come!

O, I could wish this tavern were my drum! [*Exit.*

ACT IV

Enter HOTSPUR, WORCESTER, *and* DOUGLAS.]

HOTSPUR. Well said, my noble Scot: if speaking truth
   In this fine age were not thought flattery,
   Such attribution should the Douglas have,
   As not a soldier of this season's stamp
   Should go so general current through the world.
   By God, I cannot flatter; I do defy
   The tongues of soothers; but a braver place
   In my heart's love hath no man than yourself:
   Nay, task me to my word; approve me, lord.
DOUGLAS. Thou art the king of honour:
   No man so potent breathes upon the ground
   But I will beard him.
HOTSPUR.   Do so, and 'tis well.
Enter a MESSENGER *with letters*.]
   What letters hast thou there?—I can but thank you.
MESSENGER. These letters come from your father.
HOTSPUR. Letters from him! why comes he not himself?
MESSENGER. He cannot come, my lord; he is grievous sick.
HOTSPUR. 'Zounds! how has he the leisure to be sick
   In such a justling time? Who leads his power?
   Under whose government come they along?
MESSENGER. His letters bear his mind, not I, my lord.
WORCESTER. I prithee, tell me, doth he keep his bed?
MESSENGER. He did, my lord, four days ere I set forth;
   And at the time of my departure thence
   He was much fear'd by his physicians.

69

WORCESTER. I would the state of time had first been whole,
    Ere he by sickness had been visited:
    His health was never better worth than now.
HOTSPUR. Sick now! droop now! this sickness doth infect
    The very life-blood of our enterprize;
    'Tis catching hither, even to our camp.
    He writes me here, that inward sickness—
    And that his friends by deputation could not
    So soon be drawn, nor did he think it meet
    To lay so dangerous and dear a trust
    On any soul removed but on his own.
    Yet doth he give us bold advertisement,
    That with our small conjunction we should on,
    To see how fortune is disposed to us;
    For, as he writes, there is no quailing now,
    Because the king is certainly possess'd
    Of all our purposes. What say you to it?
WORCESTER. Your father's sickness is a maim to us.
HOTSPUR. A perilous gash, a very limb lopp'd off:
    And yet, in faith, it is not; his present want
    Seems more than we shall find it: were it good
    To set the exact wealth of all our states
    All at one cast? to set so rich a main
    On the nice hazard of one doubtful hour?
    It were not good; for therein should we read
    The very bottom and the soul of hope,
    The very list, the very utmost bound
    Of all our fortunes.
DOUGLAS.   Faith, and so we should;
    Where now remains a sweet reversion:
    We may boldly spend upon the hope of what
    Is to come in:
    A comfort of retirement lives in this.

HOTSPUR. A rendezvous, a home to fly unto,
    If that the devil and mischance look big
    Upon the maidenhead of our affairs.
WORCESTER. But yet I would your father had been here.
    The quality and hair of our attempt
    Brooks no division: it will be thought
    By some, that know not why he is away,
    That wisdom, loyalty and mere dislike
    Of our proceedings kept the earl from hence:
    And think how such an apprehension
    May turn the tide of fearful faction,
    And breed a kind of question in our cause;
    For well you know we of the offering side
    Must keep aloof from strict arbitrement,
    And stop all sight-holes, every loop from whence
    The eye of reason may pry in upon us:
    This absence of your father's draws a curtain,
    That shows the ignorant a kind of fear
    Before not dreamt of.
HOTSPUR.   You strain too far.
    I rather of his absence make this use:
    It lends a lustre and more great opinion,
    A larger dare to our great enterprize,
    Than if the earl were here; for men must think,
    If we without his help can make a head
    To push against a kingdom, with his help
    We shall o'erturn it topsy-turvy down.
    Yet all goes well, yet all our joints are whole.
DOUGLAS. As heart can think: there is not such a word
    Spoke of in Scotland as this term of fear.
Enter SIR RICHARD VERNON.]
HOTSPUR. My cousin Vernon! welcome, by my soul.
VERNON. Pray God my news be worth a welcome, lord.

The Earl of Westmoreland, seven thousand strong,
Is marching hitherwards; with him Prince John.

HOTSPUR. No harm: what more?

VERNON.   And further, I have learn'd,
The king himself in person is set forth,
Or hitherwards intended speedily,
With strong and mighty preparation.

HOTSPUR. He shall be welcome too. Where is his son,
The nimble-footed madcap Prince of Wales,
And his comrades, that daff'd the world aside,
And bid it pass?

VERNON.   All furnish'd, all in arms;
All plumed like estridges that with the wind
Baited like eagles having lately bathed;
Glittering in golden coats, like images;
As full of spirit as the month of May,
And gorgeous as the sun at midsummer;
Wanton as youthful goats, wild as young bulls.
I saw young Harry, with his beaver on,
His cuisses on his thighs, gallantly arm'd,
Rise from the ground like feather'd Mercury,
And vaulted with such ease into his seat,
As if an angel dropp'd down from the clouds,
To turn and wind a fiery Pegasus,
And witch the world with noble horsemanship.

HOTSPUR. No more, no more: worse than the sun in March,
This praise doth nourish agues. Let them come;
They come like sacrifices in their trim,
And to the fire-eyed maid of smoky war
All hot and bleeding will we offer them:
The mailed Mars shall on his altar sit
Up to the ears in blood. I am on fire
To hear this rich reprisal is so nigh

And yet not ours. Come, let me taste my horse,
Who is to bear me like a thunderbolt
Against the bosom of the Prince of Wales:
Harry to Harry shall, hot horse to horse,
Meet and ne'er part till one drop down a corse.
O that Glendower were come!

VERNON.   There is more news:
I learn'd in Worcester, as I rode along,
He cannot draw his power this fourteen days.

DOUGLAS. That's the worst tidings that I hear of yet.

WORCESTER. Ay, by my faith, that bears a frosty sound.

HOTSPUR. What may the king's whole battle reach unto?

VERNON. To thirty thousand.

HOTSPUR.   Forty let it be:
My father and Glendower being both away,
The powers of us may serve so great a day.
Come, let us take a muster speedily:
Doomsday is near; die all, die merrily.

DOUGLAS. Talk not of dying: I am out of fear
Of death or death's hand for this one half year.   [*Exeunt.*

SCENE II — *A public road near* COVENTRY.

Enter FALSTAFF *and* BARDOLPH.]

FALSTAFF. Bardolph, get thee before to Coventry; fill me a
bottle of sack: our soldiers shall march through; we'll to
Sutton's Co'fil' to-night.

BARDOLPH. Will you give me money, captain?

FALSTAFF. Lay out, lay out.

BARDOLPH. This bottle makes an angel.

FALSTAFF. An if it do, take it for thy labour; and if it make
twenty, take them all; I'll answer the coinage. Bid my lieu-
tenant Peto meet me at town's end.

BARDOLPH. I will, captain: farewell. [*Exit.*

FALSTAFF. If I be not ashamed of my soldiers, I am a soused gurnet. I have misused the king's press damnably. I have got, in exchange of a hundred and fifty soldiers, three hundred and odd pounds. I press me none but good householders, yeomen's sons; inquire me out contracted bachelors, such as had been asked twice on the banns; such a commodity of warm slaves, as had as lieve hear the devil as a drum; such as fear the report of a caliver worse than a struck fowl or a hurt wild-duck. I pressed me none but such toasts-and-butter, with hearts in their bellies no bigger than pins'-heads, and they have bought out their services; and now my whole charge consists of ancients, corporals, lieutenants, gentlemen of companies, slaves as ragged as Lazarus in the painted cloth, where the glutton's dogs licked his sores; and such as indeed were never soldiers, but discarded unjust serving-men, younger sons to younger brothers, revolted tapsters, and ostlers trade-fallen; the cankers of a calm world and a long peace, ten times more dishonourable ragged than an old faced ancient: and such have I, to fill up the rooms of them that have bought out their services, that you would think that I had a hundred and fifty tattered prodigals lately come from swine-keeping, from eating draff and husks. A mad fellow met me on the way and told me I had unloaded all the gibbets and pressed the dead bodies. No eye hath seen such scarecrows. I'll not march through Coventry with them, that's flat: nay, and the villains march wide betwixt the legs, as if they had gyves on; for indeed I had the most of them out of prison. There's but a shirt and a half in all my company; and the half shirt is two napkins tacked together and thrown over the shoulders like a herald's coat without sleeves; and the shirt, to

say the truth, stolen from my host at Saint Alban's, or the
red-nose innkeeper of Daventry. But that's all one; they'll
find linen enough on every hedge.

Enter the PRINCE *and* WESTMORELAND.]

PRINCE. How now, blown Jack! how now, quilt!

FALSTAFF. What, Hal! how now, mad wag! what a devil
dost thou in Warwickshire? My good Lord of Westmoreland, I cry you mercy: I thought your honour had already
been at Shrewsbury.

WEST. Faith, Sir John, 'tis more than time that I were there,
and you too; but my powers are there already. The king,
I can tell you, looks for us all: we must away all night.

FALSTAFF. Tut, never fear me: I am as vigilant as a cat to
steal cream.

PRINCE. I think, to steal cream indeed, for thy theft hath
already made thee butter. But tell me, Jack, whose fellows are these that come after?

FALSTAFF. Mine, Hal, mine.

PRINCE. I did never see such pitiful rascals.

FALSTAFF. Tut, tut; good enough to toss; food for powder,
food for powder; they'll fill a pit as well as better; tush,
man, mortal men, mortal men.

WEST. Ay, but, Sir John, methinks they are exceeding poor
and bare, too beggarly.

FALSTAFF. Faith, for their poverty, I know not where they
had that; and for their bareness, I am sure they never
learned that of me.

PRINCE. No, I'll be sworn; unless you call three fingers on
the ribs bare. But, sirrah, make haste: Percy is already in
the field.

FALSTAFF. What, is the king encamped?

WEST. He is, Sir John: I fear we shall stay too long.

FALSTAFF. Well,
    To the latter end of a fray and the beginning of a feast
    Fits a dull fighter and a keen guest.   [*Exeunt.*

SCENE III — *The rebel camp near* SHREWSBURY.

Enter HOTSPUR, WORCESTER, DOUGLAS, *and* VERNON.]
HOTSPUR. We'll fight with him to-night.
WORCESTER.   It may not be.
DOUGLAS. You give him then advantage.
VERNON.   Not a whit.
HOTSPUR. Why say you so? looks he not for supply?
VERNON. So do we.
HOTSPUR.   His is certain, ours is doubtful.
WORCESTER. Good cousin, be advised, stir not to-night.
VERNON. Do not, my lord.
DOUGLAS.   You do not counsel well:
    You speak it out of fear and cold heart.
VERNON. Do me no slander, Douglas: by my life,
    And I dare well maintain it with my life,
    If well-respected honour bid me on,
    I hold as little counsel with weak fear
    As you, my lord, or any Scot that this day lives:
    Let it be seen to-morrow in the battle
    Which of us fears.
DOUGLAS.   Yea, or to-night.
VERNON.   Content.
HOTSPUR. To-night, say I.
VERNON. Come, come, it may not be. I wonder much,
    Being men of such great leading as you are,
    That you foresee not what impediments
    Drag back our expedition: certain horse

Of my cousin Vernon's are not yet come up:
Your uncle Worcester's horse came but to-day;
And now their pride and mettle is asleep,
Their courage with hard labour tame and dull,
That not a horse is half the half of himself.
HOTSPUR. So are the horses of the enemy
In general, journey-bated and brought low:
The better part of ours are full of rest.
WORCESTER. The number of the king exceedeth ours:
For God's sake, cousin, stay till all come in.
                          [*The trumpet sounds a parley.*
Enter SIR WALTER BLUNT.]
BLUNT. I come with gracious offers from the king,
If you vouchsafe me hearing and respect.
HOTSPUR. Welcome, Sir Walter Blunt; and would to God
You were of our determination!
Some of us love you well; and even those some
Envy your great deservings and good name,
Because you are not of our quality,
But stand against us like an enemy.
BLUNT. And God defend but still I should stand so,
So long as out of limit and true rule
You stand against anointed majesty.
But to my charge. The king hath sent to know
The nature of your griefs, and whereupon
You conjure from the breast of civil peace
Such bold hostility, teaching his duteous land
Audacious cruelty. If that the king
Have any way your good deserts forgot,
Which he confesseth to be manifold,
He bids you name your griefs; and with all speed
You shall have your desires with interest,

And pardon absolute for yourself and these
Herein misled by your suggestion.

HOTSPUR. The king is kind; and well we know the king
Knows at what time to promise, when to pay.
My father and my uncle and myself
Did give him that same royalty he wears;
And when he was not six and twenty strong,
Sick in the world's regard, wretched and low,
A poor unminded outlaw sneaking home,
My father gave him welcome to the shore;
And when he heard him swear and vow to God
He came but to be Duke of Lancaster,
To sue his livery and beg his peace,
With tears of innocency and terms of zeal,
My father, in kind heart and pity moved,
Swore him assistance and perform'd it too.
Now when the lords and barons of the realm
Perceived Northumberland did lean to him,
The more and less came in with cap and knee;
Met him in boroughs, cities, villages,
Attended him on bridges, stood in lanes,
Laid gifts before him, proffer'd him their oaths,
Gave him their heirs, as pages follow'd him
Even at the heels in golden multitudes.
He presently, as greatness knows itself,
Steps me a little higher than his vow
Made to my father, while his blood was poor,
Upon the naked shore at Ravenspurgh;
And now, forsooth, takes on him to reform
Some certain edicts and some strait decrees
That lie too heavy on the commonwealth,
Cries out upon abuses, seems to weep
Over his country's wrongs; and by this face,

This seeming brow of justice, did he win
The hearts of all that he did angle for;
Proceeded further; cut me off the heads
Of all the favourites that the absent king
In deputation left behind him here,
When he was personal in the Irish war.

BLUNT. Tut, I came not to hear this.

HOTSPUR.   Then to the point.
In short time after, he deposed the king;
Soon after that, deprived him of his life;
And in the neck of that, task'd the whole state;
To make that worse, suffer'd his kinsman March,
Who is, if every owner were well placed,
Indeed his king, to be engaged in Wales,
There without ransom to lie forfeited;
Disgraced me in my happy victories,
Sought to entrap me by intelligence;
Rated mine uncle from the council-board;
In rage dismiss'd my father from the court;
Broke oath on oath, committed wrong on wrong,
And in conclusion drove us to seek out
This head of safety, and withal to pry
Into his title, the which we find
Too indirect for long continuance.

BLUNT. Shall I return this answer to the king?

HOTSPUR. Not so, Sir Walter: we'll withdraw a while.
Go to the king; and let there be impawn'd
Some surety for a safe return again,
And in the morning early shall mine uncle
Bring him our purposes: and so farewell.

BLUNT. I would you would accept of grace and love.

HOTSPUR. And may be so we shall.

BLUNT.   Pray God you do. [*Exeunt.*

SCENE IV—YORK. *The* ARCHBISHOP'S *palace.*

Enter the ARCHBISHOP OF YORK *and* SIR MICHAEL.]

ARCHBISHOP. Hie, good Sir Michael; bear this sealed brief
  With winged haste to the lord marshal;
  This to my cousin Scroop, and all the rest
  To whom they are directed. If you knew
  How much they do import, you would make haste.

SIR MICHAEL. My good lord,
  I guess their tenour.

ARCHBISHOP.   Like enough you do.
  To-morrow, good Sir Michael, is a day
  Wherein the fortune of ten thousand men
  Must bide the touch; for, sir, at Shrewsbury,
  As I am truly given to understand,
  The king with mighty and quick-raised power
  Meets with Lord Harry: and, I fear, Sir Michael,
  What with the sickness of Northumberland,
  Whose power was in the first proportion,
  And what with Owen Glendower's absence thence,
  Who with them was a rated sinew too
  And comes not in, o'er-ruled by prophecies,
  I fear the power of Percy is too weak
  To wage an instant trial with the king.

SIR MICHAEL. Why, my good lord, you need not fear;
  There is Douglas and Lord Mortimer.

ARCHBISHOP. No, Mortimer is not there.

SIR MICHAEL. But there is Mordake, Vernon, Lord Harry
    Percy,
  And there is my Lord of Worcester and a head
  Of gallant warriors, noble gentlemen.

ARCHBISHOP. And so there is: but yet the king hath drawn
  The special head of all the land together:

The Prince of Wales, Lord John of Lancaster,
The noble Westmoreland and warlike Blunt;
And many mo corrivals and dear men
Of estimation and command in arms.

SIR MICHAEL. Doubt not, my lord, they shall be well
opposed.

ARCHBISHOP. I hope no less, yet needful 'tis to fear;
And, to prevent the worst, Sir Michael, speed:
For if Lord Percy thrive not, ere the king
Dismiss his power, he means to visit us,
For he hath heard of our confederacy,
And 'tis but wisdom to make strong against him:
Therefore make haste. I must go write again
To other friends; and so farewell, Sir Michael.   [*Exeunt.*

ACT V

SCENE I — *The* KING'S *camp near* SHREWSBURY.

Enter the KING, PRINCE OF WALES, LORD JOHN OF
    LANCASTER, SIR WALTER BLUNT, *and* FALSTAFF.]

KING. How bloodily the sun begins to peer
    Above yon busky hill! the day looks pale
    At his distemperature.

PRINCE.   The southern wind
    Doth play the trumpet to his purposes,
    And by his hollow whistling in the leaves
    Foretells a tempest and a blustering day.

KING. Then with the losers let it sympathise,
    For nothing can seem foul to those that win.

                                    [*The trumpet sounds.*

Enter WORCESTER *and* VERNON.]

    How now, my Lord of Worcester! 'tis not well
    That you and I should meet upon such terms
    As now we meet. You have deceived our trust,
    And made us doff our easy robes of peace,
    To crush our old limbs in ungentle steel:
    This is not well, my lord, this is not well.
    What say you to it? will you again unknit
    This churlish knot of all-abhorred war?
    And move in that obedient orb again
    Where you did give a fair and natural light,
    And be no more an exhaled meteor,
    A prodigy of fear, and a portent
    Of broached mischief to the unborn times?

WORCESTER. Hear me, my liege:

For mine own part, I could be well content
To entertain the lag-end of my life
With quiet hours; for, I do protest,
I have not sought the day of this dislike.
KING. You have not sought it! how comes it, then?
FALSTAFF. Rebellion lay in his way, and he found it.
PRINCE. Peace, chewet, peace!
WORCESTER. It pleased your majesty to turn your looks
Of favour from myself and all our house;
And yet I must remember you, my lord,
We were the first and dearest of your friends.
For you my staff of office did I break
In Richard's time; and posted day and night
To meet you on the way, and kiss your hand,
When yet you were in place and in account
Nothing so strong and fortunate as I.
It was myself, my brother, and his son,
That brought you home, and boldly did outdare
The dangers of the time. You swore to us,
And you did swear that oath at Doncaster,
That you did nothing purpose 'gainst the state;
Nor claim no further than your new-fall'n right,
The seat of Gaunt, dukedom of Lancaster:
To this we swore our aid. But in short space
It rain'd down fortune showering on your head;
And such a flood of greatness fell on you,
What with our help, what with the absent king,
What with the injuries of a wanton time,
The seeming sufferances that you had borne,
And the contrarious winds that held the king
So long in his unlucky Irish wars
That all in England did repute him dead:
And from this swarm of fair advantages

You took occasion to be quickly woo'd
To gripe the general sway into your hand;
Forgot your oath to us at Doncaster;
And being fed by us you used us so
As that ungentle gull, the cuckoo's bird,
Useth the sparrow; did oppress our nest;
Grew by our feeding to so great a bulk
That even our love durst not come near your sight
For fear of swallowing; but with nimble wing
We were enforced, for safety sake, to fly
Out of your sight and raise this present head;
Whereby we stand opposed by such means
As you yourself have forged against yourself,
By unkind usage, dangerous countenance,
And violation of all faith and troth
Sworn to us in your younger enterprize.

KING. These things indeed you have articulate,
Proclaim'd at market-crosses, read in churches,
To face the garment of rebellion
With some fine colour that may please the eye
Of fickle changelings and poor discontents,
Which gape and rub the elbow at the news
Of hurlyburly innovation:
And never yet did insurrection want
Such water-colours to impaint his cause;
Nor moody beggars, starving for a time
Of pellmell havoc and confusion.

PRINCE. In both your armies there is many a soul
Shall pay full dearly for this encounter,
If once they join in trial. Tell your nephew,
The Prince of Wales doth join with all the world
In praise of Henry Percy: by my hopes,

This present enterprise set off his head,
I do not think a braver gentleman,
More active-valiant or more valiant-young,
More daring or more bold, is now alive
To grace this latter age with noble deeds.
For my part, I may speak it to my shame,
I have a truant been to chivalry;
And so I hear he doth account me too;
Yet this before my father's majesty—
I am content that he shall take the odds
Of his great name and estimation,
And will, to save the blood on either side,
Try fortune with him in a single fight.

KING. And, Prince of Wales, so dare we venture thee,
Albeit considerations infinite
Do make against it. No, good Worcester, no,
We love our people well; even those we love
That are misled upon your cousin's part;
And, will they take the offer of our grace,
Both he and they and you, yea, every man
Shall be my friend again and I'll be his:
So tell your cousin, and bring me word
What he will do: but if he will not yield,
Rebuke and dread correction wait on us
And they shall do their office. So, be gone;
We will not now be troubled with reply:
We offer fair; take it advisedly.

                 [*Exeunt* WORCESTER *and* VERNON.

PRINCE. It will not be accepted, on my life:
The Douglas and the Hotspur both together
Are confident against the world in arms.

KING. Hence, therefore, every leader to his charge;

For, on their answer, will we set on them:
And God befriend us, as our cause is just!

   [*Exeunt all but the* PRINCE OF WALES *and* FALSTAFF.

FALSTAFF. Hal, if thou see me down in the battle, and bestride me, so; 'tis a point of friendship.

PRINCE. Nothing but a colossus can do thee that friendship. Say thy prayers, and farewell.

FALSTAFF. I would 'twere bed-time, Hal, and all well.

PRINCE. Why, thou owest God a death.   [*Exit.*

FALSTAFF. 'Tis not due yet; I would be loath to pay him before his day. What need I be so forward with him that calls not on me? Well, 'tis no matter; honour pricks me on. Yea, but how if honour prick me off when I come on? how then? Can honour set to a leg? no: or an arm? no: or take away the grief of a wound? no. Honour hath no skill in surgery, then? no. What is honour? a word. What is in that word honour? what is that honour? air. A trim reckoning! Who hath it? he that died o' Wednesday. Doth he feel it? no. Doth he hear it? no. 'Tis insensible, then? yea, to the dead. But will it not live with the living? no. Why? detraction will not suffer it. Therefore I'll none of it. Honour is a mere scutcheon: and so ends my catechism.
                   [*Exit.*

SCENE II—*The rebel camp.*

Enter WORCESTER *and* VERNON.]

WORCESTER. O, no, my nephew must not know, Sir Richard,
The liberal and kind offer of the king.

VERNON. 'Twere best he did.

WORCESTER.   Then are we all undone.
It is not possible, it cannot be,

The king should keep his word in loving us;
He will suspect us still, and find a time
To punish this offence in other faults:
Suspicion all our lives shall be stuck full of eyes;
For treason is but trusted like the fox,
Who, ne'er so tame, so cherish'd and lock'd up,
Will have a wild trick of his ancestors.
Look how we can, or sad or merrily,
Interpretation will misquote our looks,
And we shall feed like oxen at a stall,
The better cherish'd, still the nearer death.
My nephew's trespass may be well forgot;
It hath the excuse of youth and heat of blood;
And an adopted name of privilege,
A hare-brain'd Hotspur, govern'd by a spleen:
All his offences live upon my head
And on his father's; we did train him on,
And, his corruption being ta'en from us,
We, as the spring of all, shall pay for all.
Therefore, good cousin, let not Harry know,
In any case, the offer of the king.

VERNON. Deliver what you will; I'll say 'tis so.
Here comes your cousin.

Enter HOTSPUR *and* DOUGLAS.]

HOTSPUR. My uncle is return'd:
Deliver up my Lord of Westmoreland.
Uncle, what news?

WORCESTER. The king will bid you battle presently.

DOUGLAS. Defy him by the Lord of Westmoreland.

HOTSPUR. Lord Douglas, go you and tell him so.

DOUGLAS. Marry, and shall, and very willingly.   [*Exit.*

WORCESTER. There is no seeming mercy in the king.

HOTSPUR. Did you beg any? God forbid!

WORCESTER. I told him gently of our grievances,
    Of his oath-breaking; which he mended thus,
    By now forswearing that he is forsworn:
    He calls us rebels, traitors; and will scourge
    With haughty arms this hateful name in us.

Re-enter DOUGLAS.]

DOUGLAS. Arm, gentlemen; to arms! for I have thrown
    A brave defiance in King Henry's teeth,
    And Westmoreland, that was engaged, did bear it;
    Which cannot choose but bring him quickly on.

WORCESTER. The Prince of Wales stepp'd forth before the
        king,
    And, nephew, challenged you to single fight.

HOTSPUR. O, would the quarrel lay upon our heads,
    And that no man might draw short breath to-day
    But I and Harry Monmouth! Tell me, tell me,
    How show'd his tasking? seem'd it in contempt?

VERNON. No, by my soul; I never in my life
    Did hear a challenge urged more modestly,
    Unless a brother should a brother dare
    To gentle exercise and proof of arms.
    He gave you all the duties of a man;
    Trimm'd up your praises with a princely tongue,
    Spoke your deservings like a chronicle,
    Making you ever better than his praise
    By still dispraising praise valued with you;
    And, which became him like a prince indeed,
    He made a blushing cital of himself;
    And chid his truant youth with such a grace
    As if he master'd there a double spirit
    Of teaching and of learning instantly.
    There did he pause: but let me tell the world,

If he outlive the envy of this day,
England did never owe so sweet a hope,
So much misconstrued in his wantonness.
HOTSPUR. Cousin, I think thou art enamoured
  On his follies: never did I hear
  Of any prince so wild a libertine.
  But be he as he will, yet once ere night
  I will embrace him with a soldier's arm,
  That he shall shrink under my courtesy.
  Arm, arm with speed: and, fellows, soldiers, friends,
  Better consider what you have to do
  Than I, that have not well the gift of tongue,
  Can lift your blood up with persuasion.
Enter a MESSENGER.]
MESSENGER. My lord, here are letters for you.
HOTSPUR. I cannot read them now.
  O gentlemen, the time of life is short!
  To spend that shortness basely were too long,
  If life did ride upon a dial's point,
  Still ending at the arrival of an hour.
  An if we live, we live to tread on kings;
  If die, brave death, when princes die with us!
  Now, for our consciences, the arms are fair,
  When the intent of bearing them is just.
Enter another MESSENGER.]
MESSENGER. My lord, prepare; the king comes on apace.
HOTSPUR. I thank him, that he cuts me from my tale,
  For I profess not talking; only this—
  Let each man do his best: and here draw I
  A sword, whose temper I intend to stain
  With the best blood that I can meet withal
  In the adventure of this perilous day.
  Now, Esperance! Percy! and set on.

Sound all the lofty instruments of war,
And by that music let us all embrace;
For, heaven to earth, some of us never shall
A second time do such a courtesy.

> [*The trumpets sound. They embrace, and exeunt.*

SCENE III—*Plain between the camps.*

The KING *enters with his power. Alarum to the battle. Then enter* DOUGLAS *and* SIR WALTER BLUNT.]

BLUNT. What is thy name, that in the battle thus
Thou crossest me? what honour dost thou seek
Upon my head?

DOUGLAS.   Know then, my name is Douglas;
And I do haunt thee in the battle thus,
Because some tell me that thou art a king.

BLUNT. They tell thee true.

DOUGLAS. The Lord of Stafford dear to-day hath bought
Thy likeness; for instead of thee, King Harry,
This sword hath ended him: so shall it thee,
Unless thou yield thee as my prisoner.

BLUNT. I was not born a yielder, thou proud Scot;
And thou shalt find a king that will revenge
Lord Stafford's death.

> [*They fight.* DOUGLAS *kills* BLUNT.

Enter HOTSPUR.]

HOTSPUR. O Douglas, hadst thou fought at Holmedon thus,
I never had triumph'd upon a Scot.

DOUGLAS. All's done, all's won; here breathless lies the king.

HOTSPUR. Where?

DOUGLAS. Here.

HOTSPUR. This, Douglas? no: I know this face full well:

A gallant knight he was, his name was Blunt;
Semblably furnish'd like the king himself.

DOUGLAS. A fool go with thy soul, whither it goes!
A borrowed title hast thou bought too dear:
Why didst thou tell me that thou wert a king?

HOTSPUR. The king hath many marching in his coats.

DOUGLAS. Now, by my sword, I will kill all his coats;
I'll murder all his wardrobe, piece by piece,
Until I meet the king.

HOTSPUR.   Up, and away!
Our soldiers stand full fairly for the day.   [*Exeunt.*
Alarum. Enter FALSTAFF, *solus.*]

FALSTAFF. Though I could 'scape shot-free at London, I
fear the shot here; here's no scoring but upon the pate.
Soft! who are you? Sir Walter Blunt: there's honour for
you! here's no vanity! I am as hot as molten lead, and as
heavy too: God keep lead out of me! I need no more
weight than mine own bowels. I have led my ragamuffins
where they are peppered: there's not three of my hundred and fifty left alive; and they are for the town's end,
to beg during life. But who comes here?
Enter the PRINCE.]

PRINCE. What, stand'st thou idle here? lend me thy sword:
Many a nobleman lies stark and stiff
Under the hoofs of vaunting enemies,
Whose deaths are yet unrevenged: I prithee, lend me thy
sword.

FALSTAFF. O Hal, I prithee, give me leave to breathe a
while. Turk Gregory never did such deeds in arms as I
have done this day. I have paid Percy, I have made him
sure.

PRINCE. He is, indeed; and living to kill thee. I prithee,
lend me thy sword.

FALSTAFF. Nay, before God, Hal, if Percy be alive, thou
get'st not my sword; but take my pistol, if thou wilt.

PRINCE. Give it me: what, is it in the case?

FALSTAFF. Ay, Hal, 'tis hot, 'tis hot; there's that will sack a
city.

[*The* PRINCE *draws it out, and finds it to be a bottle of sack.*

PRINCE. What, is it a time to jest and dally now?

[*He throws the bottle at him. Exit.*

FALSTAFF. Well, if Percy be alive, I'll pierce him. If he do
come in my way, so: if he do not, if I come in his willingly, let him make a carbonado of me. I like not such
grinning honour as Sir Walter hath: give me life: which
if I can save, so; if not, honour comes unlooked for, and
there's an end. [*Exit.*

SCENE IV—*Another part of the field.*

Alarum. Excursions. Enter the KING, *the* PRINCE, LORD
JOHN OF LANCASTER, *and* EARL OF WESTMORELAND.]

KING. I prithee,
Harry, withdraw thyself; thou bleed'st too much.
Lord John of Lancaster, go you with him.

LANCASTER. Not, I my lord, unless I did bleed too.

PRINCE. I beseech your majesty, make up,
Lest your retirement do amaze your friends.

KING. I will do so.
My Lord of Westmoreland, lead him to his tent.

WEST. Come, my lord, I'll lead you to your tent.

PRINCE. Lead me, my lord? I do not need your help:
And God forbid a shallow scratch should drive
The Prince of Wales from such a field as this,
Where stain'd nobility lies trodden on,
And rebels' arms triumph in massacres!

LANCASTER. We breathe too long: come, cousin Westmore-
    land,
  Our duty this way lies; for God's sake, come.
                 [*Exeunt* PRINCE JOHN *and* WESTMORELAND.
PRINCE. By God, thou hast deceived me, Lancaster;
  I did not think thee lord of such a spirit:
  Before, I loved thee as a brother, John;
  But now, I do respect thee as my soul.
KING. I saw him hold Lord Percy at the point,
  With lustier maintenance than I did look for
  Of such an ungrown warrior.
PRINCE.   O, this boy
  Lends mettle to us all!   [*Exit.*
Enter DOUGLAS.]
DOUGLAS. Another king! they grow like Hydra's heads:
  I am the Douglas, fatal to all those
  That wear those colours on them: what art thou,
  That counterfeit'st the person of a king?
KING. The king himself; who, Douglas, grieves at heart
  So many of his shadows thou hast met
  And not the very king. I have two boys
  Seek Percy and thyself about the field:
  But, seeing thou fall'st on me so luckily,
  I will assay thee: so, defend thyself.
DOUGLAS. I fear thou art another counterfeit;
  And yet, in faith, thou bear'st thee like a king:
  But mine I am sure thou art, whoe'er thou be,
  And thus I win thee.
            [*They fight; the* KING *being in danger,*
               re-enter PRINCE OF WALES.
PRINCE. Hold up thy head, vile Scot, or thou art like
  Never to hold it up again! the spirits
  Of valiant Shirley, Stafford, Blunt, are in my arms:

It is the Prince of Wales that threatens thee;
Who never promiseth but he means to pay.
                              [*They fight:* DOUGLAS *flies.*
Cheerly, my lord; how fares your grace?
Sir Nicholas Gawsey hath for succour sent,
And so hath Clifton: I'll to Clifton straight.
KING. Stay, and breathe a while:
    Thou hast redeem'd thy lost opinion,
    And show'd thou makest some tender of my life,
    In this fair rescue thou hast brought to me.
PRINCE. O God! they did me too much injury
    That ever said I hearken'd for your death.
    If it were so, I might have let alone
    The insulting hand of Douglas over you,
    Which would have been as speedy in your end
    As all the poisonous potions in the world,
    And saved the treacherous labour of your son.
KING. Make up to Clifton: I'll to Sir Nicholas Gawsey.
                                              [*Exit.*

Enter HOTSPUR.]
HOTSPUR. If I mistake not, thou art Harry Monmouth.
PRINCE. Thou speak'st as if I would deny my name.
HOTSPUR. My name is Harry Percy.
PRINCE.   Why, then I see
    A very valiant rebel of the name.
    I am the Prince of Wales; and think not, Percy,
    To share with me in glory any more:
    Two stars keep not their motion in one sphere;
    Nor can one England brook a double reign,
    Of Harry Percy and the Prince of Wales.
HOTSPUR. Nor shall it, Harry; for the hour is come
    To end the one of us; and would to God
    Thy name in arms were now as great as mine!

PRINCE. I'll make it greater ere I part from thee;
  And all the budding honours on thy crest
  I'll crop, to make a garland for my head.
HOTSPUR. I can no longer brook thy vanities.   [*They fight.*
Enter FALSTAFF.]
FALSTAFF. Well said, Hal! to it, Hal! Nay, you shall find no
  boy's play here, I can tell you.
Re-enter DOUGLAS; *he fights with* FALSTAFF, *who
      falls down as if he were dead, and exit* DOUGLAS.
      HOTSPUR *is wounded and falls.*]
HOTSPUR. O, Harry, thou has robb'd me of my youth!
  I better brook the loss of brittle life
  Than those proud titles thou hast won of me;
  They wound my thoughts worse than thy sword my flesh:
  But thought's the slave of life, and life time's fool;
  And time, that takes survey of all the world,
  Must have a stop. O, I could prophesy,
  But that the earthy and cold hand of death
  Lies on my tongue: no, Percy, thou art dust,
  And food for—   [*Dies.*
PRINCE. For worms, brave Percy: fare thee well, great
    heart!
  Ill-weaved ambition, how much art thou shrunk!
  When that this body did contain a spirit,
  A kingdom for it was too small a bound;
  But now two paces of the vilest earth
  Is room enough: this earth that bears thee dead
  Bears not alive so stout a gentleman.
  If thou wert sensible of courtesy,
  I should not make so dear a show of zeal:
  But let my favours hide thy mangled face;
  And, even in thy behalf, I'll thank myself
  For doing these fair rites of tenderness.

Adieu, and take thy praise with thee to heaven!
Thy ignominy sleep with thee in the grave,
But not remember'd in thy epitaph!
                              [*He spieth* FALSTAFF *on the ground.*
What, old acquaintance! could not all this flesh
Keep in a little life? Poor Jack, farewell!
I could have better spared a better man:
O, I should have a heavy miss of thee,
If I were much in love with vanity!
Death hath not struck so fat a deer to-day,
Though many dearer, in this bloody fray.
Embowell'd will I see thee by and by:
Till then in blood by noble Percy lie.   [*Exit.*

FALSTAFF. [*Rising up*] Embowelled! if thou embowel me
to-day, I'll give you leave to powder me and eat me too
to-morrow. 'Sblood, 'twas time to counterfeit, or that hot
termagant Scot had paid me scot and lot too. Counterfeit?
I lie, I am no counterfeit: to die, is to be a counterfeit; for
he is but the counterfeit of a man who hath not the life
of a man: but to counterfeit dying, when a man thereby
liveth, is to be no counterfeit, but the true and perfect
image of life indeed. The better part of valour is discre-
tion; in the which better part I have saved my life.
'Zounds, I am afraid of this gunpowder Percy, though he
be dead: how, if he should counterfeit too, and rise? by
my faith, I am afraid he would prove the better counterfeit. Therefore I'll make him sure; yea, and I'll swear I
killed him. Why may he not rise as well as I? Nothing
confutes me but eyes, and nobody sees me. Therefore,
sirrah [*stabbing him*], with a new wound in your thigh,
come you along with me. [*Takes up* HOTSPUR *on his back.*
Re-enter the PRINCE OF WALES *and*
         LORD JOHN OF LANCASTER.]

PRINCE. Come, brother John; full bravely hast thou flesh'd
    Thy maiden sword.
LANCASTER.   But, soft! whom have we here?
    Did you not tell me this fat man was dead?
PRINCE. I did; I saw him dead,
    Breathless and bleeding on the ground. Art thou alive?
    Or is it fantasy that plays upon our eyesight?
    I prithee, speak; we will not trust our eyes
    Without our ears: thou art not what thou seem'st.
FALSTAFF. No, that's certain; I am not a double man: but
    if I be not Jack Falstaff, then am I a Jack. There is Percy
    [*throwing the body down*]: if your father will do me any
    honour, so; if not, let him kill the next Percy himself. I
    look to be either earl or duke, I can assure you.
PRINCE. Why, Percy I killed myself, and saw thee dead.
FALSTAFF. Didst thou? Lord, Lord, how this world is given
    to lying! I grant you I was down and out of breath; and so
    was he: but we rose both at an instant, and fought a long
    hour by Shrewsbury clock. If I may be believed, so; if not,
    let them that should reward valour bear the sin upon their
    own heads. I'll take it upon my death, I gave him this
    wound in the thigh: if the man were alive, and would deny
    it, 'zounds, I would make him eat a piece of my sword.
LANCASTER. This is the strangest tale that ever I heard.
PRINCE. This is the strangest fellow, brother John.
    Come, bring your luggage nobly on your back:
    For my part, if a lie may do thee grace,
    I'll gild it with the happiest terms I have.
                               [*A retreat is sounded.*
    The trumpet sounds retreat; the day is ours.
    Come, brother, let us to the highest of the field,
    To see what friends are living, who are dead.
               [*Exeunt* PRINCE OF WALES *and* LANCASTER.

FALSTAFF. I'll follow, as they say, for reward. He that rewards me, God reward him! If I do grow great, I'll grow
less; for I'll purge, and leave sack, and live cleanly as a
nobleman should do.   [*Exit*.

SCENE V—*Another part of the field*.

The trumpets sound. Enter the KING, PRINCE OF WALES,
            LORD JOHN OF LANCASTER, EARL OF WESTMORE-
            LAND, *with* WORCESTER *and* VERNON *prisoners*.]
KING. Thus ever did rebellion find rebuke.
   Ill-spirited Worcester! did not we send grace,
   Pardon and terms of love to all of you?
   And wouldst thou turn our offers contrary?
   Misuse the tenour of thy kinsman's trust?
   Three knights upon our party slain to-day,
   A noble earl and many a creature else
   Had been alive this hour,
   If like a Christian thou hadst truly borne
   Betwixt our armies true intelligence.
WORCESTER. What I have done my safety urged me to;
   And I embrace this fortune patiently,
   Since not to be avoided it falls on me.
KING. Bear Worcester to the death, and Vernon too:
   Other offenders we will pause upon.
              [*Exeunt* WORCESTER *and* VERNON, *guarded*.
   How goes the field?
PRINCE. The noble Scot, Lord Douglas, when he saw
   The fortune of the day quite turn'd from him,
   The noble Percy slain, and all his men
   Upon the foot of fear, fled with the rest;
   And falling from a hill, he was so bruised
   That the pursuers took him. At my tent

The Douglas is; and I beseech your grace
I may dispose of him.
KING.   With all my heart.
PRINCE. Then, brother John of Lancaster, to you
This honourable bounty shall belong:
Go to the Douglas, and deliver him
Up to his pleasure, ransomless and free:
His valour shown upon our crests to-day
Hath taught us how to cherish such high deeds
Even in the bosom of our adversaries.
LANCASTER. I thank your grace for this high courtesy,
Which I shall give away immediately.
KING. Then this remains, that we divide our power.
You, son John, and my cousin Westmoreland
Towards York shall bend you with your dearest speed,
To meet Northumberland and the prelate Scroop,
Who, as we hear, are busily in arms:
Myself and you, son Harry, will towards Wales,
To fight with Glendower and the Earl of March.
Rebellion in this land shall lose his sway,
Meeting the check of such another day:
And since this business so fair is done,
Let us not leave till all our own be won.   [*Exeunt.*